SWIFTSTAR

STAR TRIBES, BOOK FOUR

BLAZE WARD

KNOTTED ROAD PRESS

SwiftStar
Star Tribes, Book Four
Blaze Ward
Copyright © 2020 Blaze Ward
All rights reserved
Published by Knotted Road Press
www.KnottedRoadPress.com

ISBN: 978-1-64470-143-0

Cover art:

ID 115305194 © Luca Oleastri | Dreamstime.com

Cover and interior design copyright © 2020 Knotted Road Press

Never miss a release!
If you'd like to be notified of new releases, sign up for my newsletter.

I will never spam you, or use your email for nefarious purposes. You can also unsubscribe at any time.

http://www.blazeward.com/newsletter/

Packmule

Persephone

Additional Alexandria Station Stories

Siren

Two Bottles of Wine with a War God

The Story Road

The Science Officer Series

The Science Officer

The Mind Field

The Gilded Cage

The Pleasure Dome

The Doomsday Vault

The Last Flagship

The Hammerfield Gambit

The Hammerfield Payoff

Shadow of the Dominion

Longshot Hypothesis

Hard Bargain

Outermost

Dominion-427

Phoenix

Princess Rualoh

Earth Force Sky Patrol

Birth of the Star Dragon

Flight of the Star Dragon

Call of the Star Dragon

Shadow of the Star Dragon

Trial of the Star Dragon

PART ONE
WARRIORS

ONE

Daniel stood patiently and stared out the wide window at the massive ship maneuvering close to the station. Shortly, they would send a shuttle over for him.

Him. Daniel Lémieux. Chef.

And other things.

He wondered what his various ghosts might have to say on the topic, but now was not the time to dive inside himself to ask them. War was coming and he would have more than enough time on the flight outwards to do that.

The beginning of the war would take the form of that enormous horseshoe crab monster of a starship over there, thousands of years old and painted with freckles like a deranged pixie had been hired as an interior and exterior designer. That thing would become his new home shortly, because he could do something that only one other person in the entire galaxy could do right now.

Use the mental powers of the Ishtan to find people and things at distances measured in light-years.

Shortly, that ship could carry him to war.

Daniel still wasn't sure how he felt about it, but it was necessary. That described most of his life these days.

Necessary.

He glanced over at the Commander, Kathra Omezi, standing next to him as they both watched the approaching ship move into orbit. As always, she towered over him, but he was short for a male and she was tall for any human, nearly two meters and certainly an entire head above him.

Tall and athletic, with a leanness yet that was only starting to turn into muscle and mass as she aged. Skin like onyx and hair kept buzzed tight against her skin most of the time.

She had a few years yet before it would start coming in gray, but the woman was thirty-three now. No longer the terrible warrior she had once been, but only because the other leaders, older women of the tribe, had demanded that she stop taking so many crazy risks.

Kathra had responded by vowing to outlive them all instead.

She probably would.

But her world was changing, just as his was. The war was coming. Perhaps not as many light-centuries would be involved for her, but she was still overturning everything she had known in the process.

Everything he had known as well. In Kathra's case, she was pregnant finally, with a daughter that would be the next leader of the Mbaysey Tribal Squadron, although hopefully not for many decades.

Daniel Lémieux was simply going to war in her name.

He even understood why Kathra was making the choices she had. Appreciated it, as well, but it was still strange to actually be living through the consequences of those enormous decisions, like that ship coming closer.

SwiftStar.

But he was comitatus. Sworn to serve her, body and soul, like the two dozen warrior women Kathra had. And one other cook.

It was the definition of comitatus that was changing, and Daniel wasn't sure the galaxy would ever be the same.

He was merely Commander Omezi's personal chef.

Except he wasn't that anymore.

Up until now, it had been an academic discussion for the most part. Ndidi had done more of the cooking than him over the last year or so. He was just Kathra's Executive Chef now, while Ndidi Zikora was the *Chef de Cuisine*, actually running the kitchen and training new women how to cook like she and Daniel did, using mostly Daniel's original recipes plus things culled from every cookbook he had obsessively acquired while they were still in human space.

The adventures had carried him far beyond the regions the Sept Empire claimed, or the Free Worlds beyond that.

Beyond even that swath of savagely damaged worlds that were still known as K'bari space, even though the K'bari themselves were no longer a stellar civilization. At least on those few worlds where they had survived at all.

Well closer to the galactic core, Kathra's Mbaysey Tribal Squadron had located the Anndaing, bipedal hammerhead sharks who possessed the most advanced technology in the region.

Fierce merchants who carefully hid the terrible secret of what dangerous warriors they could turn themselves into if threatened. When the rare *Call to Armada* led them to assemble fleets of thousands of small ships, like terriers ready to assault a bear.

Perhaps piranha taking on a killer whale was a better image, because the Anndaing had broken many threats, including the people who had once built this frightening warship just coming into a docking orbit with the station.

The Ovanii.

Once they had been wanderers and raiders. But no more. Their legend today might remind educated Anndaing of the human stories of the fierce Vikings that had so terrorized northwest Eurasia before industrial technology. Like the Vikings, the Ovanii had possessed a wealth of nearly-forgotten culture that Daniel was slowly bringing back, but that was not today's story.

In that distant past, the Anndaing Armada had broken the Ovanii. So utterly and permanently that only one colony of the people survived today, just barely crawling back up to their own industrial revolution after millennia of barbaric darkness, when they would not accept defeat and integration into the Anndaing Merchants Guild, the government and culture that had defeated them.

What would it be like if they finally returned to the stars after so many centuries? Did they still have legends of being great star-faring warriors? Daniel had asked Wyll Koobitz, the representative of Merchants Bank, but the reports had been ambiguous.

"You are remarkably silent today, even for you," Kathra finally broke the silence engulfing them, looking down from her incredible height and smiling.

He shrugged and looked closer, but she was only three months pregnant at this point, so nothing showed yet. Except the glow the woman seemed to exude this morning.

Daniel had never been around pregnant women, but others assured him this was normal.

Erin, Spectre Two and Kathra's second in command, had the same glow whenever Daniel saw her, tempered somewhat by the woman's innate fierceness.

But it was just the two of them, him and Kathra, right now.

"I am standing on the landing pad, back on Genarde,"

Daniel looked up at the woman. "I have just sold my restaurant to my *Chef de Cuisine* for the eleven hundred or so Sept Crowns in his wallet at the time, and walked away from everything and everyone I have ever known."

She nodded, silently, understanding.

Daniel had inherited mental abilities he could not describe or explain when the two of them had killed the terrible villain known as Urid-Varg. Kathra had been Daniel enough times, been to the very core of his soul to understand all his secrets.

She knew him better than he did, because she didn't have any of the deflections or evasions a man constructs after he turns forty and has to admit to the kind of person he has become.

All the comitatus had merged with him at one time or another, but only Kathra, Erin, and Ndidi did it regularly. A'Alhakoth, Spectre Twenty-Three had done so as well, but she saw other things in Daniel than the human women did. Things that still left him unsettled.

"The future did turn out to be more interesting than just starting another restaurant," Kathra assured him with a warm smile. "Or even opening a hot dog stand on a starport concourse somewhere."

"There are days I do not believe you, Kathra," Daniel grinned back.

But he understood her. He had been her, just as she had been him. Some days, it was difficult to tell where each of them ended. Ndidi was the same way, but Kathra had originally ordered that woman to become his confessor, and never rescinded that.

Fortunately, most of the comitatus detested the thought of a male's touch. Even Kathra had gone to the sperm banks and secretly selected the father of her child for the doctors.

She and Erin had the same man, whoever he was, but Daniel had not pried.

It would be enough that the daughters born would be sisters of the blood, as well as the soul.

"Everything must change, Daniel," Kathra noted, returning to the refrain that had been her mantra since that day, half a year ago, when a Sept warship had emerged from jump right here in this system, and come that close to killing him, but for Kathra, and more importantly, Ife.

He turned back to the ship in front of him.

The design reminded him of a horseshoe crab with the long end chopped off. Armor scales around the flat and plates across the top and bottom where a frightening number of turrets could emerge for combat.

The Ovanii had built it so long ago. The Anndaing had interred it on a different planet from its crew, stored against future need.

Kathra Omezi had bought it.

Knowing the Anndaing as he did from close contact over the last year, the fact that they had sold her the ship outright, instead of making such a deal a long-term lease, told him just how serious they took the threat of the Sept.

But then, their galaxy had changed as well. The Anndaing sectors were beyond K'bari space when seen from the perspective of humans worlds. Humans had been unknown beyond K'bari space to them as well.

Until the Cargo-6 *Koni Swift* and Trademaster Crence Miray had stumbled into the Mbaysey at a system that had no name. Just a number. A milepost in the wilderness, as it were.

"Everything must change," he agreed with a nod. "But I don't have to like it."

"You'll still be cooking, as much as Ndidi will allow it,"

Kathra grinned. "And with a larger crew, she might need you now."

They shared a laugh. Before, Kathra's comitatus had required one cook, because all two dozen of them ate communally, occasionally with a handful of crew selected by lottery once word got out about the new chef Kathra had hired.

Ndidi had cooked for the rest of the crew, until it became necessary to promote the woman to be Daniel's keeper. And his friend.

Ndidi was comitatus as well, although her glasses had kept her from ever flying a Spectre fighter ship, which used to be the measure of the comitatus warriors.

But with Kathra retiring to simply command, several other women had changed roles as well. Others had been promoted, but the comitatus as it had been was no more.

Change.

"It will not be the same," Daniel echoed. "And that will be good. But I look forward to this war ending, so that I can return to a bistro, or perhaps a brasserie somewhere, and just cook."

"That will be easy then," Kathra said.

Daniel turned back to her, waiting for the other shoe to drop.

"We just have to destroy the Sept Empire."

Indeed.

TWO

ONCE, the need to wear glasses had meant that Ndidi would never be a warrior. Never join Commander Omezi's comitatus. That the only way she would be allowed to serve aboard the great flagship *WinterStar* was by taking an apprenticeship in the kitchen.

But they had seen more in her than she had known, even then.

Ndidi studied her reflection in the mirror and pulled at the jacket she wore, still uncomfortable in so many layers and long sleeves.

But Ife had insisted that her officers dress in uniforms, rather than the simple pants and light shirts everyone wore on *SeekerStar*, where Kathra kept the temperature a balmy twenty-five degrees most of the time.

SwiftStar was kept four degrees colder. At first, Ndidi hadn't understood, but now the jacket she wore made sense. She still wore the tangerine pants of the comitatus, and the black shirt, but with a turquoise jacket over that, signifying that she was an officer aboard this vessel.

Second in command even, which made no sense to

Ndidi whatsoever, except that everyone had celebrated her when it happened.

Again, maybe they knew her better than she did.

She looked at the stranger in the mirror again, trying to see what they saw.

Twenty-four years old. Short compared to most of the women Kathra had surrounded herself with. Muscular and stocky. Blind as a slug without her glasses.

Attractive enough to the women of the comitatus and crew that she'd gone to bed with more than one of them. Even Daniel found her beautiful when she looked in his mind, but the thought of a male touching her made her skin crawl. Even a friend like Daniel.

And he had other outlets, so she didn't need to worry.

She tugged at her sleeves again and the bottom of her jacket, trying to make it lay right, but it was doing what it wanted, regardless of her ideas.

Like much of the galaxy.

Ndidi took a deep breath and shrugged.

She turned and cast one quick glance around the cabin she had been assigned. Most of the ship was empty, so there were a tremendous number of rooms available, but Ife had wanted everyone centered, with the bridge just forward and engineering just aft.

The Ovanii had carried their entire tribe in fleets of ships like this, so they had suites for more than a thousand families, and the Ovanii had been as tall as Kathra on average, so the rooms were large as well.

Her personal cabin was larger than the room she had once shared with five other girls when she was just a cook aboard *WinterStar*, before circumstances had put her in charge of the main kitchen.

Before Kathra made her comitatus.

Ndidi grimaced at how far she had come, and how far

she might fall when she finally made a mistake, but she would do the best she could until then.

She emerged into the ring hallway on the port side, exactly opposite the matching room Ife had to starboard. It wasn't really a ring, running in a loop from the aft hull around the bow and back again, but that was what they had been called on *WinterStar* and *SeekerStar*, when the one hallway connected to itself if you just walked for long enough.

These didn't but you could still walk a long ways when you wanted to. Probably why Ife had the whole crew together in as compact a space as possible.

The gravity was strange as well, without any Coriolis force working on her inner ear. *SwiftStar* didn't rotate, unlike the rest of the Tribal Squadron. It had something close enough to grav field inducers like the old Sept and Free Worlds TradeStations, but much more efficient.

And set higher, which she was still getting used to. The Ovanii lived at 1.15 gravity, rather than the lower settings humans from Tazo preferred, and even that was 1.06 compared to Earth.

For Ndidi, it meant retraining herself not to catch at a falling knife in the kitchen when she dropped something. Knives, pans, pots, mugs.

They fell just enough faster that her hands would have to be retrained, and she wasn't there yet.

Yet.

Even she knew how stubborn she was. None of the other crew were more stubborn. Didn't matter if they were comitatus, flight crew from *SeekerStar*, or new recruits picked up from the various species of Anndaing space to fill out crew slots.

Maybe that was why Kathra had promoted her.

She entered the flight deck's observation lounge as the

door slid into the wall, marveling at even the tiniest bits of technology the Ovanii had had, compared to the poverty Ndidi had grown up with. Doors with power to sense you coming and open themselves without you doing it.

Lights that came on when someone entered a dark room for the first time, although she'd nearly jumped out of her skin the first time they went dark, having seen no movement from her in so long they presumed the room was empty.

Ife was already there, smiling proudly at the space. It wasn't the massive flight deck of *SeekerStar*, or even the cramped ones they'd had on *WinterStar*. Just enough for three good pilots to put SkyCamels or Spectres in here, or a reasonable professional landing an Anndaing transport, like today.

Nobody else was here but the two of them as they watched the shuttle come to rest and the outer doors close. A long pause, and air began to fill the space.

Like *SeekerStar*, *SwiftStar* did not have the correct docking ports for an Anndaing transport. This space had been designed for what the Ovanii had classified as an assault transport, according to Daniel's research.

Ndidi was learning Ovanii, along with the Anndaing she knew and several other languages she had picked up along the way. Not all of Daniel's cookbooks had been translated yet.

"You look good," Ife smiled at her as Ndidi came to rest on her left, just like on the bridge. "And you'll do fine. Think of it as a cooking competition, against the whole rest of the crew."

"Daniel's the only competition," she said automatically.

"*Oui*," Ife's smile cranked up another notch. "And on *SwiftStar*, I am probably the only one with more experience than you."

"I'm a chef by training." Ndidi almost groaned out those words, unable to help herself.

"You are a leader," Ife's voice got serious now. "A planner. An officer. And you are comitatus. Kathra does not do that lightly. If she treats me the same now, I took two decades longer than you to prove myself to the woman. I can see you commanding this ship, one of these days soon, or perhaps the second one Kathra buys or builds."

"You're crazy, Ife," Ndidi replied.

"That is beside the point, young one," the woman said with a laugh. "It is still the truth."

Ndidi let that go. In her heart, she didn't believe, but again, everyone else did.

Kathra had moved her to the very center of things and given her specific instructions that only Ndidi could carry out, more than once.

She nodded and brought her shoulders back as Daniel emerged from the ship, into the bay, and began walking this way.

Like the two of them, he no longer wore the darker clothes of *SeekerStar*'s crew, but had on the same tangerine pants, black shirt, and turquoise jacket that she did.

Officer. Still the head chef, although Ndidi would be damned if he thought he was going to keep her out of his kitchen.

That brought a smile to her face. Daniel had refused any other responsibility than fighting the Sept with the powers of Urid-Varg. That and cooking.

But he was no longer Kathra's personal chef. Or even Ife's. He had his own staff now, but the crew of this enormous vessel was only one hundred and thirty-eight. Twenty-five of those were officers, including the three of them. Fifty-eight were human, with the majority of the rest

Anndaing that had been seconded specifically by Crence Miray and Wyll Koobitz.

Two men Ndidi had learned to trust.

They knew Daniel's secret and had kept it.

The hatch opened and Daniel joined them.

He looked about how she felt, so Ndidi smiled.

They were all being called upon to transcend themselves and take on greater responsibilities than any of them had ever imagined.

That would keep her going.

THREE

IFE HAPPENED to enter the bridge of *SwiftStar* first because both Ndidi and Daniel lagged back a step. Probably intentionally, if unspoken.

Probably unspoken. She didn't think the two of them were mentally conversing, but they'd all shared beings enough times that they were adult brother and sister, as one did once you got past the fussy years and settled into yourself.

Like the ship, her bridge was horseshoe shaped, with them entering from the base. She took her place, standing next to her command platform.

Standing.

WinterStar and *SeekerStar* had no gravity at the core, so the bridge was always in freefall and you swam between rooms, instead of walking. Latched yourself to hooks or strapped yourself into a seat whenever still.

Ndidi took up her spot on Ife's left. The Ovanii called that the shield hand, and the second in command of these vessels was thus Shield. It sounded so much nicer than First Savaran, which was the Sept term.

17

Similarly, Ife wasn't the Aspbad of this ship, even though she was. The Ovanii called that person the Speaker. She liked that title better. On her right, Ngozi Obi had joined her from *SeekerStar* as gunner, except that now her official title on *SwiftStar* was Sword.

Ife presumed that Ngozi had transferred just for the title alone. Ngozi could be like that.

Daniel took up a seat on her left in front of Ndidi, where he would be opposite the sensors officer on her right. Sensors had been Ife's old responsibility on *SeekerStar* and then *WinterStar* before that. Having to understand everything that was going on around you at all times, and where the ship would move to, had made that position a useful training ground for Ife.

Which would make the future interesting, since her current sensors officer was an Anic, one of the Anndaing client species they had brought into the modern age several centuries ago.

Acqueir Chanthraphone was an erect biped, but then so were most of the species in this part of the galaxy. She was as tall as many of the Mbaysey women, who tended to be extremely tall for humans. Acqueir, like most of her kind, was rail thin. Maybe sixty kilograms nude. Gray-blue skin marked with turquoise lines and patterns under her uniform that had seemed almost like scales from a distance.

Her eyes were all pupil, glowing a soft blue that could be seen in the dark. The Anic had no body hair save for a mohawk crest similar to Erin's, except straight instead of curly, and ranging from red to lavender.

Alien among the Mbaysey, but she could still be mistaken for human in the dark, unlike Anndaing and some of the others.

And as smart as Ndidi. Possibly one that Daniel and Kathra would have to investigate for membership in the comitatus at some point, after she had proven herself in battle with them.

Now that she had brought the other two, the entire crew were on board and at their positions. Poised in silence broken only by air hissing from overhead vents and various consoles beeping to keep people apprised of their status.

"Bring up the main screen," Ife ordered. "Forward view without subtitles. Standard magnification."

Ife's primary pilot was Stina Carte, Spectre Sixteen. Another of Kathra's comitatus that had chosen to give up a life of flying Spectres for service in a new war. She was the only *Anglo* aboard, just as Daniel was the only *Rabic*, but with Acqueir, it made the bridge team just look like a federation of species.

Stina had things moving quickly. *SwiftStar* had been in their hands for four months now, since Koobitz had brought it to Ogrorspoxu from the secret base where they had entire fleets of old Ovanii ships interned. Everyone had already been training in simulators, but then they took the ship out and pushed it. Learned what it would and wouldn't do.

Ife had only ever flown in fragile Mbaysey ships. Even *SeekerStar* was a spinning top that might break if you were too hard on it.

SwiftStar had been built as a dedicated warship by an entire species of steadfast warriors. Ife would feel good taking on an entire Sept Patrol by herself.

She studied the stars ahead of them, and the edge of Ogrorspoxu just visible as the ship orbited, with the primary station above and behind them, relative in orbit.

"Open a channel to Kathra," Ife said. "Conference mode and put her on the main screen."

Video communications. Just another mark of the former poverty of the Mbaysey, like so much else. Gravity fields everywhere. Magical doors. And seeing someone's face while you talked to her.

Ife smiled as the screen activated and the Commander was there.

Ife could see the transformation that had already taken place in the woman, after just a few months. The glow. It was unlikely that they would return in time for the birth of the next Commander, but the future of the Mbaysey would be assured.

SwiftStar was just the sword reaching out to teach the Sept better manners. Ife would need a whole squadron of such ships as this, the tiny Dueler-class vessels that were already massive. She would need Assailants, and maybe even one of the remaining Battlemasters, if she was truly going to carry out Kathra's dream and actually break the Sept.

Ife's dream, as well. And that of all the rest of the women who had ever lived on Tazo. Who had grandmothers and aunts still marked with the barcode tattoo that had meant they had once been property of a Sept lord.

Kathra seemed to be studying them for a long moment. Committing faces to memory, perhaps, if they failed to return home.

Ife was not possessed of such doubts, but her job was to bring this team to safety.

And blow up Sept shipping.

"Range deep and deadly," Kathra began. "Even the Free Worlds has not yet been moved to resistance, but they have spent decades denying this day. Without us, their time will come, and come quickly, so you will be my sword and my shield. The Sept must finally be taught to know fear. To understand it deep in their souls where it gnaws at them in the quiet darkness. You cannot stop a Septagon by facing one, but you can cut his throat from behind. Do that, and then return. I will prepare them for war here."

The line cut at the far end and the screen returned to stars. Ife felt her heart surge hard and loud at those words.

"Stina," she croaked, pausing to swallow past a dry tongue. "Break us out of orbit. All ahead full."

"Executing," Stina replied, equally shaky in her tones.

It had come down to this.

The Mbaysey were finally sailing out for war.

FOUR

Kathra was standing on the bridge of *SeekerStar*, supervising things when they came out of jump in the Kanus system. Obioma was still merely piloting. However, when Kathra wasn't around Obioma had moved up to something like the command position Ife had mostly held.

They were all growing into new roles. The Commander wasn't going to be flying her Spectre into battle anymore, and Obioma was going to become *SeekerStar*'s Speaker one of these days.

The woman was good, else she wouldn't be here, but Ife had run things before this.

Thus are we all growing up.

Kanus had not changed in the two months Kathra had been gone this time. Nor would it with A'Alhakoth acting as her representative, dealing with any problems that might come up. Another woman growing into a role, and doing it well.

The Tribal Squadron was currently off harvesting from one of the nearby uninhabited neighbor systems that had largely sheltered Kanus for so long. With no other inhabited world nearby, the Anndaing had marked a large region of space off-limits for the longest time, only admitting the Kaniea to stellar civilization two hundred years ago when the Merchants Bank felt they were finally advanced enough.

"We have arrived," Obioma announced in a flat voice.

Kathra grinned at the older woman. Like Ife, it was a polite way of telling her Commander that she knew what she was doing and could the woman please go away?

"Contact the station and let them know we're coming over," Kathra said as she unbuckled and thrust off toward the rear entryway. "And tell Erin as well."

"Will do," Obioma called after her, but Kathra was already moving.

Her center of gravity had not changed yet, but she could just imagine herself and Erin navigating zero gravity while heavily gravid with their daughters. Someone would no doubt record the whole thing and use it to embarrass them later.

Probably turn the two of them into training videos for newbies.

Kathra made a note to keep up her yoga and weight training as long as she could into this pregnancy, just so Erin looked sillier on the day somebody finally ambushed them with cameras. She was the Commander, after all.

She rode down to gravity on the lift, contemplating a future date when she didn't need to necessarily live on a ship that used simple physics for gravity. When poverty wasn't the single most important defining characteristic of the Mbaysey.

Already, they were wealthier than they had ever been, the result of being able to charge premium prices for exotic foods from human lands. Eventually that would even out as Kaniea learned how to make similar things to what the ClanStars produced, as well as started importing raw materials and seeds from the Free Worlds, but Kathra knew those sharp old women in charge. They would treat every chicken like an industrial secret to be guarded with one's life.

Every bottle of beer would be fined down twice now, just so nobody could get their hands on the specific yeasts necessary to replicate the flavor.

Every little bit to keep that profit margin up for one day longer.

At the same time, *IronStar* and *ForgeStar* would continue doing what they did. Gas giants and asteroid fields were always good for exotic materials that could be traded, and the iron and nickel that made up most of space would be used for ship repairs or traded to stations in ingots.

That trade instinct had gotten them off Tazo originally. Out of the Sept Empire. Out of Free Worlds space. Maybe out of the Anndaing Merchants Guild space at some future date. She just needed enough money to fit out a new *FactoryStar*, the kind that could manufacture the sorts of advanced electronics that she could no longer replace at a TradeStation.

Then she might never need another planet for the rest of her life.

Erin met her down on the flight deck, perhaps looking a little extra fierce today, since they had been the ones left behind while others went out to fight.

That had always been the definition of the comitatus, but not anymore. Kathra had promised the old women that she would out-live them all. Erin had always promised to have a sister for Kathra's child.

The comitatus would have to adapt.

Yagazie's dream would live on into the next generation, even if that meant that fierce children like her and Erin had to turn into mothers, safely back from the fighting that others would do in her name.

Kathra studied her oldest friend in the galaxy. Saw the grin under that fierce glower.

Erinkansilemi Uduik. *Erin.*

Lighter skinned than most, the result of the slaver blood that ran in her veins that she proclaimed to the entire universe with the tattoo on her cheek. Grandmother Ezinne's mark, reproduced exactly.

Not that Erin would ever be the property of a Sept nobleman, but they would recognize that mark on her before she killed them.

The mohawk had been trimmed in the last day or two, cut so precise that it looked like a hat the woman wore. The sides weren't shorn, but had speed lines shaved into the tight buzz. Kathra agreed with Erin that it added to her fierceness.

The mechanical leg, from the replacement knee down. The Anndaing had offered her a cybernetic replacement, but Erin had rejected that out of hand. She had grown accustomed to the replacement and had no interest in being off her feet even the week that healing would take. To say nothing of having to learn to walk again.

Plus, like Kathra, the woman had grown up poor. Economy was as deeply ground into Erin as Kathra, and the need to come back for tuning, replacements, or upgrades tied her to Anndaing space, when *SeekerStar's* machine shops would do just as good a job with the current version.

Erin smiled as Kathra crossed the space to where Spectre Two was lined up next to Spectre One for emergency combat launch, even here at Kanus.

But they'd thought they'd be safe at Ogrorspoxu, too.

"So how hard will it be to add a cradle instead of the front gunner's seat?" Erin asked as Kathra got close. "Not like we have missiles to throw at someone, so we don't ever use it."

Kathra laughed. Erin wasn't going to give up the combat

flying without a direct order. And even then not until Kathra did.

"We're supposed to be respectable matrons now, you goof," Kathra replied, walking right up and hugging the woman. She'd always been focused on being The Commander before, and it was only now that she could just be a person.

The Kaniea and the Anndaing still expected it of her, but that was a cloak she could put on when she docked at the station.

"You first," Erin laughed as they broke and headed for their flight ladders.

Both Spectres were docked for launch. Attached to the outside of the third rim, where the spin of the ship itself would hurl them into space as they disconnected and lit their engines.

Kathra opened the top hatch and climbed down the ladder to the compact interior. A Spectre was a two-woman ship, with a small head and kitchenette aft, for longer patrols. The front seat, where a missile and electronic warfare specialist would sit, was almost never used, except when one of the women was ferrying someone between ships.

On Spectre One, only Daniel ever joined her.

But replacing the seat with a cradle for an infant was silly.

Maybe a booster when her daughter got older and could understand the sights out the cockpit window…

"Spectre One, ready to launch," Kathra called on the line as she finished her pre-flight.

"Spectre Two, ready to launch," Erin echoed a moment later.

"Both craft, you are clear for flight," Obioma replied. "Launch in twenty-four seconds and you will be aimed at the station itself."

Kathra waited, and then fired everything. Sure enough, the station appeared around the rim of the hub as she jumped forward and out, Erin right behind her and sliding off to one side.

Kathra checked her scanners for any ship with a blue-shift. Obioma no doubt had all guns unlocked as well, remembering just how easily another *SeptStar* could sneak into Kanus space and attack.

It only took one lucky shot, same as they had done to Yagazie.

Kanus flight control might have had the same thoughts, because they seemed to have cleared nearby space as well, leaving a bubble of emptiness around *SeekerStar*.

"Spectre One, this is Spectre Twenty-Three," a friendly voice came over the line, speaking in Spacer rather than Anndaing or Kaniea. "Docking vectors have been assigned and transmitted."

A'Alhakoth ver'Shingi. The first Kaniea, the first true alien to join the Mbaysey, although others had since followed. The only one in the comitatus.

So far.

And Kathra's Ambassador to A'Alhakoth's own homeworld.

Normally, A'Alhakoth should be on the ground, staying at the estate of her parents, so Kathra was surprised to find her in orbit. But she'd also been gone for two months, and left A'Alhakoth in charge in her absence.

Hopefully, the latest news was good.

FIVE

A'Alhakoth was Kaniea. The planet below her had birthed her originally, but she no longer considered it her home.

Kanus was just a place now.

It still felt weird admitting that to herself, even after being here for a year now, but she had changed when she went up and out, beyond all known space to the place where she met Erin and Daniel.

She told herself that she would not miss the man when he went off to war. That was a lie, but not a bad one, as they were both comitatus. Both sworn life and soul to Kathra Omezi and the dream of the Mbaysey.

But she would have liked to have gone with *SwiftStar*.

Kathra knew that. Knew everything, as they had become one with Daniel's help on more than one occasion, so that A'Alhakoth knew what the Commander needed her to do here in her absence.

As the junior-most member of the comitatus, Kathra had still put her in charge.

The Mbaysey's Ambassador to the Anndaing Merchants

Guild, from their own representative here on Kanus. She doubted that Morgan Wilzae had ever expected to be important.

An assignment to Kanus as trademaster had been something of a posting in the boonies for the old shark. A place where career bureaucrats were sent after a lifetime of service as a reward, rather than an important banker from Ogrorspoxu drawing the short straw.

But Kathra had put her foot down resolutely enough that even the Anndaing had not argued.

Kathra's embassy would be at Kanus, and nowhere else. Her Ambassador would be A'Alhakoth ver'Shingi. Theirs would continue to be Morgan Wilzae until his normal retirement date, still a year in the future.

That the sharks at the capital had agreed told A'Alhakoth just how important they considered the humans to be.

And now Kathra was back.

A'Alhakoth had been up on the station when she'd been expecting them, because there was news to be shared, and not necessarily shared even down on the planet.

The station was easier to secure. That might be important.

Morgan met her in the conference room closest to the docking station where Kathra and Erin were arriving shortly. He looked more gray than normal, even for a shark, but that was only partly due to his age.

As Anndaing went, he was something of an elder statesman, thrust into the role of a lifetime by the chance of Kanus becoming one of the fronts in a war very few people knew about.

At least so far.

A'Alhakoth had no doubts that it would change soon, but Kathra had tasked her with being smarter than everyone else. None of the comitatus warriors Kathra had left her with knew Kaniea culture well enough to read between the lines.

And A'Alhakoth had not had enough time to recruit spies from her own people.

She looked around the chamber. Small and homey. Businesslike, only in the sense that both Anndaing and Kaniea expected a meeting room to remind everyone of a salon, rather than something like the human office Kathra maintained.

Nice carpet on the floors. Pseudo-wood paneling on the walls, with several landscape paintings. A side table for tea, coffee, or arl, depending on one's needs and preferences.

This room could be equipped with a table, had they been sharing a meal, but A'Alhakoth knew that Kathra would prefer to meet first, and then share in a larger meal with important locals and any comitatus that were on station.

And A'Alhakoth had specifically left Kam, Nkechi, and Obi out of this loop, much as it pained her. Not because they could not be trusted, but because they were being watched.

Nobody should have realized A'Alhakoth was here until they heard her voice on the radio, and even then they might not understand.

So she took one chair and put Morgan across from her. Kathra and Erin got shown in by a steward from the ver'Shingi estate who had served her father for a decade before even A'Alhakoth's oldest brother had been born, so the man could be trusted to keep his mouth shut.

Kathra looked once around and settled her eyes on A'Alhakoth.

Erin was in combat mode already, but it was unnecessary.

Should be unnecessary, at least today.

"Please, Kathra, sit," A'Alhakoth said, gesturing to the two chairs. "I might simply be paranoid and everything turns out to be nothing."

Erin grunted and took one of the side seats, with Kathra across from her. Morgan had his back to the only door, but he was the only one unarmed right now, anyway. And the only male.

Kathra came to rest, but did not relax.

She watched instead.

"Anndaing space is generally on our side," A'Alhakoth began, looking for the right words to convey the flavor she needed, across her fifth or sixth language. This needed to be said in Spacer, not Anndaing. Morgan could follow along well enough now.

"But?" Erin asked, eyes on the door and the Anndaing ambassador equally.

"I have spent a great deal of time around the Se'uh'pal," A'Alhakoth explained. "Traveling away from Kanus originally as their guest and then as a worker on a second vessel later. I have a rather low opinion of them as a culture, but partly that might be being Kaniea raised around Anndaing."

"What have they done?" Kathra asked.

"They have done nothing, as yet," A'Alhakoth said. "But Crence Miray and *Koni Swift* have broken the long monopoly that Se'uh'pal hulls had on trade farther out on the rim from Anndaing space. And forced them to change their runs, so that they no longer skirt wide around the long gap that everyone calls K'bari space and through the Bhaorajj."

"I imagine that has irritated any number of captains," Kathra chuckled. "They do not like having healthy competition."

"Just so," A'Alhakoth said. "Moreso, because now other Anndaing ships have started making long fast runs, mostly to Thrabo and Tavle Jocia, but you did sell the Merchants Guild a complete and rather detailed map of the Free Worlds. Our shark friends have made inroads in at least two dozen systems, while the Se'uh'pal are only now adapting."

"How did they used to make those runs?" Erin asked, relaxing a little as she assumed that no assassins were imminent.

"Through Grishn space and then across that gulf to Bhaorajj worlds before heading outwards to the Free Worlds," A'Alhakoth said. "That was the path I traveled originally, meeting aliens even weirder than Anndaing."

How else to describe the Bhaorajj? Creatures like centaurs of legend, but made of a spider body, with an upright torso emerging from an abdomen with six legs, the whole covered in feathers rather than fur, for reasons she had never learned. Stolid folks for the most part, they fit in well with the utterly amoral Se'uh'pal, trading both directions with general disdain for everyone else.

That was part of the reason that humans had never made it as far as Anndaing space in any great numbers.

"So what is the problem today?" Kathra asked, growing serious.

"Ugly rumblings, but nothing I have been able to isolate," A'Alhakoth said. "However, I do believe that you should curtail some of your public activities, at least for a time. Someone only has to get lucky once, and if they have no wish to live afterwards, they will take stupid risks."

"The Se'uh'pal are not inclined to suicidal activities," Kathra pointed out. Both Erin and Morgan nodded.

"True, but you have met my brother Goli," A'Alhakoth. "Once. Before he took my father up on the offer and retired to something like a communal monastery in the mountains. There are many others like him in this system. Goli's zealotry leads him to isolation, but others may not be so circumspect."

"Why do humans trigger such outrage?" Erin asked. "The Anndaing have been here for two centuries."

"Very few of them live on the surface, Erin," A'Alhakoth replied. "And then mostly in the large cities, where they are engaged in trade. Humans, and the Mbaysey, threaten a much more visceral change to Kaniea culture."

"Comitatus," Kathra said the word aloud as if that summed up everything.

In a way, it did. A'Alhakoth nodded.

"You have told the men that they aren't good enough to even be considered warriors in your new world," A'Alhakoth confirmed. "While also challenging the women to want more than just a happy marriage and family, perhaps with a job for a few years before the children arrive, or after the youngest are adults."

"Daughters will ask their fathers or brothers *why not?*" Kathra smiled savagely.

"Indeed," A'Alhakoth. "Not all of those men will be as open minded as Linga ver'Shingi was, with a youngest daughter of six children who could want for more from her life. For those of a lower social class, the cultural threat is even greater, because Kaniea culture retains the trappings of aristocracy."

"And humans are enough like Kaniea to represent a dream any daughter could aspire to," Kathra concluded the thought. "Or a threat to any son."

"Exactly," Morgan spoke up now, showing his colors. "We have heard rumblings of discontent, but they hide from any direct search."

"What would you have me do?" Kathra demanded in a polite voice.

"Exercise care, Commander," Morgan replied. "Nothing more. By now *SeptStar* has made it home and imperial agents and provocateurs have begun to be detected in numbers at places like Thrabo and Tavle Jocia. My own diplomatic messages have passed along such hints of intrigue, with them aimed at Ogrorspoxu and Kanus. The capital is not at risk, as my people still have volumes of lessons we could teach the Se'uh'pal on intrigue, but the Kaniea are..."

"More backward?" A'Alhakoth suggested when the elder diplomat faltered.

"I would not wish to give offense," he backpedaled.

"I would rather have the truth," A'Alhakoth said, almost in perfect harmony with Kathra saying the same thing.

They glanced at each other. Kathra smiled warmly and A'Alhakoth blushed. She nodded to the Commander.

Kathra turned her attention to Morgan.

"Would the defenses here at Kanus be sufficient for an attack by a *SeptStar*, or perhaps a squadron of such vessels?" she asked. "My forces have by now crossed the K'bari Reaches and begun to explore the dark corners of Free Worlds space for the place from which *SeptStar* crept. And that ship was specifically built by someone intimately familiar with *SeekerStar* and *The Haunt*."

"I do not know, Commander," the man admitted. "Our fear in the past has always been piracy. Such things are rare, because a pirate would have to face the combined wrath of the Merchants Guild, so few will risk it. But outsiders will not be bound by our standards. Especially if they see the war as a cultural affair, and not merely an economic one."

Kathra fell silent. A'Alhakoth nodded grimly as the woman thought. All of this had come up in just the last few weeks, so perhaps nothing was advanced enough to be a threat.

But her brother Goli was just one such example of the risks Kathra faced. And the Se'uh'pal. And the Sept.

A'Alhakoth had no good answers for her Commander.

Kathra surprised her by smiling.

"Perhaps it is time Alla learned a few valuable lessons," she said.

"Alla?" A'Alhakoth asked. "My eldest brother?"

"Yes," Kathra said. "Let us summon him, and I will make him an offer he can't refuse."

SIX

Daniel had spent much of his time over the last few months wondering how the Ishtan had found him. Nominally, that was an academic question, since the last four survivors of that terrible species had finally been killed.

But they had not vanished.

Before dying, they had been mentally joined with a Sept aspbad named Hadi Rostami. The same who had been aboard Septagon *Vorgash* before. Daniel had recognized his signature.

Before, the man had been a background flavor in the greater mélange that had been Septagon *Vorgash*. A soft lemon sorbet next to the brighter tastes and textures that had been the naupati, a creature he knew as Amarin Pasdar. That one had been a jalapeño stuffed with pepperjack cheese and a spicy cream sauce poured over the top.

Rostami had survived the battle. Worse, he had been changed by the Ishtan beforehand. Before they died and somehow flooded the man's mind with their own energy.

Now his signature across the light-centuries was like a flourless chocolate torte, with a smooth transition of tastes that somehow ran laterally through so many different textures, from the crust to the mousse atop.

Rostami had fled the battle at Ogrorspoxu, and Daniel had been an hour recovering from the terrible migraine induced by the death screams of the semi-immortal Ishtan.

Rostami might be his equal for mental power. It was hard to say. Daniel had been greatly reduced in power by the destruction of the Star Turtle. Again, by *Vorgash* and Rostami.

And even at his greatest, Daniel had been no match for Urid-Varg. Nor had the Ishtan, which was why they had spent thousands of years stalking the creature and perhaps aiding his enemies when such folk finally grew tired of worshiping such a terrible god.

SwiftStar sat in the darkness deep between systems. Most people were uncomfortable to not be close to a star. Better to be right near orbit of some inhabitable planet with which you could share news and humanity.

The Mbaysey lifestyle had begun to rub off on him.

The ship was dead silent. Not for any particular reason other than it was late in the day and much of the crew kept to normal hours.

SwiftStar drifted in the darkness, a great panther idly waiting by a game trail for prey to wander by.

Daniel listened to the song of the stars themselves, since there were no human minds close enough to even detect the buzz of their conversation.

But Rostami was out there somewhere. A year had passed, so he should have made it back to his Sept masters by now and been sorted out.

What would they make of him? Or would he tell anyone the terrible secret he bore?

Daniel understood the left hand of evil. Rejected it outright, which was why Kathra Omezi and her comitatus had not put him to death. Why they watched him like hawks still.

Rostami had the ability now, too.

Daniel considered what a high Sept officer might do with such power.

With the sort of power they both had, you could just shut a woman's mind down while you ravaged her body. Or leave her awake as a passive witness, screaming silently in her mind but trapped in her flesh and unable to fight back. When that got boring, the touch made it possible to make her participate with an outward appearance of willingness.

And if you were really a rapist, you could truly make her enjoy it.

Finally, you could make her dependent on it.

Evil, simple as that.

Rostami would not have the ability to speak so many lost languages. Nor the ancient memories stretching back some twelve thousand years.

But he could still twist minds as he needed.

As he desired.

A sound caused Daniel to glance up from his inward ruminations.

Acqueir, the Sensors officer.

Alien, but friendly.

Anic, which made her a biped easily mistaken for a skinny human.

Daniel had dated his share of fashion models back on Genarde, when he was younger and famous.

They were birds of a similar feather.

But the models never had eyes that glowed quietly in the dark.

The bridge lights had been turned down some, with most of the crew off shift and the ship at rest.

Acqueir took up her station, almost opposite from the

place he normally sat, and began checking things. He didn't think she was due on duty, but hadn't bothered memorizing the duty roster. Except as he needed to cook, but even then, he had a handful of excellent assistants now.

None of them as good as Ndidi, but probably all better than Ebube, most of the time. And even that wasn't entirely fair. She wasn't a bad chef. She just worked directly off of a recipe, without ever stretching herself beyond it and finding art.

Daniel realized that he and Acqueir were alone on the bridge. He wondered if that was accident, circumstance, or something else, but didn't bother reaching out with his mind to listen to her emotions.

He could do that, and did when he thought it was necessary. Just smell the dreams and fears someone gave off if they weren't focused on mental silence.

Sounded like too much work today.

Acqueir turned to him as he looked at her.

It was hard determining where those eyes were actually focused, since they were just glowing, sky-blue orbs, but he felt the impact. That cute, upturned nose was aimed at him like a weapon, and the pointed tips of her ears were horizontal and reminded Daniel of a primitive sensor array beaming signals outward. Her mohawk was fuchsia and needed to be cut, as it flopped over and almost touched one ear now.

She had gray skin with interesting lines in it that always looked like varicose veins. With her build, she should have had spots like a giraffe, but he kept that thought to himself.

"What do you see, out there?" she asked simply.

Not many women, and far fewer men, knew his secrets. But Ife had insisted that her officers be brought in from the cold.

That included Acqueir.

"Right now, nothing," Daniel gestured outward with both hands. "We are too far away for minds to even be a sound in the background."

"Then what are you listening for?" she continued. "Or to?"

"The stars themselves talk," Daniel said. "Solar wind intersecting with galactic wind, so at times it can be almost like standing on the shore listening to the waves."

She paused. Cocked her head just the slightest bit, like she didn't believe him and was trying to see through whatever fables he was spinning.

Daniel had never merged with this woman.

It had not been necessary. Might never be, but that was not his decision to make. Both Ndidi and Ife knew the truth, and could order him to do a great many things, if they thought it essential.

Daniel was just a tool.

And a chef.

"And when we get closer?" she asked.

"There is one person I seek," Daniel said. "The distance is enormous, and my skills still raw, but somewhere out there is the human known as Hadi Rostami."

"The other one like you," she nodded to herself.

"Perhaps," Daniel deflected her words. "We share a similarity in capability, but not in temperament. He would have already turned himself into a god by now."

"And you will not," she declared in a tone with some level of reserve.

But she didn't know the truth with the intimacy of the comitatus.

Of the Commander. Or her command officers. Women like Erin, Ife, Ndidi, or A'Alhakoth.

He caught himself wistful at the last name.

A'Alhakoth was still too young as yet, barely an adult by

Kaniea standards, so he felt like a dirty, old man, watching her. He was aware that she did not feel the same way, but they had never acted on that earlier conversation.

Perhaps circumstances had kept them separate. Perhaps Kathra needed him focused on a more important task for a time.

Certainly, none but him could stop Rostami. The others might be lucky enough to kill the man. And they might not.

Well, Iruoma would not succumb easily, but the others weren't nearly as stubborn.

"I will not become a god," Daniel repeated the line.

Everyone who knew of his power secretly had that fear. Or the greed.

Women could not grasp this power, masculine as it was. Kathra had convinced the Anndaing that it was a human thing, so they would eventually seek a human they could suborn.

Or not. How did you trust that you could continue to control someone after you have made him a god?

"Are you pair-bonded?" Acqueir asked suddenly, her eyes seeming to take on a brighter glow than he had seen before.

Daniel had to think back and translate the term in his head. That wasn't easy when you spoke so many languages.

Married. But far more than that. Anic pair-bonded at a deep level. Mental, emotional, even physical to a certain extent.

"I am not," he replied.

Anic were close enough to human in shape and overall biology. He had studied her through that lens more than once, but a male on an Mbaysey ship was subordinate to any woman, regardless of her rank.

And *SwiftStar* was an Mbaysey vessel. Acqueir Chanthraphone was an Mbaysey warrior, for all that she was Anic.

"You have not had relations with any woman on this vessel," she stated with the sort of certainty that told Daniel she had also been paying close attention.

"Most Mbaysey do not enjoy the touch of a male," Daniel shrugged.

A few experimented with such perversions, as they saw it, but Areen was not here, and he had never found a polite way to break through to Yejide that he knew her dark secret. Nor had any of the other women, which surprised Daniel. He had expected one of them to take the warrior aside and tell her.

Maybe they had, and she had just never taken that one step forward.

Daniel would have welcomed her, but it was not his place to speak.

And A'Alhakoth had not joined *SwiftStar*.

Daniel wondered if Acqueir was going to proposition him now. It was her prerogative, not his.

Instead, she just nodded and turned her attention back to her screen, as if the question was entirely academic.

It might be. He chose not to impose his mind upon her space to discover otherwise.

Not his place.

Instead, Daniel reached out to the stars around him, seeking Rhages in the immense distance.

SEVEN

Hadi sat and wondered, studying the man seated across the table from him almost as much as he did the world around him. They were on Rhages. Imperial capital of the Sept. He and Amirin Pasdar, the famous naupati, were having tea, on a balcony overlooking a view in paradise.

More Earth-like than Earth itself was how Rhages was billed, an Eden as the ancients might have known it, before millennia of industrialization had permanently damaged the homeworld.

Hadi was unsure how true that line might be, but he did know that Rhages had intentionally been kept pure from the very beginning of colonization. Looking around, he could smell a cleanness in the air that was not there on Earth, regardless of where he had previously looked.

The sky overhead was a sharper blue than he could imagine an ancient Earth having.

Even the Imperial government did not intrude on the planet itself, mostly being kept on the great moon overhead that had reminded early explorers of Luna when they found the place.

That dull cinder of a moon was covered over with domes now. Bureaucrats who were sufficiently important were brought there from all over the empire, before the most important ones finally earned themselves a place on the luscious, green planet below.

As a mere aspbad, Hadi Rostami would not have been brought here. In his failure to destroy either Kathra Omezi or Daniel Lémieux, he should have been kept at a great distance.

Possibly exiled, or at least shunned.

But he had successfully navigated his way back to Amirin Pasdar, himself in a sort of genteel exile at one of the family palaces at the imperial capital.

After all, the Pasdar were one of the Seven Clans, the very *Sept* themselves that had given the empire its seven-fold name, as they had exploded out of the Persian Highlands on Earth centuries ago and taken the whole world, en route to conquering more than half of human space.

The other half still lay waiting.

But Hadi knew the mind of Amirin Pasdar, seated across from him now in his own quiet meditation as they both enjoyed the pleasant view. Had known the man well, even before his mind lay open before Hadi like a book on a nearby table.

Vorgash had destroyed the Star Turtle while they commanded it, even if Kathra Omezi had escaped them. Her terrible allies were no more, leaving just her to hunt down now. That Amirin had commissioned a warship to continue to harry her deep into the galactic interior showed initiative on his part, especially as he had returned to Sept space with all the details instead of abandoning his command to set off with a harpoon in one gnarled hand.

It became Rostami's mission after that. His failure, none of which could be laid at Pasdar's feet.

Casualties on *SeptStar*'s flight to imperial space after the battle had been terrible. Many men had later succumbed to the implacable, mental assault of those Ishtan monsters. Five men had died directly during climax of the battle itself. Seven more had chosen suicide later. Certainly they had taken their own lives, without the assistance of an aspbad who had a terrible secret to hide.

At least the final report showed such as the cause of death.

No man alive could gainsay such a finding, with the exception of a rebel cook hiding deep in alien space.

Hadi studied the balcony onto which servants had previously conducted him before leaving them to what they thought was probably a fiction of solitude, with so many servants bustling about. It was a semi-enclosed arcade of the ancient style, perched elegantly on a cliff-side, with nearly two thousand meters of tumbling hillside drop visible beyond the rail, down to a river flowing heartily to the sea.

The weather was spring-like at this latitude, with a few scudding clouds and a hint of green crispness to the breeze that reminded Hadi of a home he couldn't actually remember.

Cultural home, maybe. That place where Sept itself had been born.

The ancient paradise in the Persian Highlands.

Hadi sipped at cool water cut with lemon juice. Across the small table, Amirin did the same. They had remained silent thus for several minutes after Hadi had been admitted.

Unspoken between them was the assumption, at least on Amirin's part, that the servants who bustled around them were not to be trusted, reporting to their own masters every hint of suspicion.

Hadi smiled.

They would only report what he would allow. That much

control he had acquired as his ruined ship had limped home. Hadi had learned to destroy minds and men around him to keep his secret.

Everything had been blamed on the Ishtan.

As it should.

"I do not understand how it is that you were allowed to see me without minders," Amirin finally murmured in a low voice as he looked around and noticed that they were alone.

Hadi took a look as well and reached out with his mind, his new powers, making sure that the servants found a reason to remain busy back in the suite itself for a few minutes, leaving the two of them alone on the patio with the breathtaking overlook.

"You have met the Ishtan," Hadi replied evasively, listening to the way his words drifted quietly away on the warm breeze.

Amirin studied him now, perhaps seeing something that he had missed earlier.

"You say they are destroyed in the official reports," Amirin emphasized the last few words.

"They were," Hadi agreed. "Before that, they did things to me to help ensure that I could continue your quest after they had destroyed the cook."

"What things?" Amirin's voice grew hoarse with suppressed emotion.

"They made me over into them," Hadi said. "In certain ways."

He had finally learned to control it, at a certain cost to other minds around him. Hadi reached out now to his naupati and grasped the man's mind. Perhaps his soul.

In a blink, they were standing on the Command Node of Septagon *Vorgash*, high in orbit of Tavle Jocia, except that it was all an illusion.

"What is this?" the naupati roared in surprise.

"A place where we can talk without listeners," Hadi replied calmly.

They were back in their formal uniforms as well, instead of the casual robes of the extended palace. That alone marked this as mere façade.

Amirin walked to the front of the space and reached out a hand to touch the transparent portal. Hadi followed, standing close as the man spun back to him with a harsh, calculating look.

"They have made you Ishtan," Amirin accused him.

"A lesser one, perhaps," Hadi agreed. "They gave me powers similar to what the chef has, so that we could continue chasing the rest of the Mbaysey when the Ishtan were done with us, done with their task."

"Then how was *SeptStar* so badly damaged?" Amirin asked. "I have seen the official reports. Are the aliens that much more advanced?"

"They are in some ways, and not in others," Hadi shrugged with his mental body. "*Vorgash* would be as irresistible there as anywhere, but a Patrol would be at risk. I have come to you to talk about the future, Amirin. Our future as the Sept."

"We must destroy Omezi," the man rasped heavily. "And whatever allies she seeks."

"Indeed," Hadi agreed. "But I had many conversations with the Ishtan, both before they altered me, as well as after."

"Conversations?" Amirin asked, turning now to focus his will on the man who had been his aspbad, his chosen command officer to oversee that tremendous killing machine known to the galaxy as *Vorgash*.

"They were immortal, Amirin," Hadi said.

Here, in the privacy of his mind, he felt comfortable talking to the man as something of a peer. Amirin Pasdar was a naupati. In his youth also a highly decorated Sardar, a ground commander of an elite combat unit.

And he was Pasdar of the Pasdar themselves. A power within the Sept.

But he was merely human. Hadi Rostami was something else, at least for another five or so years, depending on what the aliens had said.

He didn't know if he yet trusted a scientist to try to understand what had been done, with the idea of extending it, or replicating it in another.

Was the galaxy prepared for humans with such psionic powers?

"Immortal, yes," Amirin agreed. "I spoke with them at some length of their great quest over the millennia."

"And I spoke to them of the future," Hadi countered. "To them, the Sept Empire was a single grain of sand, pushed up onto a beach for a time, before some future storm washed it back out to sea."

Amirin paused to study him. Naupati Pasdar had chosen Hadi specifically for his bureaucratic and scholarly background, providing the sorts of administrative backbone that kept *Vorgash* running at the highest level for so long. Without him, systems had begun to return to merely impressive.

That had made Hadi smile.

"How long does the Empire have?" Amirin asked, finally understanding the image of timelessness.

Perhaps he had spoken of similar things with those deathless, pink snakes in his own time.

"A few centuries, at most." Hadi relayed the image that the Ishtan had planted in his mind, a great and complicated ideogram that somehow managed to sum up the entirety of the Sept Empire in a few, simple strokes of a brush. "After that, chaos returns and drags them back down."

"But?" Amirin asked, hearing the catch in Hadi's voice.

"When they altered me, they gave me other options," Hadi said. "I can reach into another man's mind and change it, Amirin. Even now, your servants have all found ways to keep themselves busy, each certain that someone else has us under close observation and they can relax."

"Any man?" Amirin asked, voice aghast.

But he had been part of the Ishtan mind. Pasdar knew the truth.

"If I am close enough to them, yes," Hadi said. "That allowed me to get here, when various bureaucrats might have perhaps said no. I simply demanded the chance to make my case in person, each of those times, and as an aspbad, it was granted. Once I was in front of a particular bureaucrat that had the power, I simply reached into their mind and changed it."

"Why are you telling me this?" Amirin's eyes grew big. Then narrowed with devious intent.

"Because the Ishtan also said that you were highly likely to attempt to make yourself emperor, given time and circumstances," Hadi said. "And likely to succeed. I have seen it. They saw it in you, and then in my memories when we became one being."

"One being?"

"I am Ishtan in human form now, Amirin," Hadi finally admitted. "We were one when their physical forms were destroyed by Ram Cannon fire, so I absorbed that surge of energy representing their deaths. I am not sure, but they may have even found ways to embed themselves in me for as long as I live, or at least as long as I retain this power."

"It will fade?"

"So they assured me at the time, that after no longer than seven years I would return to what I had been before," Hadi said. "But that was before they died. I do not know how long I—we—have now."

"So they gave you the power, knowing that you might return and try to stop me from conquering the Sept?" Amirin's eyes took on a dangerous hue, the one that reminded Hadi of how the man got that terrible scar on his forehead and back across his shaved skull, when a rebel's blade had just missed his eye socket.

"They gave me the power knowing that I might return and assist you in overthrowing the Sept, Amirin," Hadi said, relaxing and opening his arms.

In this mental space, the naupati could not injure him. But he needed the man calm enough to make rational choices.

Hadi wasn't sure he was even sane any more, at least by human standards. Or that Amirin Pasdar was, either.

"Could we overthrow Sept?" Naupati Pasdar asked in the sort of command voice for which he was known.

"We could, quite easily," Hadi said.

"But?"

"They could not predict the outcome," Hadi continued. "On the one hand the Empire is already doomed to fall in a few centuries. Your success might push that off as much as another thousand years."

"Or?"

"Or we might bring the entire thing down around our ears," Hadi heard himself say. "That was the price we would have to pay, for the power they would put in our hands."

EIGHT

She had annihilated asteroids. Melted comets. Even blown up small moons in otherwise uninhabited solar systems.

But she had never actually killed anyone, on duty or even accidentally.

Ndidi knew that was going to change today.

Some cultures saw killing as a moral failing. Others saw it as the right of the strong to oppress the weak, as long as weakness was detected.

Today's killing would fall into a category that Ndidi knew was righteous. And not just because the people she would be killing were Sept.

Not all of the Sept was necessarily evil. The Mbaysey had been Sept until thirty years ago. Citizens tied to a small reservation on an unimportant planet. Mbaysey men had gone off to find jobs in factories or serve in the military, leaving the women behind to run things.

Yagazie had led them into space and left the need for men behind as well, so none of the men she was going to kill today were Mbaysey.

That wouldn't have changed one iota of her plan, but it was still good to know.

Those men were all Sept. They all deserved to die at this point.

Ndidi Zikora was simply going to be the instrument of their destruction.

She looked around the bridge. There were only two men present with her today.

Daniel, because he was Daniel.

Comitatus, in every sense of the word, even before Ndidi had joined him and the other women. And the bloodhound that had led them to this quiet solar system, uninhabited and forlorn.

The Sept had built themselves a base here. Ife had calculated the subsectors where the Sept had to have built themselves a base in order to threaten Ogrorspoxu, but Daniel had located it, listening in the darkness until he found the sound that ten thousand men made when they dreamed about conquering the universe.

The other male here was Myler Bolazt, Stina's Anndaing Assistant Pilot, occupying a secondary station across the bridge and close to Daniel, where he could take over if something happened to Stina.

He had also earned his spot on this crew, impressing Wyll and Crence, as well as Kathra and Stina.

High praise, for any man.

All the rest were women.

Mbaysey, either by birth or conscious decision.

Ife was in her command station, overseeing everything, but turned and staring at Ndidi now, her hard face inscrutable with the coming actions.

The old woman had ordered her to take command for this, saying it was time for her to strike the first blow.

Kathra and Ife had put Ndidi here.

They saw things in her that liked to hide from Ndidi in the mirror.

She took a deep breath.

"Sword, bring all your batteries to readiness," Ndidi called to Ngozi, four meters away.

"We are prepared." Ngozi had turned serious, but she had been there at Ogrorspoxu when *SeptStar* tried to kill Daniel.

And the woman had killed the last four Ishtan, giving her even bragging rights on Iruoma, as long as she didn't press too hard.

"Systems, prepare all engines and generators for red-line output on my command," Ndidi said into the open microphone feeding her words back to Tanuss Barleyne, the Chief Engineer.

That woman was a Wisp, another piscine species like the Anndaing that had become land dwellers in the ancient past. A biped with a horn like a unicorn or one of Daniel's Upynth, except that this one glowed when she was emotional. It was something like an Terran anglerfish in that, monsters that prowled the deeps with a light on the end of a tentacle, but Tanuss was almost as nerdy as Joane Obiakpani, Spectre Five, who was now her assistant.

"All systems live, Trademaster," Tanuss replied automatically over the line, forgetting in her excitement that she wasn't on an Anndaing combat merchant.

Ndidi wondered if the main engineering space was lit up by the woman alone, from the enthusiasm in her voice.

Ndidi turned her attention to Acqueir Chanthraphone, the Anic woman who had been required to impress no less than Ife herself to sit on this bridge today. "Sensors, prepare to achieve weapons lock as soon as we come out of jump."

And Ife was the expert on sensor systems.

"We will be coming out low and passing under the target

from close range, raking left to right," Ndidi reminded the woman. "We should have surprise, but that is not something we can count on."

"Locks ready to cast, Shield," Acqueir replied crisply, glancing back with those blue eyes that were so utterly cool looking.

Ndidi turned to Stina, glancing over the other way at Myler as well, just so the male knew she meant business. "Pilot, your target has been designated and confirmed."

"Confirmed," Stina said simply.

"All hands, stand by for combat." Ndidi turned and looked both ways from her station before coming to rest on Ife's smile and warm nod. She took a breath and swallowed past a tight throat. "Execute."

SwiftStar leapt out of the universe like a hound on a rabbit's trail.

NINE

Coming out of jump, Daniel was as blind as *SwiftStar*'s sensors, but he reacted faster than those ancient electronics and found the station parked exactly where he and Ife had earlier placed it.

The Sept built stations like this as arms extending outwards from a central hub. However, none of the old Mbaysey had ever lived in a part of the world that ever saw snow. Their reservation had been equatorial, just like the ancient, Central African homeland that their ancestors had known.

But that station reminded Daniel of a snowflake as he watched it come into being.

A cylindrical core with eight docking stations off of that. Each facing had an extension of some sort outward, and then a Patrol craft docked to the outside of that. Daniel had no idea what the various volumes connecting outwards might be, but he presumed either storage for raw goods, or machine shops capable of repairs. When he listened for minds, he only heard them at the center, or around the outer rim.

SwiftStar had surprised them.

Normally, a Sept Patrol was composed of ten vessels, escorts working as a team for the larger ships in the fleet, each themselves small enough to chase after things like the Mbaysey Tribal Squadron. The ships were compact and uncomfortable. A vessel with a crew of forty crammed into a space where Daniel would have thought twenty claustrophobic, but the ship was a flying mass of machinery with a few corridors and rooms tucked in. However, it did let them have full grav fields, long range, and three cannons as heavy as anything short of the Ram Cannons on *SeekerStar*.

Ten such ships, the ubiquitous *Patrol*, was enough to threaten even *SeekerStar* and *The Haunt*, so Kathra had always been forced to flee. Especially in the days when all they had was *WinterStar*, much smaller.

Today, he was flying in a modernized and refitted Ovanii Dueler. Twice again longer than a Patrol ship. Ten times wider, even if much of this vessel was unused space.

It was also a dedicated warship, purpose-built by a species who made a living as marauders dangerous enough to cause the Anndaing to rouse from their ancient, mercantile torpor.

Two of the Sept ships should be out on a standard patrol circuit, well away from the station itself and protecting the approaches that a normal attacker might have had to rely on, if they didn't already know the exact coordinates of their target ahead of time.

That left eight docked. Daniel did not know the first thing about navies, but Ife and others had assured him that a random two would be able to launch and respond in short order, and that two would be so completely off-line for repairs and maintenance that they would do nothing but watch as the battle unfolded around them.

That would leave four that might be a problem, two that might be a risk, and two more that might come down from their patrol to engage at the end of the battle.

Ife had laughed. The others seemed heartened by that.

Daniel had shrugged and told the women what he had seen.

He was only a bystander today. A witness to history, as it were, right up to the point he needed to fix them what Ife assured him would be a victory dinner.

Ndidi was handling things. Her and the women she and Ife had brought.

It felt wrong, going into battle without Kathra and Erin, but this was his future.

And it was just the beginning.

"All cannons lock as you bear. Fire at will," Ndidi called.

Unnecessarily, as far as Daniel could tell. Ngozi never once looked up from her screens, stabbing buttons and typing furiously. Acqueir was similarly engaged, sniffing at the station to see which ships might be a threat. And which might be easy kills.

Her aura reminded Daniel of the butcher who had regularly supplied his restaurant with freshly-slaughtered pork, back on Genarde. A workman-like fellow with a sharp cleaver and a rude joke on his lips.

The guns rattled the hull as they fired. The whole ship vibrated with the energy as each weapon built up a tremendous surge of power from the banks of generators rear and then dumped the capacitor out to lase it into the target.

The Patrol was not the target today. Those ships were simply things in Ngozi's way, as near as Daniel could tell. He watched a passive relay from her screen flow by on his, while listening to the space around them with half his mind for sudden changes that might represent unforeseen problems.

Any warning he could give would be critical, even if Rostami was nowhere near. That man's signature was distant and faint. Earth, perhaps, but more likely Rhages. Both were the same rough direction from here, stars that might be twinned in a telescope if you cared enough to filter out all the others in-between.

Ndidi's mission, given to her by Ife and Kathra, was to destroy the station itself. Without it, the Sept would be that much more limited in their ability to threaten the Free Worlds or Anndaing space. Patrols would have to load up as much food as they could stuff into whatever crevices were available, and then race back to whatever was the next station in the chain that eventually reached to the Sept Empire's borders.

They certainly could not flee to a Free Worlds station. Not unless they wished to be taken prisoner and possibly exchanged home later, minus their ships.

The Free Worlds would not welcome those *salauds*.

Daniel watched the first bolts hammer into the underside of the station. Ndidi had purposely come in low, but on a plane with the station itself. That let Ngozi fire into the center without having to shoot around docked Patrol vessels.

The station did not appear to be armored. That might have been an oversight on their part.

At Ogrorspoxu, *SeptStar* had been sheltered by better armor than either *SeekerStar* or *Windrunner*. Specially-hardened plates strapped over the skin of the vessel to absorb incoming fire and protect the vessel.

Ngozi's bolts were hammering raw steel skin, venting air, vapor, and large pieces. More bolts streaked in, punching into gaps already opened.

Daniel wondered if the woman could actually cut the station in two, like a chef boning out a big piece of meat.

Ngozi had the right cleaver for the job.

"Target coming live and preparing to counterfire," Acqueir called out.

On his screen, Daniel watched the Anic woman highlight one of the Patrol ships suddenly. He didn't know what it was she saw, but Ngozi immediately shifted more than half of her turrets onto that one vessel and began sequencing shots into it.

This looked more like the battle he had lived through, and the pirate escapades he had heard about from the comitatus women, as well as the Anndaing merchants.

Bolts hit the Patrol ship like nails being driven into concrete, rather than a knife carving a warm brie. But again, *SwiftStar* was an order of magnitude more powerful, more dangerous, than one of these ships.

And Ngozi was old enough to remember Tazo.

The targeted vessel began to bleed. Air and other fluids leaked through the armor.

And then something exploded.

Daniel wasn't watching with a camera, so the scanner just marked a haze and turned the icon red, but he heard the explosion with his mind.

Forty men got snuffed out as their ship died.

He had always been assured that it was impossible to make a ship actually explode in combat. That beam fire was like fighting with ice picks, where your enemy eventually bled to death.

Apparently, you could put a steel shaft through someone's heart. Maybe a reactor had failed, overloading itself and taking out a neighbor, who went in a sudden chain reaction.

One limb of the station peeled back like the ancient cartoons where a trick cigar exploded in someone's face.

Ngozi poured all her fire into that gap, blasting chunks off the central hub as Daniel watched.

"Daniel, find me the outer two," Ndidi snapped at him, breaking the mesmerizing images of death on his screen.

Reminding him that he had a mission here. Not as important as the other women, but relevant nonetheless.

He closed his eyes and flung his mind out into the void.

Nine and Ten, Ife and Ndidi had called them. Somewhere out there.

SwiftStar had not gotten close enough find them, once they knew where the station itself was.

Acqueir was looking, but only with a portion of her concentration, because she was focused on the station.

Daniel went hunting. Instead, as ordered.

There was one. Medium range, relative to what the women had taught him. Capable of turning and racing down to engage *SwiftStar* coming out of its attack pass, if their commander was sharp and on the ball.

He reached out a…it wasn't a mental hand. Tendril? Tentacle?

A length of psionic rope, perhaps, placing an image and a location in Acqueir's mind, so that she could send a pulse that direction.

He tasted a moment of raw panic from her, before she understood what it was he had just done to her.

Now, where was the other one?

Daniel could not find anything.

Frantic, he turned and sought closer, but there was nothing. Nobody.

Were there only nine vessels? Could there be?

This was where the chef was out of his depth. Daniel had no experience in warfare. None, except the kind settled with a bake-off and occasionally a presenter talking along to the camera for the folks at home.

Ndidi was busy. Focused like a gem-cutter on her task.

He reached out to Ife instead, mentally tapped her on the shoulder, then pulled her into the mental living room he shared with all women when they first entered his mind.

He didn't remember it from his youth, but it had that sort of feel, with a picture window looking over a tiny front yard with a picket fence and grass.

Ife looked just as fierce here as she did on her bridge, even with Ndidi as the one holding the greatsword.

He projected nearby space as he could understand it.

"I can't find them," he said. "There appear to only be nine Patrol vessels here, plus the station."

Daniel couldn't help that his voice had begun to sound a little frantic. Lives were at stake.

Friendly lives. The Sept just needed to die so they would stop being a threat to innocents.

"Show me," Ife said, much more calmly.

He merged himself with her, showing the woman the memories of the last two seconds, which had felt like hours at the speed he was thinking right now.

"Good enough," Ife said simply. "They are not here. That one ship cannot stand against us."

"Oh," Daniel said, letting go so that both of them dropped back into real space.

He had not considered that something might have happened to cause the other ship to not be here. Maybe it was escorting cargo ships home. Or needed more maintenance than the station could provide. Something that would draw it to relative safety on the fateful day, when Ndidi decided to kill all his fellows.

"One located," he said aloud. "Acqueir has them. The tenth ship is not present in system."

Ndidi turned and stared at him for a long beat.

The smile that came over her face would probably utterly terrify anyone that didn't know the woman as well as he did. The glasses almost made her look like a demon right now.

"Pilot, slow us down and curve *SwiftStar* hard around our orbit," Ndidi called out. "Maintain range instead of moving away."

Stina grunted something that Daniel took as an assent.

Ife looked over at Daniel and smiled serenely.

That was almost more frightening than the look Ndidi was flashing the world.

"Sword, begin killing Patrols and ignore the station," Ndidi ordered. "Track number Nine and prepare to engage if he closes. Let me know if he starts to run."

Anybody could flee from this slaughter relatively easily. However, there were no planets or stars nearby, which made it the perfect place to establish a secret base from which to invade your enemies.

At the same time, that base could not escape. Only those nine ships.

Six now.

Kathra would eventually need to build something similar, except that it would be more heavily armed, larger, and most likely bring with it a contingent of Anndaing ships who would move out and trade with any nearby systems as soon as they were allowed.

"Targets sequenced," Acqueir called over the buzz of the room.

Ngozi just kept typing, but Daniel heard the occasional rude comment from the woman.

She had spent a career on *WinterStar* and then *SeekerStar*. She had fled, time and again, from Sept incursions because a Patrol like this was more than the Mbaysey could challenge.

Until today.

Daniel could smell the paybacks wafting through the air, from human, Anic, and Anndaing in equal amounts.

SwiftStar began pounding another ship into scrap.

TEN

"Bᴜᴛ ꜰᴏᴜʀ ᴏꜰ ᴛʜᴇᴍ ᴇꜱᴄᴀᴘᴇᴅ," Ndidi snarled.

She couldn't help herself.

"Yes," Ife agreed with a calmness that Ndidi found almost more infuriating than the escaped ships.

At least Daniel and the others had the courtesy to look chagrined, seated around the conference room table as the officers reviewed the outcome of the battle.

Ife leaned forward and put her elbows on the table.

"So you only destroyed five Patrol vessels, and then shattered the station itself into pieces from which those four who temporarily escaped us might come back, but I'm not sure what they might do besides rescue no more than a handful of survivors."

She paused and Ndidi finally felt the terrible rage the woman had been masking for so long.

"Even if I had the necessary crew to take that many people prisoner, I would not," the Speaker said with a voice like glass grinding into an open wound. "That might let them mistake this for an honorable war. They need to fear their extermination instead."

Ndidi bit back her response. It would look pale and childish compared to that.

And everyone here knew it.

"Plus, only four of them escaped," Ife said. "Broken, even if they do find their fifth. All they can do is convey to their Sept lords that a strange, alien warship appeared out of the gulf and crushed them. Assuming I don't chase them down to their next location and annihilate it before more of them can escape."

Ndidi sucked a breath down deep into her chest. Ife's rage was what the elders brought. The women who had been born on Tazo.

Ndidi had been born in space after Yagazie convinced the others to build enough ClanStars to leave.

To no longer be attached to any planet where Sept lords could threaten them.

Ndidi had spent less than eight days combined in her entire life on the surface of any planet, including time on Kanus and Ogrorspoxu.

She was a star child. Part of the Mbaysey Star Tribe.

Ndidi let the silence drift. It was technically her meeting, since she had been in command of the attack. Ife was merely supervising.

Daniel and Acqueir had handled the role of seeking exceptionally well, working as a team. Ngozi had practically signed her name on the various pieces of steel they had left scattered back there. Stina had flown *SwiftStar* like a Spectre, rather than a massive warship.

"Okay, so the mission was a success," Ndidi conceded, letting go a breath slowly enough that it didn't turn into a sigh. "One station located and subsequently destroyed. Survivors escaped to relay the message to their naupati and their emperor that someone takes offense to Sept incursions into this zone of space."

"Will they know it was us?" Ngozi asked, her eyes still raging, even as she smiled.

"I doubt it," Ife broke in now. "We did not identify ourselves. They should draw a logical conclusion, which will subsequently be ruptured when their spies return with information about what Anndaing vessels look like."

That got a rude laugh around the table.

Like the sharks that built them, Anndaing merchants and warships tended to be long and sleek, with a hammerhead design for the bow. On warships, the two ends of the hammers tended to be weapon emplacements, giving them a tremendous arc of engagement, while a Cargo-6 like *Koni Swift* had the bridge on the right and spare space on the left. Crence Miray had added a library and salon/lounge for his crew over there, but many trademasters lived in personal opulence instead.

A few added a half-sized cargo pod dock, like the smaller pony kegs of thin beer that Clan Ihejirika supplied to *SeekerStar* occasionally.

"Yet more angry aliens?" Daniel asked. "Beyond the few that the Se'uh'pal might warn them about?"

"Do we know who is out there?" Ndidi asked back.

She liked the way the man felt comfortable enough to just shrug at her. Ndidi had been around enough Anndaing, plus her Wisp and Anic crewwomen, to understand that other cultures had to deal with the masculine tendency to talk too much. To have an opinion even when their ignorance bade them shut the hell up.

Kathra did not tolerate it. Daniel was woman enough, and comfortable enough. The other few men, like Myler, had learned quickly, on the sharp edge of her and Ife's tongues.

"This is the northern edge of K'bari space," Daniel said. "At least looking at it with a standard presentation map at small scale. Inward, I suppose is the correct term?"

Several women nodded at him, Ndidi included.

"*Bon*," he continued. "So the Bhaorajj are not all that far from here as those things go. If you cut straight across, intent on ignoring the Free Worlds in building your network, you might get close to the Upynth sector of worlds. Is that secret enough, or have they already begun building up a network to attack the Free Worlds?"

"Do they hate you folks enough to ignore the Free Worlds?" Acqueir leaned into the conversation now. "Are the Mbaysey enough of a threat, especially if they have allies now, that the Sept need to come this way instead of going after the rest of the human worlds?"

Ndidi studied the Anic woman. It was a cogent question, and one that none of them could answer. Perhaps nobody could answer at present, except that Ndidi suspected that the Anndaing Merchants Guild might have already begun putting spies in the right places to know.

"We don't know," Ndidi answered after a beat. She turned to Ife. "Do we run home now and perhaps find out what they know? Or do we sail across, looking for other places we might attack?"

"For now, we'll head outward just a bit more, to see if they have any other bases close by," Ife decided. "But not for long. Kathra needs to know what had happened so she and the others can plan. The Anndaing will need to know as well. Plus we might recruit some Upynth to our cause, if the grand war with the Sept over human supremacy has finally begun."

Ndidi nodded. She had handled the attack well, but there was so much more to learn from Ife and the others. Especially since she was the youngest person on this ship and some of the others had been serving in Kathra's navy since before she was born

But Kathra and the others believed in her.

Maybe she needed to, as well.

ELEVEN

Kathra studied the man who had joined her aboard *SeekerStar* for the trip to Ogrorspoxu. With Daniel gone, Alla ver'Shingi, A'Alhakoth's oldest brother, was the only male aboard the vessel right now.

The Kaniea was still finding his footing in space, as it were. Even more so here in her office, with her and Erin.

He had his father's height and the strong build of youth. In that, most Kaniea males were so similar that they cast the same shadows.

Alla had been raised as an eldest son of noble families on both sides, the one expected to take over the estate when his father retired, and the title when the man passed on some distant, future date.

Kathra knew that Kaniea lived longer than humans, and aged slower. At twenty-four, A'Alhakoth was the same physical age as Ndidi, but was only now barely considered an adult on Kanus. Alla was in his forties, but just approaching the prime of his life, with perhaps twelve or fifteen decades ahead of him.

Still, he had learned politics from a male Kathra had

come to respect. And not just because Linga had done such an exceptional job providing A'Alhakoth with the tools his youngest daughter would need to thrive in a hostile, usually-male-dominated galaxy.

They were in Kathra's office today. Erin was in her chair on the right, as she always was. Both of their pregnancies were just enough advanced to show the tiniest bulge if they were naked.

Kathra hadn't lost one step of her physical fitness yet.

"I'm still not sure I understand why my presence is so critical to your mission, Commander," Alla tried to sound helpful instead of obstinate.

"Perhaps I'm just feeling evil, Alla ver'Shingi," she smiled at the man, watching his discomfort grow, even as she had no heat to her words.

"Kaniea are not unknown on Ogrorspoxu," he offered, circling back to that argument again, like a dog worrying a bone, hoping that they had missed a bit of meat earlier.

"And they are not common, either," Erin smiled serenely, playing the same game Kathra had begun.

It helped that for all his size, Alla was shorter than both of them. He still had the greater mass of a Kaniea male, but Kathra had half a head of height on him.

"And my sister would not be better suited?" he shifted. "Especially in light of the situation?"

"Oh, I expect to swap you and A'Alhakoth at some point, Alla," Kathra nodded. "But for now, she serves me better by reminding all of Kanus that they need to trade with a woman, even as they build up relations with your house. I presume that you will be maneuvering for better marriages for Kilga and Trelga than you had previously expected?"

He laughed, and Kathra watched some of the nervous tension bleed out of the male.

"Yes and no," he replied with an enormous grin. "It is not

that people don't have faith in you, but many are concerned that you will be a threat, Commander. We've had a few quiet conversations, but no house wants to necessarily tie themselves to ver'Shingi if we are about to fall on our faces, challenging the lords of the galaxy."

Kathra and Erin chuckled in turn. Nobody would want to be first. Nobody would want to be last. One brother would likely marry a pioneer, the other a powerful princess.

"And that's why you are necessary, Alla ver'Shingi," Kathra explained. "Until a year ago, you didn't even maintain a trading house with the Merchants Guild. Now you are suddenly among the most prominent of the Kanus families. Whether for luck or notoriety, as you noted, remains to be seen. At Ogrorspoxu, you will be even more interesting."

"By being a merchant trader?" he asked. "I still feel like I'm missing something."

"By being my ally, Alla," Kathra said. "The Mbaysey have few friends at Kanus, but that changes at Ogrorspoxu, for reasons that I might not have chosen to mention when we were still at Kanus."

"And it is finally time?"

He sat up straighter now, aware that *SeekerStar* had transitioned to jump, out and away from his home and his people.

And anyone that might have overheard such a conversation earlier.

"The Mbaysey need to trade, Alla," Kathra said simply. "The ClanStars are largely self-sufficient, but we need inputs of bulk grains and advanced electronics, as a rule. Food and technology, where we can produce enough of the rest. In turn, excess metals and exotic gases can be traded. In the past, that happened at TradeStations, either in Sept Space, while we still skirted those edges, or out in the Free Worlds."

"Yes, I have heard many stories from your women," Alla

nodded, growing more confident, perhaps, as he glanced over at Erin.

His confusion had been a necessary ploy for a time. But she needed him now.

A male.

And not even one Daniel had been able to merge with to truly know. But for all his expertise on Kanus, Alla ver'Shingi was still a neophyte in the ways of truly cutthroat politics, such as the old women of the Mbaysey engaged.

Usually without literal knives.

"So the tribe will not generally trade directly with the friendly merchants at Ogrorspoxu," Kathra explained.

"No?"

"No," she shook her head firmly. "For the next year or however long, the plan is to maintain Kanus as the center of our operations, trading with Kaniea merchants."

"Pardon my bluntness, Commander, but that seems rather stupid," Alla stated, growing so bold as to speak like one of her women.

But they were in the privacy of Kathra's office, aboard *SeekerStar*, in jump.

No witnesses would tell tales later.

"You could get much better trade rates at one of the Anndaing worlds, even if not the capital," Alla continued. "And have a wider selection of goods for yourself. Kanus is a lovely world, but we lack the industrial might to challenge even third-tier systems like Agliv, to say nothing of Ogrorspoxu."

"Today, yes," Kathra said. "What happens if all Mbaysey trade flows out from Kanus exclusively?"

"Those pretty merchants will have to come to us for all the exotics you supply," Alla replied. "Middleman issues will cut off at least a fifth of the profit you might make otherwise."

"Indeed," Kathra agreed. "My clan elders put it at closer to a quarter, and I'm more inclined to accept their math. Getting them to agree was the hardest part."

"Then why do it, Commander?" Alla asked. "If I may be so bold, possibly so rude, it seems stupid."

"The ver'Shingi are now our allies, Alla," she answered quietly.

His whole face fell into confusion. He truly looked like A'Alhakoth when that happened.

"And not just the ver'Shingi, but all of the Kaniea," Kathra continued. "Thus, my approach to trade needs to generate the greatest benefit for a much wider array of folks, and not just twenty-four pissy, old women. Most of those middlemen will be Kaniea, at least initially. That gives them a jump on the Anndaing trademasters who will arrive later."

"You would give up that much profit...?"

"To make sure all my allies benefited," Kathra completed the thought. "Yes. The arrival of the Mbaysey into Anndaing space is not all that disruptive, even with the problems the Sept will cause. But for the Kaniea, it will be a revolution. I need to make sure my allies are stronger than my enemies there. I do that by making everyone rich, rather than just a few."

"And you need me at Ogrorspoxu because I will become the face of Kaniea trade, as well as Mbaysey." His eyes suddenly lit up with realization. "Which A'Alhakoth could not do, because she is comitatus, and thus an extension of your will. That's frighteningly huge in scope, Commander."

"Yagazie, my mother, demanded that the Mbaysey be free, Alla ver'Shingi," Kathra felt her tones grow dark. "That required a stubbornness you may have never yet encountered. Later, it required ingenuity and luck. Now, it requires friends with a view to the profit that they might make."

"And that, measured over generations, Commander," Alla

almost gasped. "Are you truly intent on disrupting Kaniea and Anndaing culture on that scale?"

"It becomes almost necessary, Alla," Kathra said.

"Necessary?"

"The Sept are coming," she reminded him. "They have already come this far once. Next time, it may be battle fleets intent on subjugating all non-humans beneath a Sept boot. I will need allies when that occurs. But more importantly, I will need friends."

TWELVE

Crence Miray had come to like Tavle Jocia, on this, his third big trading voyage into Free Worlds space.

Anndaing were still wildly exotic creatures, especially as this deep into the Free Worlds you were mostly dealing with humans, rather than places like Thrabo, where the species mix was much wilder.

But Crence knew that Thrabo would become a hive of scum and villainy soon enough. A worse hive, maybe. Multi-species hive. He didn't figure all his cousins showing up like locusts to trade would improve things. Every con artist, grifter, and pirate who could scrape together the cash would head there, looking to get rich. From both sides of the border.

Which was exactly why Crence had taken *Koni Swift* all the way to Tavle Jocia instead, clear in the heart of the human realms. Nobody else was dreaming as far ahead as he was.

Or hadn't been. Like everything, that was going to change.

He considered the need to upgrade himself to a Cargo-12

soon. Maybe even move up into the bulk traveler category and start hauling huge amounts of goods.

No, stay down in the light freighter range with a 12. Bigger than that and you needed to be dealing with stations, rather than individual merchants. Too easy to get locked into bulk grain or fruit transport, rather than exotic goods where you could command stupid margins, purely on being weird and new.

Nobody got rich hauling maha seeds by the kiloton.

Koni Swift had docked yesterday. It helped that after a year, the locals on this station had added a warehouse wing capable of docking a standard Cargo-6 and putting up temporary seals around the bays to extract the cargo boxes without him having to break out the tug and move things around.

Let the local stevedores do it. He wanted to walk the decks, and maybe have a few chats with people. Be seen publicly, in case anybody wanted to set up private meetings on the ship later.

Alten and Dane had accompanied him, like usual, with Jine back on the ship in command for now. Crence had a corner booth in a favorite restaurant, somewhat isolated from sound, but big enough that most of the folks in here could see the alien Anndaing eating.

The place was packed, as usual. The owner appreciated Crence bringing the crowds here, and the spillover had started bringing random tourists, too.

Greasing the wheels of commerce as many ways as he could.

Dinner had been slabs of meat from some sort of ground ruminant. One of the bigger ones, with horns coming out of the sides of its head in dangerous ways. Long since domesticated, but Crence hadn't found anyone willing to set up a ranching ship for him yet, let alone fly a whole crew of trained humans out to someplace like Acran.

That was coming. Maybe as soon as the next trip, depending on how this one went.

Anndaing weren't as addicted to steak as humans, but the exotic would work in his favor for a while, and then he could sell the ranch off to other investors once it became a general thing. Maybe get Daniel to provide a whole recipe book for folks back home.

Across the way, a human entered the restaurant and made eye contact with Crence.

About damned time.

Crence had wondered if the man had gotten lost, or had forgotten.

He tracked the man walking to the bar and taking up a stool instead of approaching. Humans had to actually turn their head that direction to stare, but they didn't have eyes on the sides of the their skulls, so it was generally easy enough to sneak up on them.

Crence kept his head turned towards Dane and continued to talk about nothing.

One eye tracked the man across the room.

"Is that?" Alten asked vaguely, also one eye roaming.

"It is," Crence replied, enjoying his dessert.

Bread pudding in a sweet cream sauce. Tasty, even if he'd had to get the local chef to make a slightly different version.

Human tolerance for alcoholic poisons was still frightening, even to an Anndaing merchant who liked to skirt the edge.

"Should I go up to the bar and get the next round of drinks?" Dane asked.

"No," Crence decided. "We'll let this run for a bit. Might be issues we don't know about."

Like, why the man hadn't just walked over and bowed to introduce himself. Many humans had, leaving behind a funny little piece of card stock with contact information printed on it.

"Is anybody else paying attention, Alten?" Crence asked quietly.

Again, two eyes that could move independently allowed the Anndaing to stalk all manner of prey, rather than having to face it.

"Nothing obvious," his bodyguard replied.

Crence nodded. As good as he could do right now.

The downside of celebrity was that anyone wanting to meet with him came in for some level of scrutiny.

That could be a problem when you wanted to build a spy network.

The human sat at the bar and ordered something.

Crence caught the flash of cash passing in response to the glass being delivered, along with the quick glance this way from the bartender, gone so fast that Crence almost thought that he imagined it.

The bread pudding gone, he settled back and enjoyed some tea. Joane Obiakpani, Spectre Five, had gotten him hooked on the human beverage. But it was generally available in any establishment in human space, where fermented boullo juice was going to be a rare delicacy that might not even be available right now, except from what bottles he had specifically brought for Rodrigo, the owner of the establishment.

A few minutes passed and the human waitress returned with more hot water.

He thought she was human. The shape was female, which itself was so weird, but the coloration range available to the species was just impossible. Kaniea were blue. Anic were gray. Humans seemed to be all the rest, if he looked wide enough.

Call her human. Good enough.

Fresh pot of tea, just steeping.

Crence caught a hint of writing on the napkin that she had placed under the pot as she set it down and he nodded to the woman.

Not even safe to be seen talking to him? How bad had it gotten?

Were they already reduced to delivering secret messages by dead-drops instead of passing coded messages and data chips in handshakes?

Crence had hoped that his opponents weren't that sharp.

But apparently, the battle had gotten more dangerous since the last time he was here.

THIRTEEN

DANIEL DIDN'T NEED to be on *SwiftStar*'s bridge to listen to the cosmos. He had done it the first few times just because it put him close to Acqueir or one of her assistants when he located something, so he could immediately give her a vector to program into her systems.

At the same time, it also invoked his ghosts perhaps a little more than he was usually comfortable with, since they had all belonged to galactic species before they had been taken. Each felt the call of those distant stars.

Besides, it was unnecessary for him to actually be here to listen. And he felt more comfortable aft in his kitchen.

Always, he returned to his kitchen. That was where Daniel found peace.

After five years in space, there was no one place he could call home. Certainly he didn't ever expect to be welcomed back to Genarde, unless the Sept picked that to be his final prison world, if they ever caught him and didn't just execute him as a traitor to the species.

WinterStar had been destroyed. *SeekerStar* left behind. Ogrorspoxu was truly a lovely place, but just a milestone.

Not a destination.

But *SwiftStar* had a kitchen he could claim. Even for just a little while.

It helped that the space itself was several thousand human years old. And yet, everything in here made perfect sense, once he made adjustments for being four decimeters shorter than the chef who had lived here before him.

The convection stove. The heating element top. The rapid-cooker that used microwaves in a narrow band to heat water in something.

Even the cutting board had been made from a wood he couldn't identify, but looked remarkably similar to the one he had left behind on Genarde.

It brought back his past. And distracted him from thinking about his ghosts. Or stepping deep inside himself for someone to talk to.

Daniel sat on a bench and listened to the universe instead.

He wasn't cooking anything right now. The evening crew had finished cleaning an hour ago and gone on to whatever they did when he didn't need them. The morning crew was fast asleep now, alarms set so they could come and start the bread rising for morning in a few hours.

The lights were at half right now. Daniel had even turned off the music he occasionally played in the background to dull the sharp sounds of kitchen staff hard at their art.

It was just him most of the time, so everything was a symphony. Even the few times he had managed to drag Ndidi back here to help him, they had been halves of a whole in this kitchen. Right hand and left, like a violinist.

Or a single chef.

The interior hatch between the kitchen and the dining hall opening caught his attention. He was not immediately visible to someone standing in the doorway, but he saw their shadow as they paused.

"Daniel?" a voice called quietly across the darkness.

He recognized her, surprised that no light had accompanied the woman into the room. And unsure what that meant.

"Here," he called back, remaining seated.

The bench wasn't all that comfortable, but he didn't feel like rising.

Tanuss entered, her horn starting to glow just a little. Enough that he could track her as she moved around various counters designed for a chef like him to deliver food across to his assistants to carry out to tables.

Tanuss was a Wisp. The species had an official name, but the ancient legends of the Will-o-the-Wisp transcended many cultures, and the anglerfish design had occurred on a variety of worlds. Only one had cast them up onto dry land as bipeds and then raised them to intelligence, though.

"Sitting in the dark?" she asked, muting the glow of her horn as she came into sight.

"Being alone and quiet," he replied as she paused, right at the edge of entering this side of the counter, the place where the cooks worked.

"Would you prefer your privacy?" she asked.

"No," Daniel said. "Company would be good. Better than my ghosts. Can I get you anything?"

Daniel looked closer at her now, studying the woman's body and its language.

Her skin was gray in the light, with iridescent patterns in pink and lavender that only superficially looked like scales. More like a tattoo artist having fun with geometric designs, turning her into a Shia mosque, like a few Daniel had known in his travels.

Physically, she gave the impression of being long and

skinny, similar to Acqueir, but she wasn't. Standing, he had perhaps two centimeters on her eye to eye, but her horn was taller than he was.

Petite. That described her.

Tanuss stepped more fully into his space. Her horn gave off a tentative light now. Enough to read in bed, perhaps, in an otherwise dark room.

She stepped around his question, it seemed, and found a bucket that had been filled with an Anndaing equivalent of tomato sauce at one point, turning it over so she could sit.

Like the other officers, she wore the flame colored pants and black shirt that had been the comitatus uniform, with the blue-green jacket over that. The fabric clung to her in interesting ways as he watched.

The Wisp were erect bipeds of a similar model to others. She had small breasts, compared to many human women, and thinner curves, but he assumed that was her ancient aquatic heritage.

"Perhaps some juice?" he asked as she settled. "I had contemplated cracking open a bottle of red wine, but could not find the enthusiasm to drink all of one by myself."

"Juice would be nice," she said in a quiet, careful voice.

Daniel rose and made his way to the walk-in refrigerator, pulling a glass jug off a shelf and returning to the outer world. Unlike the other officers, he dressed like a cook unless he had a reason not to. Black pants. Long-sleeved black shirt with the doubled cloth that hid the gem on his chest.

Tonight, he still had his apron on, but he hadn't gotten it all that messy cooking dinner, so it didn't need to be washed until probably after lunch tomorrow.

"Did I interrupt anything?" Tanuss asked as he handed her a glass.

"Brooding," he replied with a shrug. "Nothing useful. It is better that you came down to rescue me, most likely."

Her horn's glow got a little brighter as she sipped.

"What brings you to my domain?" he asked with a tired smile as he found his place on the bench again.

"I was wondering about humans," she said. "I have only known the Mbaysey, and they are much of a type due to their shared culture. You are something much different."

"*Oui*," he nodded. "Although I am not sure that I qualify as human anymore, if you wish to be technically correct."

"That is the best kind of correct," she smiled, just as nerdy as Joane, or Adanne Eguminyo, back on *SeekerStar*. "Do you think you are a god, Daniel?"

"I would be a very poor example," he laughed. "One who had achieved godhead by accident, and was unwilling to do anything with it."

"And using the power does not thrill you?" she asked. "Does not fill you with a desire to make the galaxy better?"

He had had this conversation with many women on this ship, especially Ife's officers. Even merged with most of them superficially, as a way of them understanding what he could do. At the same time, Daniel had not shared his inner self, like he had with Kathra, Erin, or Ndidi.

He did not need these other strangers having the keys to his soul. The comitatus would be enough.

"I am a cook, not a philosopher, Tanuss," he replied. "Better or worse are all slippery slopes that all tend to end up in some flavor of evil. I have done enough bad things on my own. Having godhead would not make it better. On the contrary, it just makes my mistakes so much deadlier for the rest of the universe."

"The left hand of evil," she nodded.

"*Oui*," he said. "But even that is just a little thing. Imagine doing that to a planet. A culture. An entire species. That was what Urid-Varg was. I have no desire to emulate him."

"But you retain the gem," she pointed out.

Daniel looked at her harder now, wondering what her angle might be. What deeper question the woman sought answers for.

Her voice gave nothing away.

"No female can use it," he reminded her. "And no other male would be safe with such temptation. I have not cast it into the heart of a star because the Commander forbid me that relief. At some point, she will change her mind and free me. Until then, I am a slave to Urid-Varg's ego, but I can at least put that *branleur's* power to use thwarting the Sept. Destroying those *salauds*, perhaps, if I am lucky enough."

The fire in his voice surprised him a little. Daniel had wondered occasionally if he was too phlegmatic to rage like that, but he supposed that most topics simply did not raise any great passion in him.

Were he a Wisp, he expected that his own horn might be glowing painfully bright right now.

Tanuss surprised him by setting her empty cup down on a nearby counter and standing. He stared blankly up at the woman as she walked closer and suddenly sat down in his lap, straddling him like they were already lovers.

She took his own cup and put it somewhere behind him out of sight on a counter.

"Are you ever lonely, Daniel?" she asked in a quiet voice, her legs behind him on the rear of the bench.

Her own horn was brighter than it had been. It did not convey any particular emotion when it lit up, so much as measured the power of feeling behind it. Tanuss lit the room, so he kept his eyes down on her mouth and neck, watching her gill slits flutter ever so slightly.

A Wisp was a land-creature, breathing air, but they retained gills, and could stay under water for as much as an hour if they weren't exercising strenuously.

He wondered how she might react to a kiss on her neck, just below the jawline.

But she had asked a question.

"I am alone," he offered.

"That is not the same thing," she countered, both elbows resting on his shoulders now, with one hand in his hair and the other caressing the back of his neck. "I am the only one of my kind on this vessel. And females out-number males by a drastic proportion."

"On *SeekerStar*, I was usually the only male aboard," Daniel nodded, wondering how serious this woman might be. "Same as *WinterStar*. But the Mbaysey are generally homosexual by culture. There were only a few women who might ever consider laying with a male."

"Have you ever lain with a non-human?" she asked, leaning close enough now that his face could be pressed into her chest if either of them desired.

Daniel considered A'Alhakoth. She had expressed an interest, but Daniel had been hard pressed to step past himself. The Kaniea woman was just barely an adult by her own culture, and he felt like a dirty, old man even watching her walk.

Anndaing females were almost externally identical to males, and mostly alien in shape. Anic pair-bonded, but he hadn't done enough research to understand if they might dabble outside that bond. Perhaps Acqueir had considered pair-bonding with a human? Or could she retain such a bond with a male he had not heard of, while exploring things with a mere human?

"I have not," Daniel answered.

She had asked if he had, not if he had explored the occasional fantasy of actually doing so. Different question.

"Might you?" she asked now, her horn brighter than he had ever seen it. "With an alien?"

Idly, Daniel wondered what that horn might look like when she was in the throes of a particularly good orgasm, if it was glowing like this now.

"People are people," he shrugged, leaning close enough to kiss her on the base of the throat.

She purred like a cat when he did, so he continued.

Hopefully, the woman had done her own research before pursuing this path. Not every species was capable of the act in such a way that one or both found pleasure.

But people were people.

None of the other women had suggested or offered before now, but he didn't know if they had been warned off, heard stories suggesting that Areen was a threat, or just didn't like men. Or at least humans.

Her hands came up around his head and Daniel supposed that perhaps the only Wisp in the crew might be as lonely as the only human male occasionally got.

FOURTEEN

IFE CONTEMPLATED the chamber assigned to her as Speaker. It was huge, but Ovanii had been a large species, and she had grown used to the compact confines of *WinterStar*. *SeekerStar* was better, but still small.

Ndidi appeared at the door and rapped on the frame before entering. Like Kathra, Ife kept the door open most of the time. Too easy to get hidden away from things out on the ship. Even one as sparsely inhabited as *SwiftStar*.

Ndidi sat without comment. They frequently came to rest thus, but both of them tended to be quiet people.

It was only the war that had put them here.

"How soon until Ogrorspoxu?" Ife asked to break the silence.

"Mid-evening tomorrow, if all goes well," Ndidi replied.

"How long do you expect us to be in for repairs?" Ife continued.

She had all the answers from Ndidi's reports, but staying on top of those things was the job of the Shield, and Ife had decided to follow many of those same patterns with her own crew.

The Mbaysey had no similar structures for a military force, once you got past the original women of Kathra's comitatus.

"Less time than originally scheduled," Ndidi offered, her voice slightly resentful.

"The armor is properly regenerating?" Ife asked.

"It is, even as old as those systems are," the Shield replied. "Nobody understands how it was done."

"Oh, I am quite positive that any number of Anndaing scientists understand the process, Shield," Ife said. "They do not use it to build their own vessels, but could, given enough time and the right threat to their trade."

Like, say, a Sept fleet building up for an invasion.

The Ovanii had taken simple steel, like everyone else used for their exterior armor, and done something to it. Harder, though it wasn't quite as durable as it could be, but it also reverted to pattern, given enough time and a low-voltage electrical current flowing through it.

In colloquial terms, it would slowly heal after a battle, assuming you had enough time and power.

The Sept defenders had gotten violently rambunctious in that first battle, once they recovered from their surprise, but *SwiftStar*'s armor had protected the ship from most of their bolts. The few that had gotten past had run into that face-hardened hull, where the outer skin protected a complicated honeycomb of cubic chambers each a little larger than dinner plates, themselves filled with a strange gel that would harden when the pressure dropped.

Not a single shot had penetrated a chamber where crew or non-existent passengers might have been at risk.

Conversely, Ndidi had killed five Patrol vessels and a floating warehouse, the first time she had ever been in a real battle.

"So we have succeeded in our initial task." Ndidi relaxed enough to even rest her shoulder blades on the chair. "What is next?"

"That is a political decision," Ife replied. "I have my theories, but Kathra will decide."

"That is a given," Ndidi nodded. "What would you do?"

"I would skirt the edge of the Free Worlds," Ife said. "Let Daniel search from that space, until he found that particular smell that he knew to be Sept, and then fall on them again. After that, I would probably get creatively weird."

"Weird," Ndidi echoed the word, making it almost sound like a question. Or not.

Ife treated it as such. She was feeling old and treacherous tonight, where Ndidi Zikora represented youth and skill.

"Bring along someone from one of the really exotic species from the backside of Anndaing space next time," Ife smiled. "Head to someplace like the Upynth sector and establish diplomatic relations."

"Someone not human," Ndidi nodded, seeing the pattern. "Not Mbaysey, but instead just strange, alien travelers from the darkness who happened to destroy a Sept station randomly, and nobody will be able to connect the crime to Kathra, because nobody will recognize an Ovanii ship."

"If they did, then we have a much more interesting problem on our hands, at the very least," Ife suggested.

"Daniel did find that book of Ovanii poetry at Thrabo," Ndidi reminded her.

There, the young woman had an advantage, because she had been closer to Daniel mentally and emotionally.

"Indeed," Ife echoed. "But I find it unlikely that we could easily connect Upynth space with Thrabo. Too far apart. But yes, some Ovanii person had to have escaped the

Anndaing's terrible wrath in the distant past. Perhaps a whole ship like ours, or even a sector fleet. We'll worry about that when we get there."

Ndidi fell silent, but Ife could see a question unasked in her eyes. She waited for the Shield to find the words.

"I would like to add a ground combat element to the ship, going forward," Ndidi finally said.

Ife blinked in surprise. That wasn't even in the top ten things she had been expecting her Shield to bring to this meeting.

"Why?" Ife asked, turning into the taskmaster/schoolmaster now with a dangerously-bright student on her hands.

"I want prisoners," Ndidi said. "Intelligence gathering using Daniel's tools will only tell us where they are. I want to know why. And what they plan. If we give them the option to surrender instead of having to fight to the death, we also gain the ability to steal their ships, or at least all their food. Eventually, *SwiftStar* will either need to return to Anndaing space along the long sail, or find a means of purchasing supplies from a forward system. The Bhaorajj hate everyone equally, so they will sell information about us to the Se'uh'pal or the Sept without qualm. Nobody understands the Upynth all that well, except perhaps Daniel. Kathra wanted to become a pirate. Thus, I need Kam, Iruoma, and Nkechi, plus troops they train."

Ife had participated in long conversations along those lines, but that was when the Commander expected to be raiding in *SeekerStar*, which was fragile and tiny.

SwiftStar gave them many other options. Surprise was just the most fun.

She nodded to the youngster as a placeholder. All of what she'd said had made sense, but it would represent a significant upgrading of Kathra's war. Especially if they took prisoners.

Ife would not be of a mind to just execute them after they had told her everything she wanted to know, so it would be necessary to put them someplace safe. And eventually give them back.

Ife would never deal in slaves. No Mbaysey would countenance that. Grandma Ezinne and Erin were good reminders.

"The Anndaing left the Ovanii on a series of inhabitable worlds, well away from their own systems," Ife thought aloud now. "But that was an element of their original surrender. What would you do with Sept males surrendered into your custody, Shield?"

Ife liked the way Ndidi fell into herself to think, rather than immediately respond glibly. That was part of the reason the woman was inner comitatus. And Shield of *SwiftStar*.

She thought.

"We could land them at a Free Worlds TradeStation," the Shield also thought aloud. "By then, they would already know they faced the Mbayscy, and not whatever aliens we might spoof them with. Leave them with enough money to perhaps survive so that they could find a ship upon which they could work for their passage. They are just males, after all."

"Not all of them," Ife countered.

"No?" Ndidi's confusion returned.

"No," Ife growled. "For that first battle, we were not taking prisoners, so we freed the woman aboard by killing them."

"There were women aboard those ships?" Ndidi gasped.

"Sex objects for the crew," Ife let her anger override Ndidi's surprise. "Generally a ratio of one woman to ten men, so a Patrol ship might have three to five. They are not crew."

"Now I really want Kam clearing a ship," Ndidi growled angrily, her face a terrible mask as her voice got hard. "Why was I not told?"

"It was not important, and might have caused you to withhold the blade," Ife said. "I needed to see that my Shield was as deadly, as exceptional as I thought she could be. The Sword was already a killer, but nobody knew what Ndidi Zikora could achieve."

Ndidi suppressed her growl. Then she fell silent, and Ife could already see plans forming and being discarded.

"Mbaysey women are the most comfortable in zero-gravity, once I have destroyed that *salaud's* generators," she said in an ugly tone that Ife approved of. "But there will not be enough of them for my needs. We may have to open the boarding teams to an imbalance of males, Anndaing and whoever else we might recruit. A'Alhakoth's people make good warriors, from a cultural standpoint. A few Bhaorajj might be fun, if we can convince them to use their specism to our advantage."

"You are Shield, Ndidi," Ife said. "I will leave the planning in your hands, but also the task of convincing the Commander of the need. Was there anything else to discuss?"

"No," Ndidi replied, rising quickly and making her way to the door. "I have much to think about."

Indeed. The old Mbaysey remembered the years where Sept officials might arrive and demand an annual tribute of women. Some were assigned for a time to warships such as Ndidi had just destroyed. Others, the most beautiful ones like a young Ezinne Uduik, had been delivered into a worse form of servitude.

Until Yagazie managed to convince a judge that the Mbaysey should be exempt.

The new generation had been generally shielded from that knowledge. They were the future, and didn't need the scars.

But Ndidi Zikora was going to be Kathra's supreme commander one of these days. Of that, Ife had no doubts.

Ndidi's rage would be a grand, terrible thing.

And the Sept had it coming.

FIFTEEN

CRENCE HAD MADE it back to the ship with the note stuffed in his pocket, never once looking at it, beyond that first glance to confirm that the paper had been wrapped around a small chip no doubt filled with information too sensitive to even speak out loud.

He was in his office now, with Jine, while Dane had the bridge.

"Bad news?" Jine asked as he sat.

"Dunno," Crence replied. "One of my spies was late, and then delivered this via friendly courier rather than even by hand, so someone watching in that restaurant was unfriendly to our mission. Or maybe just to us."

He pulled out the special human reader he'd originally traded Kathra Omezi for over a year ago. The function was identical to an Anndaing version, if a little thicker, but the input slots were all different.

One of these days, he'd hire a team of engineers and a factory to turn out a model with Anndaing slots on the left and human on the right, just so everything could be read and watched without swapping, but he wasn't there yet.

Electronics like that had as low a margin as grain, and he was making better money bringing Anndaing readers and vid chips to the bottomless human market right now.

At the same time, the political thrillers and romance novels he was hauling home for human language lessons were a zwölf a crate these days, especially old used ones he could pick up in a station bookstore.

Because the language hadn't changed appreciably in decades, old books worked just fine.

He plugged in the chip from the spy and called up the menu. The usual amount of bulk files. What you got when you paid a competent spy good money to listen for rumors for six months and compile them all.

And a single file at the top marked **READ ME FIRST**.

Not a good sign.

Never a good sign, when dealing with low-level espionage such as this. Everything was supposed to be about as exciting as doing crossword puzzles or watching paint dry.

This felt like a ticking bomb.

He cracked it open and started to read. Everything was in human, which took a little work, but he was pretty fluent by now.

Crap.

Too soon.

Damn it.

Crence finally understood the human term for grinding one's teeth. Anndaing would be dripping blood if they did that, but they flexed their hammer forward and down, and maybe rocked it back and forth if the news was especially bad.

This might qualify.

"Crence?" Jine asked.

Crence had already forgotten his Nightflier was even in the room.

"I pay the human to stay on top of trends while we're gone," the trademaster replied. "Gives us a leg up on what to bring next time. What to set for current prices or demand in barter. The usual industrial espionage you do before you set up an official trade office somewhere."

"Got it," Jine nodded.

"Someone has dropped a stupid number of new humans on this station in the last forty days," Crence continued. "My spy thinks they are Sept agents, but they aren't doing the right things for spies."

"Like?"

"For one, they're too obvious for his tastes," Crence said. "He presumes, and I agree, that they were probably waiting for us to get back so they can have a chat."

"Do they know about our connection with the Mbaysey?" Jine asked astutely.

"Gods, I hope not," Crence said, wracking his brain to remember if anybody had accidentally said anything suggesting a connection to the Mbaysey Star Tribe. "Best I can guess is someone figured out the Anndaing connection to the Kaniea. Omezi has that one in her comitatus now. Maybe somebody talked at Thrabo, and the news got here."

"Or maybe one of the other trademasters has it in for you?" Jine pressed.

Crence snarled an obscenity under his breath. That made a lot more sense, especially if he was seen as the golden fin back home.

Maybe, just maybe somebody was jealous of his connections to Merchants Bank.

Without understanding the implications.

Or worse, they did, and had decided to get him out of the way of their trade.

"Thrabo," Crence nodded. "Somebody talked. Someone

else put three and three together and got a fin. We might be blown."

"Just like that?" Jine's hammer flexed forward in surprise.

"Espionage only works as long as nobody suspects you of being a spy, Jine," Crence reminded the shark. "And we are. You know that much."

"That much," the nightflier agreed hesitantly.

All Jine Riffin had ever wanted was to fly. That was why Crence had hired him in the first place. Might be time to cure the shark's ignorance.

"I—we—work directly for Merchants Bank, mostly under the table, Jine," Crence explained, spelling it out for his nightflier for maybe the first time. "For Wyll Koobitz directly, if you want to be exact. He's probably more powerful than most of the Board of Directors, because a lot of those are sinecure positions. Wyll and Obaj Gendrah and a finful of others are the day-to-day power behind the throne."

"Figured that much," Jine agreed warily.

Crence nodded. The shark wasn't as dumb as he liked to come across, but Jine just wanted to fly. That was why Dane did most of the other work. The shadowy stuff.

They might be past the point where such ignorance was to anybody's benefit.

"So we do deals and missions under the table for Wyll more often than not," Crence continued. "The job that found us *SeekerStar* was actually not one, but it turned on its fin as soon as I realized we had a new, space-faring species at hand. That's why we ran so hard for Ogrorspoxu. Wyll sent me here to gather more intelligence."

"Why's Tavle Jocia so important, Crence?" Jine asked, cocking his hammer to the left.

"Shipyards," Crence said. "*SeekerStar* got birthed here. So did *SeptStar*. Wyll thinks that the Sept Empire might skip conquering a lot of the worlds closer to home so that they can attack this place and hold it."

"What's that give them?" Jine asked, still wrapping his head around politics instead of jump vectors.

"A serious forward base if they wanted to cross K'bari space *en masse*," Crence grimaced.

"Oh, shit," Jine burst out. "Attack us?"

"That's always an option," Crence said. "You need bases out in the dark zones if you want to get serious, but having a shipyard this far forward lets you repair damaged ships, or turn out new ones. The locals won't mind as much if they're getting rich, but it cuts the Free Worlds almost in half."

"What do we do?"

"Nothing," Crence came down hard. "We're about two days from having a new load of stuff to head home. This time, we'll hard scan every damned thing that goes into one of the pods, and the ship itself once we're away from the station, but we act like we don't know anything. Am I clear?"

"You got it, boss," Jine said. "There was some station leave for folks in a few hours. Should we cancel that and tell people to move up their schedules here?"

"Good idea," Crence said. "Let the pups know that we're leaving early, but not why. And nobody leaves the ship any farther than the dock without my approval."

"Alten will be happy," Jine opined. "We coming back later for another trade voyage?"

Crence shrugged at Alten's happiness. That shark was a combat operative. Crence would have preferred to sail in a galaxy that didn't need them, but he knew better.

"That's up to Wyll and Obaj," Crence said. "But I wouldn't tell your girlfriend we'll be back to see her in the spring."

"Either of them," Jine laughed.

Just like a sailor. A fin in every port. Or maybe more than one.

But yeah, we won't be home to see you in the spring, darling. Unless we're maybe bringing the Armada with us.

SIXTEEN

Hadi studied the latest human that fate had cast across his path as they entered this luxurious office. Rhages, as far as he could tell, was primarily made up of expensive meeting rooms that had side bars filled with expensive alcohol that should have been forbidden. This one was no different than the others, except that the bottles all seemed to be of the finest, most expensive kind.

Hadi followed Amirin into the room and kept his face pleasantly bland as he surveyed the inhabitant already there.

Many of the earlier people Hadi had had to deal with had been merely *Vuzurgan*, if the grand nobles of the Sept Empire could be *merely* anything.

But they were human, all of them.

Even Amirin, standing at Hadi's side as they came to rest just inside the latest meeting chamber that the slow grind of bureaucracy had introduced.

Normally, the next step on a bureaucratic path such as the one he and Amirin were pursuing would be a Shah, the planetary governor of whatever place Hadi had found himself.

But this was Rhages.

The Shah of Rhages was the Emperor himself. All of the land under their feet belonged to the holiest of men. Even a fat, drunkard slug like the current inhabitant of that throne.

But they were not dealing with the Shah. Nor an emperor.

Hadi had studied what official records he could locate of the Star Tribe known as the Mbaysey, and of Kathra Omezi. The woman who had inherited her authority from Yagazie Omezi when the Sept had assassinated the mother.

Both women had been protected by a tightly-knit warrior group known as comitatus, harking back to the ancient bands of sworn warriors who had once accompanied their lord into death.

The *Keyaksar*, the Emperor, *Padishah* Dana Bahram Tabatabaei himself, had a similar group around him, but while the *Anusiya*, the Companions of the Emperor, claimed to be comitatus, Hadi looked at the man across the table and rated him nothing more than another drunkard.

Most of the Anusiya seemed to fall into the same category.

The Ishtan had stolen many of Daniel Lémieux's memories of Kathra Omezi's comitatus. Hadi probably knew those women better than any other outsider in the galaxy. Those women were fierce. Warriors.

Not drunks and playboys.

Erin would have sneered at these men. Rightfully so.

With each passing moment, Hadi understood that the Ishtan had been right about the Sept.

Or his blinders had finally been removed, allowing him to see the truth of the palace.

The decadence, the moral decay that surrounded him.

Sept had once been the seven great clans that conquered the ancient homelands. Then came to represent the seven continents of Earth as they moved outward to conquer all the colonies of men.

And non-men.

Great clan names.

Tabatabaei. Aghaei. Sardari. Nasri. Mirzadeh. Sidiqi.

And Pasdar. The man beside him. One of the few worthy of the ancient respect.

The Sidiqi across the way was probably only impressive to the servants from whom their continued employment required such a thing. Even in his own mind, Hadi Rostami refused to call the man comitatus.

He would not insult the capable women around Kathra Omezi so.

Wealth. Decadence personified. That was the impression the Sidiqi drinking companion conveyed as Amirin made small talk with the man.

As a commoner, silent Hadi, seated off to one side and back, barely rated notice.

But Amirin Pasdar had changed over the last year.

The mighty warrior, so dour and intense, had shifted somewhat to the side in the man's body. He was not gone, but Amirin had learned to conduct himself more like a courtier and less like a man with a brutal, ancient knife scar marring his forehead and skull.

Each of the fools before this, Hadi had merely implanted the need to see that Amirin Pasdar and his servant be moved along to a more important person.

This was something of a penultimate step. There weren't more important men left.

They had reached the opening move in a much larger game.

Hadi reached inside the Sidiqi's mind and simply watched the man.

Up until now, twisting someone's mind had not been all

that risky, as they were all faceless bureaucrats who would not matter tomorrow.

The Sidiqi had a name. And a power base. Hadi would need to move more carefully, in case Amirin needed the man intact later. Companions of the Emperor might yet be of some value to the next one to sit on that throne.

The Sidiqi's mind suddenly turned a corner away from mere pleasantries and grew exceptionally serious as Hadi watched.

"So I am given to understand, Pasdar, from the Argbadh no less, that you think we should alter our plans," the Sidiqi said suddenly "That we should ignore the Free Worlds facing us and move on instead to the threat of the new aliens your servant found."

It spoke volumes that the very *Commander in Chief* of the Sept Navy, the *Argbadh* himself, was rated as nothing more than a servant in this man's mind. But then, thus were all men who were not born *Vuzurgan*, in the eyes of those who were.

Hadi refrained from sneering at the fool across the desk.

Barely.

"Not entirely ignoring them," Pasdar deflected politely. "But perhaps adapting the plan somewhat."

Neither Amirin nor Hadi knew what plans the great powers of the empire had. Or the Andarzbad for that matter, the councilors to the *Padishah* who might only be mere commoners like men such as Hadi Rostami might aspire to.

Wheels within wheels.

"Tavle Jocia," the man said bluntly.

Among their kind, that sort of approach was almost an insult. Hadi watched Pasdar refuse to rise to the bait. But Amirin also knew full well that Hadi could twist this Sidiqi if it became necessary. Shatter him, perhaps, like other men whose minds had failed as Hadi learned to control his power on the flight home.

"It does represent one of the crown jewels of the Free Worlds," Amirin smiled. "Ownership of it gives us significant influence over the worlds we have not yet conquered. In time, with the right Shah over them, it might become a dab of honey on a leaf, delightfully enticing the others into joining for the trade benefit, rather than requiring an object lesson in power."

Hadi was impressed. Amirin Pasdar had truly learned to act and sound like these fops, even as Hadi Rostami had merged personalities with Amirin Pasdar enough to see past the elaborate façade.

"Shah?" Sidiqi asked disdainfully. "You?"

"Oh, no," Pasdar smiled warmly and shook his head. "I see a more military role for myself in our glorious future. Our mighty Keyaksar should appoint one of his closest allies, one of his favorites to such an important job. A man with military background, certainly, but also a capable politician who can bring the restless natives around. The system itself is rather wealthy and sophisticated. It could bring much reward to such a man. Much more valuable than one would expect, given its location. I was pleasantly surprised during my recent jaunt there."

All *Vuzurgan* were expected to serve in the military at some point, if they could. Absolutely, if they had any aspirations to sit at the foot of the dread Padishah and drink his wine.

Amirin might have been describing the Sidiqi before them, but the same words probably encompassed all of those men, at least at these rarefied levels.

"Oh?" Sidiqi asked obliquely, suddenly more polite in his demeanor.

Hadi reached out a delicate finger now and nudged the Sidiqi's mind. Not much. And nothing out of character.

Enough to tempt a man like Sidiqi to consider suggesting to their Lord that he be made a Shah of a newly-conquered world like Tavle Jocia, where the great wealth of those shipyards and trading houses might flow into his coffers, rather than one of his rivals at Court.

Not every man is led astray by his penis, after all. Some can be had for mere gold.

"Indeed," Amirin replied to the Sidiqi lord. "It was my hope to find allies at Court who could see the long-term benefits of perhaps approaching some of the Sept Empire's problems with something other than a hammer."

Another seed planted. Hadi made sure that it was well buried in the fertile soil of a man who already had his doubts about Emperor Dana Bahram Tabatabaei.

Subtlety and guile, rather than immense rages and scorched earth.

Amirin Pasdar would need many allies when he made his move to eliminate the current fool seated on that throne.

It would be even better if men like this Sidiqi thought that such support was their own idea.

SEVENTEEN

Daniel studied *SeekerStar*'s dining hall as he walked into it, amazed at the social and emotional changes already visible in the faces and the eyes of those present, and the implications going forward.

Both Kathra and Erin were well along in their pregnancies now. Even starting to show, however slightly. Daniel could sense the second being each was carrying as a sort of generalized bundle of love and need, but neither child was far enough along to be a person yet.

But both women glowed. Daniel had been around very few happily-pregnant women in his time. Partly, that was an occupational hazard, as he hadn't been the least interested in being a father then, and was due to get his booster updated soon enough that it wouldn't be an issue again for another half decade.

Assuming Kathra didn't order him to abstain for several months while he made contributions to the tribe's sperm bank. His power could not be transmitted, but he supposed that brains and force of will might offset size and color.

The Commander would make those decisions. Not him.

Ife and Ndidi carried themselves like warriors now. Not like the old comitatus women, who tended to be jaguars resting as they considered whether or not to eat you, but hardened soldiers ready to go into battle at the drop of a pan.

Wyll Koobitz surprised Daniel by also being present, at what he would have expected was a private Mbaysey planning meeting.

But then again, the larger situation might mean war with the Anndaing, so Merchants Bank would want their fin in the soup as well.

Daniel caught Kathra studying him closely as everyone got settled. He almost felt like a stranger, entering into the comitatus dining hall aboard *SeekerStar*, which was always where Kathra did such things.

Perhaps because of that she had cleared the room and the kitchen behind it of all crew, and put a sign on the door for the comitatus itself to remain outside until admitted.

That probably frosted a couple of them, but again it wasn't Daniel's decision, so he wouldn't have to deal with the fallout.

It wasn't even his kitchen anymore. Nor Ndidi's.

But Kathra's eyes had a sharp appraisal when she looked at him. Not hostile but digging some into his soul.

He smiled wanly at her and asked with his eyes if they should have their own quick meeting.

She nodded tightly, a response which frightened him even more that just talking in front of a group such as this.

So he took her into that living room that hadn't been his childhood home. Daniel assumed by now that it must have been some vid he didn't remember from his youth.

Kathra sat on the couch. He put himself at the front window, with the sunlight to his back and the shadows cast before him.

The scene outside seemed to feel like a cold fall day, even as Kathra was brightness and joy to look at. Perhaps he was just feeling old as two of his favorite people were becoming mothers.

"Commander?" he asked tentatively.

"I wanted to see how you were doing," Kathra answered, unfolding those impossibly long legs and standing, putting her nearly two heads above him.

Her smile brought him comfort he had not realized he had been lacking.

"*Bon*, I think," he said.

She stepped close enough that he had to tilt his head back to look into her eyes.

"You seem calmer, more at peace than you have been since the day you first walked onto my deck," Kathra noted.

Daniel paused and turned inside for a moment.

"Yes, I would agree," he nodded.

She held out her hand as an invitation, and Daniel took it, merging with her for a long moment so that she could step inside him and find whatever it was she was looking for.

At this point, words between them were frequently unnecessary.

Kathra stepped back after an instant that might have lasted an eternity.

"Are the Mbaysey that great a trial for you?" she asked compassionately, returning to the couch and stretching comfortably upon it. "I can smell Tanuss on your skin."

"That is an occasional fling," Daniel shrugged, taking the seat in the corner of the room. Close to her, but still separate, if that was possible. "But the Mbaysey maintain a different relationship with Daniel the Chef, Kathra."

"Oh?"

"I must subvert myself to you, to them, at all times," he continued. "That is a good thing, because it keeps me grounded in myself. Keeps me from ever accidentally turning into a mad god. But Tanuss approaches me as an outsider. Another alien who is alone and perhaps lonely. With her I can have a relationship of equals, such as we have carved out, from time to time."

"Have you ever merged with her?" Kathra asked.

"*Non*," Daniel replied. "Not until you or one of the few others who could do so decided to order it, or allow it."

"Will it continue?"

Daniel shrugged.

"Others have considered such a thing from time to time, but not pursued it," Daniel answered. "We are all adults."

"And you do not consider A'Alhakoth an adult?" she pressed.

Daniel grimaced. Too much soul-searching with no good answers. Kathra knew that as well as he did. Probably better, since she would not have any evasions about it to deal with.

Intellectually, he knew A'Alhakoth was considered an adult by her own kind. But it did not help his peace of mind that she and Ndidi were almost exactly the same age, and he considered the second woman something of a daughter or favorite niece.

"I had wondered if you might have assigned her to *SwiftStar*, but then I did the logistics in my head and realized that you had everyone in the exact spot where they would do the most good for your cause," Daniel replied finally. "And each of us serve your will in all things."

"If I could spare you, I would send you to Kanus for a time, just so you two could sort it out," Kathra offered. "Or spare her."

"Do you really need her at Kanus, Kathra?" Daniel flipped the question on its head. "Would it be better for your cause if you and Erin returned to that world and truly made it the center of your operations, commanding the tribal squadron from the fringe as you intend? I've seen your plans. Forcing all the trademasters to come to Kanus would certainly change their own math."

"And send her with *SwiftStar*?" Kathra grinned. "Let you build up your harem?"

It was an old joke with no heat and instead much respect and love.

"Ife will explain. Or Ndidi," Daniel said. "We need an alien to confound the Upynth. They might know the Anndaing, but the Kaniea ought to be new to them. Tanuss would be a candidate, as would Acqueir, but both would need to become comitatus in order to succeed at such a deception."

"Has the Anic approached you, too?" Kathra grinned.

"I am, at best, confused by Acqueir's behavior, but I have not dug deep enough into Anic culture to know the truth," Daniel retorted with a lopsided grin.

"And that is why you must submit to me, Daniel," she laughed, deep and warm. "Otherwise, too many women might turn into groupies around you."

He shrugged. Daniel found himself short, slight, and largely forgettable, if everyone was not involved in a competition involving the kitchen.

Did women find that sort of expertise arousing?

Maybe. Certainly human women had chased after him. But Anic? Or Wisp?

"Yes," Kathra answered the unspoken question as if she could read his mind. But then, she was already inside his mind right now, so maybe she could.

He shrugged.

"My will is not my own, Commander," he said simply. "Nor should it be."

"As long as you remember to like yourself at the end of the day," she said.

Daniel nodded to the woman, and dropped them back into the universe.

EIGHTEEN

Kathra took a breath and considered all the sudden implications and slight hints of flavor she had picked up from Daniel in that eye blink. How much that he knew or suspected. How much was merely conjecture by an intensely intelligent person.

She glanced around the meeting hall. Three long rows of painted aluminum trestle tables in a flat gray where the comitatus ate and planned as a single entity. The table by the door to the kitchen, where food and various beverages were set out for the women to grab as they needed. The little side table, empty now, where Daniel or Ndidi had occasionally surprised people with brownies or other treats.

So much was going to change.

Only Erin had caught the moment Kathra and Daniel went elsewhere, but she didn't say anything. The two of them were largely inseparable right now, anyway, and had been for more than three decades at this point, so Erin might as well be her, as far as outsiders might be concerned.

Comitatus.

"Ndidi, since you commanded the assault, I will start with your report," Kathra said simply. "Then Ife. Finally, what we need to do as things begin to change around us."

Her plans would change, of that Kathra had no doubt. She was a major player on a complicated game board, but there were several others involved who were at least as smart as she was. Possibly as driven.

Certainly as mean.

Ndidi had to be prompted to go into a full blow-by-blow report, but Kathra was showing the woman off, both to herself and to Wyll. Most people did not realize how near perfect Ndidi's memory was.

Kathra wanted Merchants Bank impressed by the young woman, against future need.

"You took no prisoners at all?" Wyll asked, slightly aghast from the tone of that shark's voice when Ndidi finished.

Ndidi turned to the male and let some of her hidden anger come to the surface. "Black swan."

Wyll flinched from that rage.

"A what?" he asked delicately.

"A human, cultural idiom, sir," Ndidi explained tightly. "Swans are white birds. A black one is so rare and unpredictable that it cannot be accounted for in any plans. *SwiftStar* was playing the part of a random, alien encounter with something powerful, dangerous, and vindictive, come from out of the dark to destroy them without any conversation or even warning. At some point, it will become known that the ship is Mbaysey, and we will have to change our behavior, because I will want prisoners to interrogate. First, however, the Sept needs to discover fear."

Kathra alone of the group had spent enough time around the Anndaing spymaster to appreciate the minor flexing of his hammer, and how much of a reaction that was from the usually-imperturbable male. A human would have leaned back unconsciously, eyes wide and mouth possibly fallen open.

"And prisoners?" he asked carefully.

"Next batch, I want to know their souls, sir," Ndidi sounded like the voice of doom. "I have recently come to understand aspects of Sept culture the Mbaysey do not generally talk about in polite company, such as how many women I likely killed in the assault, and their apparent role aboard such vessels."

Kathra noted that Wyll started to ask, caught himself, and glanced to her with his nearer eye. Yes, that would be a conversation for the two of them to have at another time. They had not told the Anndaing in general, but that would probably serve to rally many people to her side, when it came out.

The Anndaing were merchants, not specist-supremists. Holding someone in slavery was already anathema to them. Sexual slavery would light an ugly bonfire when Kathra was ready for it.

That day was coming.

The Commander turned to Ndidi and noted the white-hot rage lying so close under the surface. Just behind those thick glasses. She watched it recede as the silence stretched and the young woman got better control of her emotions.

Kathra had wondered when Ife would tell Ndidi about the women the Sept would keep on such vessels. Apparently not until afterwards. Probably to keep the young chef in glasses focused on a singular, destructive task.

The males of the galaxy might not be safe when Ndidi had her own command, one of these days.

"Ife, what is your next step, having bloodied their noses?" Kathra asked.

"That was why it was necessary for us to return home, having completed our first mission, Kathra," the Speaker for *SwiftStar* answered obliquely, waiting for Kathra to nod before she proceeded. "We can seek after other such bases, probably buried in quiet parts of the Free Worlds, but that requires us to maintain a massive logistics train, especially if we add a ground combat force to the crew."

Ife paused and Kathra took a moment to look at everyone else. Daniel was a little gray around the edges, but holding up well. There must be some element there that she hadn't explored in merging with him.

"Second, we can establish our own bases of some sort, but that requires significant resources from ourselves or our allies," Ife went on with a nod to Wyll. "Finally, we could bypass the Bhaorajj entirely and make contact directly with the Upynth in their home sectors. If the person negotiating with the Upynth was not human, it might be some time before the Sept learned the truth."

"Candidates?" Kathra asked, again glancing over at Daniel and feeling his discomfort grow, like an oyster rapidly building up a pearl.

"On my current crew, my Anic sensors officer, Acqueir Chanthraphone and my Wisp engineer, Tanuss Barleyne," Ife answered.

Kathra suddenly saw why Daniel was quietly grinding his teeth.

And why he would accept any decision she made, however it might affect him personally.

Comitatus. Sworn body and soul.

Whatever the cost.

It wasn't always your body that you had to give up in her service.

Neither of those women was comitatus. That could

change, but then Daniel would have to subvert himself to them as he did with all her women. Merge with them and let them see all of his secrets.

And he would, of that she had no doubts.

Kathra also saw why his suggestion about her moving to Kanus permanently would perhaps play into such a complicated mélange of personalities.

It would free up A'Alhakoth to become the alien Ife needed, a Kaniea who might possibly be known in Upynth space, but very obviously was not a human, whom they would know. And one already comitatus.

Daniel might be free to continue the occasional dalliance with the alien Wisp, or the Anic. Or he might find a way to finally work things out with A'Alhakoth, but Kathra had never until this moment considered that Daniel would have to subvert himself fully to the Kaniea woman as comitatus.

On top of everything else, they could never have a relationship of true equals. The Wisp offered him that. The Anic might.

And if Kathra made either of those women comitatus, and she would need to if that was the part they were to play, Daniel would suffer.

He saw something in her eyes now, but he was closer to her in some ways than even Erin. He smiled wanly and nodded, just the slightest bit.

Because he would do whatever she ordered, without question or hesitation.

Suddenly, Kathra had a better understanding of how easy it could be to become a mad god herself. How Urid-Varg had come to be in the first place.

If nobody could stop you but yourself, you had to remember not to treat everyone around you as mindless game pieces to be moved on a board at your whim and need.

At least if you wanted to retain your humanity.

Kathra drew a heavy breath and popped her shoulders, aware of how high they had crept without her realizing it.

"I will need to interview both women personally," Kathra said of the two officers. "In addition, I will need to consider sending A'Alhakoth, as she is already vetted fully and can speak with my voice."

Daniel's flinch was probably indiscernible to anybody but her. Possibly Erin saw as well, considering the strange and delicate relationship those two had as something like adult siblings.

The others missed it, even Ndidi, who had been Daniel's confessor at one point. But Ndidi had her own demons to wrestle with now, and didn't need to try to save Daniel at the same time.

Kathra leaned back and considered how much of the comitatus she might send along with the next mission.

She would need to also meet with Areen privately, as that woman had occasionally dabbled with the *Rabic* male, although never particularly seriously.

Kathra might end up having to completely surround Daniel with women who might look on him with favor, but she also knew that he would likely retreat behind a glassy shell if she did that.

But that was a problem of personalities, and she would have to solve it herself. She turned to Wyll now and focused on him.

"I think it is time that Merchants Bank took more of a public stand," she said simply. "You've read the basic reports, and there is much information I can fill in, if you would like to accompany us to Kanus."

"Kanus?" the man asked. "I had thought that you intended to continue to base *SeekerStar* here for the time being."

"I had," Kathra replied. "But my war is going to get larger, faster than I had anticipated. Probably faster than you planned. We will need to make decisions soon."

"Decisions," he echoed her word.

"I cannot destroy the Sept alone, Wyll."

PART TWO
PIRATES

"You're sure?" Crence asked, his entire head rotated to study Jine in the pilot's seat.

"Sure? Absolutely not," the nightflier replied sarcastically. "Do I look telepathic?"

"Okay, fine," Crence harrumphed. "Patterns of probability?"

"I know almost as many humans as you do, Crence," Jine said. "And I've flown with you for a lot of years. If that isn't a pirate stalking my tailfin, then the silly eel is spotting for one, somewhere nearby. Narrow beam comm laser or something."

Crence studied the screen again as the other ship was slowly backing away from the station, almost perfectly in synch with *Koni Swift*.

Tavle Jocia was a mess in orbital space. Jine's systems were currently tracking nearly seven thousand large objects in close space, between stations, freighters, satellites, and country craft that only flew semi-ballistically around the planet itself as ground transport.

How in the three hells the nightflier had picked out the purple one as a potential problem, Crence had no idea.

But that was also why he continued to employ such a lousy poker player.

Crence muttered the sort of profanity that would have gotten his teeth polished with fresh sand, were his mother around right now to hear it. A Cargo-6 wasn't a speed demon by any stretch of imagination.

He'd known people who carved out cargo capacity to put in faster engines and bigger generators, including that one silly shark who suffered a breakdown at least once a week.

But when everything worked, that crazy bastard had the fastest sled in the galaxy.

Koni Swift was a fat, happy turtle, loaded up with trade goods and set to make one hell of a profit when he got anywhere friendly. Didn't even have to make it to Ogrorspoxu. Even Acran would make his quarter. The capital would simply make his decade.

Assuming he didn't get his silly ass jumped along the way by pirates who thought they could take him. Worse, if they thought that, they were probably right.

"How do we lose him?" Crence asked plainly.

Jine scratched at his chin. Never a good sign. Meant he was up to no good.

Even worse no good than usual.

The sort of thing that might get them a fine and stern talking to at Ogrorspoxu. Maybe short prison sentences.

Crence liked it already.

"I do not like to fly predictable," Jine began, almost evasively.

His hammer flexed defensively when both Crence and Dane started roaring with laughter.

"Not funny, you two," he continued after they had gotten the giggles under control.

"Sorry," Crence prompted him, wiping tears from his left eye.

"So, we've been flying this like good little merchants," Jine said. "Follow all the rules of local navigation and crap like that, right?"

"Indeed," Crence nodded. "I presume you want to get silly?"

"Wyll would have my pilot's license," Jine replied.

"He's not here, and if there are pirates stalking us out of Tavle Jocia orbit, then the war might have already started and we need to get home to report, by fin or by frenzy."

"Kinda my thought," Jine nodded now. "I'm assuming a stern chase to home systems now, since someone will have told the humans where those are, even if they can't really talk Anndaing all that well."

"My guess as well," Crence sobered. "The chain of systems and stops is pretty well established and published on our side, since we need to stop and listen for emergency traffic in case one of the others breaks down in K'bari space."

"So I want to pull a Mbaysey move," Jine said.

Crence felt his eyes close to popping out.

"What?"

"Those women fly like pirates a lot of the time, right?" Jine asked.

Crence hadn't seen it, whatever his silly nightflier had, but now might be the time to get a little desperate.

"Go on."

"Trademasters like to know where they are at every moment," Jine turned his head enough that both eyes could look this direction, showing Crence just how serious the shark was. "Lazy, predictable sorts of folks. I plan to set the usual path, just like we always do. Hop out to the spot at the edge of the system we've used on the previous trips, so we're clear of everything before we take an hour and plot the next jump across the pond."

"With you so far," Crence nodded soberly.

"The drives can actually be charged in about thirty-eight seconds if every generator is running flat out," Jine's voice also got serious now. Deadly serious. "I can't approximate anything narrower than a twenty-degree cone of uncertainty when we land, even on a hop this short, because the nose comes out kinda askew from jump wobbliness."

Crence felt himself pucker at the thought of *jump wobbliness*, but he had hired the best expert he could find for a reason.

"And?" Crence asked.

"And then I simply light the drives again as soon as they charge, not even bothering to try to baseline anything more than that cone," Jine said. "We hop. Whoever's there hops right behind us, presumably, because they're already expecting us—me—to panic. Second jump is a medium one. Maybe fifteen light-years. Long enough I have time to back-map from the sensor snapshots and estimate our path."

"Okay?" Crence just uttered sound to keep Jine talking at this point.

"We land somewhere," Jine continued, growing more and more serious. "And jump again thirty-nine seconds after that. Maybe the pirates have followed in time to see us go. Maybe not. Land and hop a fourth time as soon as we're somewhere. Again, just point and fire. Nothing but star plots to feed into the nav system, along with distances. Worst case, I have a sphere of uncertainly about sixty light-years across. I can keep bouncing if they manage to stay with us, but I'm swimming for my life here, and they aren't. At some point, they give up and go after easier prey. Or we identify them as an enemy warship and go into Armada service. That happens, and I maybe bend my plot to Thrabo and see if that stupid eel wants to take on all the friendlies there. Ought to be maybe twenty ships there, Cargo-2 and up. Enough guns to dissuade anybody feeling frisky. Unless he wants to be on the inside of a feeding frenzy."

Crence paused to swallow.

He didn't ask how long Jine had been planning something like this. Probably since the first time he looked at the night sky and wanted to fly. They were all like that. Every nightflier he'd ever met.

Craziest bastards in the galaxy, bar none.

Most of them never turned into piratical rascals at any point in their careers.

Maybe Kathra Omezi was going to need to hire a second warship at some point? Jine would be perfect for that role, if today was any indication.

Crence turned to Dane to get his attention. Both of the other sharks quieted.

A chasm opened up in Crence's mind.

All this over a ship that just happened to back out of the station at the same time as *Koni Swift*, headed on a roughly parallel track outwards.

Enough to cause Jine Riffin to stand his fin straight up and get twitchy.

Worse, it was catching.

"As of this moment, we are in Armada service," Crence declared officially.

Every trademaster had that authority, but the Board would review his actions later and decide whether or not to strip Crence Miray of his Trademaster credentials for it, with the bonus exactitude of hindsight that only an Anndaing's hammer-wide eyes could bring to the table.

"We will consider that ship and any others we encounter to be hostile warships until I declare otherwise," Crence said calmly, knowing that the flight recorder would pick it up and possibly damn him for all time.

"Jine, execute your plan."

TWENTY

CRENCE HAD Dane's sensor output echoed on his boards as *Koni Swift* dropped out of that first jump, the one that took them to the edge of the Tavle Jocia heliosphere.

The guns were already unlocked.

Might as well be ready to unleash a pocket feeding frenzy on the bastard if this turned out to be an ambush.

A clock started counting down on the wall in big, yellow numbers as soon as the stars returned.

Thirty-seven.

"Anything?" Crence asked the room.

He didn't care who answered. Just that both Jine and Dane were paying attention. Aft, the rest of the crew was at battlestations, just like the emergency drills now held every month since they'd first run into Kathra Omezi and come to understand that the galaxy might have gotten more dangerous than they expected.

"Negative," Dane called.

Crence flexed his fingers and tried to keep his fin from standing straight out backwards. It tended to rub the sides raw on the chair if he was too tense.

Today he might be too tense.

Thirty-one.

"Contact!" Dane yelled. "Shit."

"What?" Crence snapped.

"He's good," Dane said. "Jine, twenty-two points aft, up six. Closing hard and fast."

"Screw you, human," Jine snarled under his breath.

Crence watched the shark pull all his nightflier magic out and start punching it into the keyboard. Weirdly, his fin was totally flopped over right now, but Jine was like that when things got finicky.

Koni Swift rolled hard on a side axis. Enough that even over the grav system Crence felt the coils inside his head turning upside down for a moment.

The engines lit hard from what had been relative rest earlier. You didn't need power going through jump. The engines handled that. Better to be slow and maneuverable, in case something was in the way at the moment when you appeared.

Jine had just redlined the engines while turning to bring the ventral guns to bear. Crence didn't understand why, since dorsal had more firepower and better armor, but it also suddenly put the human pirate below them and to his side as *Koni Swift* pushed hard against a new vector.

Must have learned something from Daniel or one of the women, because the ship behind them didn't push down as hard, trying to chase.

Two-dimensional fighters? Silly buggers to go all in with a shark, then.

The hull rattled as a shot slammed into rear armor. Lights flickered as the aft turret opened up, rapid firing a staccato counter.

Seventeen.

"Second contact," Dane called. "Eel brought friends. Oh, and he came in high and off to one side of the first verk."

Koni Swift began to dive away from both of the human pirates.

Crence assumed human. *Pirate* was pretty obvious from their behavior.

The second ship was larger. Looked meaner, too. More like a warship and less like a human-style freighter.

Nine.

The hull rang again. Pretty solid shot. Fancy shooting, too, coming out of jump like that. Must have been parked close in the darkness, which made sense, since Jine had gone outward on the usual trajectory, like he didn't know there were troublemakers out here.

"All hands, party time," Jine's voice came out of the speakers.

Crence would have expected something more formal. Less casual, at least.

But this was Jine. The craziest nightflier Crence had ever considered hiring to fly him around a hostile galaxy.

Crence felt a lurch as Jine spun the nose up hard, slipped a little right on the gyros, and Dane fired a few, almost-random shots at the original stalker.

One.

More fire incoming and rattling the hull. Sustained. That was a warship. No freighter had enough generators to push that many guns at the same time without the engines exploding pretty quickly.

Zero.

"Jine?" Crence snarled nervously as nothing happened.

And then they were gone.

TWENTY-ONE

A'Alhakoth studied the note again. It had come from her father, of all people, and was the thing that let her know *SeekerStar* had abruptly returned to Kanus.

How had he heard about it, even up here on the station with her, faster than anyone else who could have sent a message?

But then she smiled. She was used to thinking of Linga as merely her father, a middle-aged, middle-tier Jarl, the lowest rank of nobility among the Kaniea.

The man must have either created or upgraded a spy network when he was forced onto the larger stage by the return of the prodigal daughter and all her friends.

All of her exceptionally dangerous friends.

A'Alhakoth's new family.

She looked quickly around her quiet office in the diplomatic and cultural section of the station. Noted the art her parents had provided from the family hall. Two potted plants in corners in front of her where they would occasionally provide fruit.

A'Alhakoth was not, thank the creators and destroyers,

responsible for handling any of the trade between the various factions involved: Mbaysey, ver'Shingi, or Kaniea. At the same time, she was Kathra's Ambassador, so every problem eventually came to her, even from the dangerously-smart old women who commanded the various ClanStars, which surprised her.

But A'Alhakoth was comitatus. An extension of Kathra's will. These women respected that.

And they damned well better, after demanding that the Commander refrain from serving on the front lines any more.

Interesting. The note also said that *SwiftStar* was flying in formation with *SeekerStar*.

What did that say about her specific future?

A'Alhakoth was unsure, except to send a quick note to her assistant, canceling every one of her current commitments for the next several days and asking to reschedule.

These merchants understood *force majeure*.

She rose and made her way across the station to the trade section, where her father was present instead of Alla, although she wondered if her brother might be returning aboard one of the ships.

A'Alhakoth didn't get to see her father as much as she might have preferred. She could generally only be seen with the man on formal occasions, rather than regularly and privately, if she wished to present as a neutral diplomat. Father understood that.

Still, she felt like a child again, sneaking into his office when he was working and she was eight. A finger to her mouth to shush the secretary before the woman could reach for the internal comm. Secrecy and privacy were called for right now.

That worthy nodded, but she was also a family retainer, a

middle-aged woman who had been with the house for longer than A'Alhakoth had been alive.

A'Alhakoth nodded back and smiled. She stepped to the door to the inner sanctum, feeling tiny and mischievous all over again.

Where do the children go?

She was adult now. Supposed to act like one. And an Ambassador and a Comitatus Warrior for the Mbaysey as well.

Screw that.

She waited for the hatch to slide silently to the side and slipped into Father's office quickly enough that it shut again behind her almost immediately.

He was deep in his papers. Always papers, even on a station in geo-synch orbit, as part of an interstellar culture. Amazingly, Linga looked younger now than she remembered him then, if that was possible. Certainly rejuvenated by the effort of joining modern society directly, rather than just preparing all his children for whatever the fates would cast at them.

Including Mbaysey.

He glanced up. Nothing moved but his eyes, then they flickered back down.

She stood perfectly still.

"Last time you did that, you at least brought me one of your cookies," he observed, speaking down into his paper.

A'Alhakoth grinned and blushed at the memory.

She had. And had forgotten.

"Daniel will be here shortly," she replied, stepping close enough to take the closer chair and sit, like she had then. "And Ndidi. I'm sure we can convince them to make a batch."

Linga put down his report and smiled, studying her.

She was dressed comitatus style, with the tangerine jacket

that matched her pants, rather than the turquoise that Ife and Ndidi wore while aboard *SwiftStar*. And had her pistol on her hip, as always.

"Better this way, even without the cookies," he apparently decided. "Is there something special that brings you to my door without them? Besides the return of *SeekerStar*?"

"*SwiftStar*," she replied, letting her voice sound like an eight-year-old runaway for a bit longer, even as adulthood intruded. "Something has changed. The original plan was not for Ife to come here."

"I saw no reports of significant damage to the vessel," he said, not offering the source of that report.

Or what spies he might have.

Nor should he. They would be Alla's spies eventually, not hers.

And A'Alhakoth had her own that she didn't share.

"So what fears drive you?" Linga asked.

"Not fears," she countered. "Again, you did not mention other warships or fleets accompanying them, so the news is more personal. Mbaysey."

"I gathered that as well," he nodded, leaning back now to study her. "The war has finally intruded enough that Kathra is adjusting her plans."

A'Alhakoth shrugged.

"Pointless speculation, when she will be able to tell us in a few hours," she offered. "But change is likely, on a scale important enough to affect the Kaniea."

"And you, dear daughter?" he smiled. "Come to hide from your nanny with cookies?"

"Next time I will bring us a plate to share," she promised with a grin. "I had truly forgotten that part, or I would have stopped by the kitchen on my way here. What happens to trade if the war does intrude?"

"Kanus is protected against pirates." His eyes got a

distant look. "Sept fleets could presumably sneak all the way across the K'bari gulf, but would require time to build up a network of bases, and I must presume at this point that the Anndaing are fin-up against such an occurrence, although nobody has mentioned it to us poor provincials. Similarly, preparations to invade the Free Worlds have been effectively muted."

"Invade?" A'Alhakoth gasped.

"Indeed, daughter," he smiled grimly. "If a war is to be fought, better it be handled over there, where the Free Worlds can still assist us in resisting the Sept, rather than waiting for the humans to conquer so many systems and add them as resources on their own side. We might not call it an invasion, especially as we're trying to help and protect them, but the outcome does not vary much. Anndaing merchants and their squadrons patrolling Free Worlds space and offering trade. A different kind of master for the humans, perhaps, as you understand what Merchants Bank would be like as an overlord, but the Free Worlds would be hard pressed to resist us either. Unless they finally organized themselves into a thing, rather than merely an idea."

A'Alhakoth absorbed his accumulated wisdom, wishing she had a cookie to share and wondering if Kathra qualified as the nanny already searching the manor high and low for her missing charge. Tomorrow would presumably change everything.

"And the Kaniea?" she asked. "Will they join such a war willingly?"

No more the prodigal daughter, she was thinking and speaking as Kathra's ambassador now, charged with overseeing the needs of the Mbaysey.

Especially if war was called for.

"There will always be a small set of folks for whom it appears to be a grand adventure," her father replied, leaning back now and fixing his eyes on some distant, invisible horizon. "At the other end will be the usual pacifists demanding that intellectual negotiation is the only logical solution. Kathra Omezi will fall somewhere in the middle, if she recruits among our kind."

"Will the Anndaing fight?" A'Alhakoth probed. "For outsiders who have brought their wars here?"

"Again, you will have a spectrum," he nodded. "With the added factor that the Anndaing might decide to extend their trade network to include some portion of the human worlds, to say nothing of the concerted efforts probably already underway to investigate the K'bari worlds known to still harbor intelligent life. Both sides will need rest and repair stops, if such a war is to be anything more than a series of piratical strikes over hideously-long sailing distances."

"Are we facing another one of those wars for the future of the galaxy?" A'Alhakoth asked, shifting into a historic mode with a historian who still had a whole library of ancient tomes down on the planet below them.

"I find it a prescient symbolism that the Anndaing sold Kathra an Ovanii warship," he grimaced. "Especially since Urid-Varg is no longer capable of his swath of devastation. I have terrible nightmares of what might have happened had that monster decided to simply conquer the Sept and use that as his next grand empire."

A'Alhakoth shivered. She had seen the Conqueror directly in Daniel's mind. Learned more of that being's history than anyone else in Anndaing space who wasn't human.

The galaxy might have been doomed, had humans gone on another one of their great religious crusades against non-believers with an immortal mad god to lead them.

But for an Algerian chef and a fire suppression cylinder.

"Thinking of Daniel?" her father asked, drawing her back to the surface.

"What?" she asked, blushing.

"You have a particular smile on your face when you talk about him," Linga said. "Like now."

"He's not Kaniea," she protested.

"That only matters if you wish children, A'Alhakoth," her father said nonchalantly. "And you are Mbaysey now, so not even then, as you'll be able to have a Kaniea child from the sperm banks when you are ready."

She felt the blush reach all the way down to her toes seemingly. This was not the conversation she had envisioned having with her father today.

Or was it?

SwiftStar's return in the company of *SeekerStar* meant everything was changing. At the very least, she would get to see Daniel again. Perhaps talk more directly about things that had only been hinted at and teased ere now.

What did she want? Even A'Alhakoth did not have the answer to that, but she knew that Kathra, Erin, and most importantly Daniel believed in her as comitatus. That was sufficient.

"The galaxy will change tomorrow," she answered simply with a shrug.

"Oh no, daughter," Linga replied with a tone she usually associated with the ancient religious prophets pronouncing their doom on the world. "It begins now."

TWENTY-TWO

As BEFORE, Hadi Rostami should have been held back at one of the many social barriers that served to isolate the centers of extreme power from mere underlings like him. Only the noblest born were supposed to be allowed near the Keyaksar, the *Padishah* Dana Bahram Tabatabaei.

Indeed, in the various hallways and even at the entry to this vast chamber, many men had been of a mind to prevent Hadi from gaining that access, even moving quietly in Amirin Pasdar's wake like a remora. Each man had, in turn, come to the conclusion that no harm would come. Pasdar needed his aide to accompany him, after all, to handle all the little tasks a great commander like that needed to delegate, so he could handle grand planning.

Or something like that.

For each victim, Hadi had framed his nudges slightly differently, on the off-chance that such blood-sworn enemies as these men ever actually stopped fighting each other long enough to compare notes later.

Every once in a while, Hadi despaired at what he was doing. At this range, he could almost smell the terrible rot at the core of the Sept Empire. All that wealth being wasted on the finest wines and whiskeys, in a culture that supposedly forbade alcohol of any kind.

Then there were the dancing girls. Every size and shape and color. Not all of them were even human, if you looked close enough. But extremely pretty.

Every single one was young, too. Far too young, as Hadi saw it.

While they might hide the fear and despair from ever marring their eyes or makeup, he was privy to their minds by watching the emotional signatures as they came and went, or just lounged in the background until some Anusiya felt an urge and grabbed one to drag into a nearby chamber.

There were moments he considered warping these men hard enough that they drew blades and set upon one another, just to wipe out such a nest of vipers and make the galaxy a better place.

Certainly, the Ishtan would have already done so.

He couldn't remember, back when he had been human, how Hadi Rostami might have reacted to the overt depravity these men seemed to revel in. The florid complexions marred by broken blood vessels in the face and nose from so much alcohol consumption. The rich foods spilled mindlessly on the floor for servants to wipe up lest it mar someone's utterly-luxurious slippers.

The victims these men demanded.

Yes, the Ishtan would have wiped Rhages out and then sat back to see if the infection had been successfully excised, or if other men needed destroying.

All other men.

In that, he felt closer to Daniel Lémieux than any other being in the galaxy. And Kathra Omezi was a glorious study in professional command and leadership, compared to the fat toad seated on the throne at the far end of the vast auditorium Hadi had been admitted to.

He looked down the long hall, lit by stained glass windows and skylights vaulted far overhead. Bodies moving like tides, while an Emperor sat atop a distant throne and occasionally shared jokes with a selected few allowed to stand near him on that distant stage.

The man shared the same coloration of all of them. How many cousins, however many removed, were in this place waiting? All dressed in sumptuous silk robes rather than the more plain cotton that had been tradition.

At least in the age of tradition.

Hadi worked hard to keep his face utterly serene and noncommittal in the face of wanting to do terrible things in here.

They all had it coming.

Amirin moved like a shark among tuna, with Hadi a relentless remora in his wake. Hadi didn't bother even listening to the conversations, as nothing useful or important would be discussed here. These powerful men were here to enjoy themselves and the power they had accumulated. To flaunt that wealth and supremacy.

Instead, he merely planted seeds as he followed in Amirin Pasdar's wake. Mostly extending and reinforcing the wonder that a hard-ass killer like Pasdar had turned into such a courtly and intellectual figure, no longer considered socially awkward as a result of the immense drive and hunger a younger version of the man had had for military glory.

It didn't take much to deflect the Anusiya. Each saw Amirin as a threat, but Hadi made him also seem like a potential ally that could be drawn into each fool's camp to help defeat some other court rival at whatever games worthless dilettantes like these participated in when they had nothing better to do than rape alien children.

Taking the Ishtan power and using it like Urid-Varg might have done called to Hadi more and more every day he spent on Rhages. Every hour.

And yet, he needed these shits, even as Hadi watched one of the Anusiya conclude a conversation with Amirin, empty a wine glass off a passing tray in one gulp and then fling it over a shoulder before grabbing a handy girl from a nearby bench, literally dragging her by the arm until her longer legs allowed her to catch up.

Amirin turned and leaned close to Hadi, putting a hand on his arm like he was leaning in to mutter something in an ear. It was a code they had worked out to let Hadi know that Amirin had something he wanted to say without witnesses.

Hadi leapt them both up to that imaginary bridge of *Vorgash* that he kept in his head as a way of retaining his sanity.

Gone were the long, flowing court robes reminiscent of a desert nobody else on this planet could have survived for longer than a day. Well, the women who were slaves here were probably tougher than he was. And many of the mostly-invisible servants.

Hadi limited his sneer to the Andarzbad and the Anusiya. The Councilors and Companions. And the Keyaksar himself.

The two of them were back in naval uniforms, fit and severe.

"It was too bad the Ishtan didn't have a disease they could unleash on Rhages," Amirin snarled as he paced, Hadi on his wing as usual. "Wipe this place clean."

"Urid-Varg would have suggested anti-matter bombs," Hadi noted dryly. "The Ishtan in my soul echo that proposal. It was part of the reason they intended to depart after assisting us in destroying the chef."

"And they still think that it could be saved?" Amirin asked.

"Never saved," Hadi corrected. "You could take it from these men and attempt to replace it with something else. You might be successful. And you might end up burning it to the ground, either accidentally or with intent."

"The latter has its appeal, Hadi," Amirin continued to pace, his hands behind his back now and clenched, lest the man's utter rage be unleashed on a wall, even in this imaginary place. "I had no idea."

"Nor I," Hadi echoed. "What does this do to your planning?"

"Originally, I had intended to have you open a path by which a quick palace coup might allow me to seize power, calling on relatives and allies to deflect and defeat the others," Amirin continues. "More and more I think that most of this palace deserves to be simply put to death as quickly as possible. The Sept have become fouled by their continued existence."

"And a coup would not help?" Hadi pivoted mentally, allowing all his bureaucratic training and expertise to shift into new patterns.

"I need the ability to excise them, like the drunkards they are." Amirin stopped pacing and turned now to face him. "Expose them to an unforgiving public and rise on the shoulders of the fleet, who I will need, at that time when it becomes necessary to expose this place to the sorts of sunlight that will likely cause many of these fools to shrivel and die, like a slug under a pile of salt."

"Successful military campaigns have historically been one of the cleanest stepping stones for a general or other top commander to remove a corrupt ruling dynasty, back when Earth forces were ground combat oriented," Hadi noted. "In the modern age, a naupati would fulfill a similar role, which is why they are drawn exclusively from the ranks of the Seven Clans. The only exception is when a truly exceptional commander is adopted or married into one of the clans, in the rare instance where they weren't born there already."

Hadi paused and began to pace himself, feeling Amirin stand still but pivot to watch him.

"Does this end the entirety of Sept as a ruling caste?" Hadi asked rhetorically. "The Seven Clans have traditionally exercised power and been enough of a limiting factor on each other to keep things under control. Have they all become so thoroughly corrupted by the exercise of power that Sept have themselves become a parasite on the Empire they originally founded?"

"Any other person hearing those words would have you executed immediately, Hadi," Amirin smiled at him. "It is indeed a good thing that we have privacy to speak. How long until someone notices?"

"We could be here for about an hour and a little less than a second would pass out in the physical world," Hadi replied. "How much time do you need here?"

"Far less than that," Amirin decided, stepping to with the sort of decisiveness that Hadi had come to expect. "We need to twist a couple of minds here to make them happy to send me off on some fool's errand in the distant hinterlands, where I will be far removed from the centers of power and risk and less of a threat to them."

Hadi nodded. Twisting minds was a perfect way to describe his continued existence.

If only there were some way to twist enough of them, quietly enough that nobody realized before he was done. But the Ishtan had not given him that much power.

Wisely, on their part.

"What place do you think will give you the accumulated glory necessary to decapitate the Sept and generally wipe

Rhages clean of the taint of Dana Bahram Tabatabaei?" Hadi asked, letting his mind roam over the options.

"The same one we have already been suggesting to fools along the way," Amirin smiled. "The beating heart and brimming bank of the Free Worlds. We need to go off and conquer Tavle Jocia."

"Will that be sufficient to build your legend?" Hadi asked. "I had understood offering various fools the chance to become Shah of the place as a way to deflect and distract them. Will we still follow that path?"

"Indeed," Amirin smiled like a wolf at the edge of the firelight, eyes aglow in the cold darkness. "And it will draw Kathra Omezi and her allies to me, where we can destroy them as well."

TWENTY-THREE

Daniel missed having Erin flying him around. Between her and Kathra, Daniel hadn't flown more than a handful of times with any other Mbaysey pilot in years.

Stina Carte, Spectre Sixteen, had volunteered, but Ife was treating *SwiftStar* like a proper military vessel, at least as they all understood it, with all her senior officers acting like grownups. That meant they were all in the back of a small Ovanii transport that had originally been modified for Anndaing, and then a second time for humans.

The seats still had gaps down the middle for fins, but were pretty damned comfortable for the finless, too. It helped that everyone had legs roughly the same length. And ceilings that might have felt cramped for an Ovanii warrior were vaulted to a short human.

Daniel glanced around as the ship docked with *SeekerStar* and began to be pulled into the flagship's maw. The color pattern in here was that same mix of bold with polka dots or geometric shapes designed to offset the color in a happy way. Fierce, ancient warriors who also happened to be poets and playwrites.

At least the women with him were serious.

Ife looked like one of those ancient harpy eagles, the grandest and fiercest of their kind, as she turned and smiled back at him.

Beside her, Ndidi looked young, but not harmless nor soft. Almost a clone of her Speaker, save for those glasses that had kept her out of a Spectre cockpit when she was younger. Acqueir was reading something on a personal slab. Tanuss woke from a quick nap with a twitch.

Joane, Ngozi, and Stina looked somehow martial in ways the others didn't. Daniel put that down to them somehow reverting to the old comitatus, rather than the crisp professionalism that they had these days.

Vacation home to see the family, as it were.

"Ready to cook a big, comitatus dinner?" Ndidi asked with a smile as the various clamps locked on.

"Ebube might be offended if we took over her kitchen," Daniel grinned back at the woman.

"Tough," Ndidi shrugged. "We're going to gather everyone up. Maybe not tonight, but soon. All the old comitatus. All the new one. All the players. Maybe even the old women, but I doubt that. Kathra will probably wait a week and let that Kaniea, Linga, host us for something."

Daniel shrugged as well. Too many options to even guess at. And unnecessary, as they were about to board the flagship and get it directly from the Commander herself.

Instead, he wondered about who else might come from Kanus itself.

No, that was a lie. He was wondering what A'Alhakoth would say when he saw her. What he might say to the young woman. She was a woman. He had to keep reminding himself that. She could walk right up and kiss him, and it would be entirely appropriate, even as weird as it might feel.

Merde, he was a mess.

Ife rose and tugged her jacket into a perfection that spoke of a deeper understanding of good tailoring than Daniel had ever achieved. The others unbuckled and rose as *SeekerStar*'s spin gave them gravity after the freefall they had felt in approaching.

"We are Mbaysey," she announced simply. Fiercely. Even extending her terrible gaze to the alien women, Tanuss and Acqueir. "They step to the side for us, not the other way around."

Daniel nodded. As did the others. Ife had always been the quiet, competent type on *WinterStar* and *SeekerStar*, but that had masked an unbreakable toughness underneath.

It had taken her becoming comitatus to show that to the rest of the galaxy.

He went last. Not for any particular reason. The others would have let him into the line earlier had he pressed.

He just felt last today. The slowest moving, however quietly afraid of what he might find on that deck when he arrived.

Or who.

They didn't do anything formal when he emerged, like arranging themselves into lines or such. Instead, all the local comitatus were there, standing around and looking tough at each other, however wicked and sidelong the grins might be.

Even the usual catcalls were muted, but he didn't let that derail him.

Daniel made his way through the mob of various bodies, most of them taller than he was, if not giants. The only other male on this deck was Wyll, which was somehow appropriate, it being *SeekerStar*.

Even Ife had left the male assistants back on *SwiftStar* to maintain things, going so far as a Deputy Assistant Engineer, so that she could bring both Tanuss and Joane.

It felt more like a council of war than anything, but he

had no idea what even a terrible warrior like *SwiftStar* could do against a Sept Empire that fielded hundreds of Septagons in battle.

But this was Kathra Omezi. Other fools had made the mistake of challenging the woman. Most of them were dead now.

Periwinkle skin caught his eye. Cobalt-blue hair.

She stood behind Kathra and off slightly to one side, almost invisible behind the much taller Commander.

A skull more triangular than a human, seen face-on, with a prominent forehead partially hidden by bangs, and intense, navy eyes staring at him. A head that tapered down past dominating cheekbones to a tiny, delicate jaw.

She smiled. It was a private, knowing smile that looked like it should be more at home on a much older person.

Daniel had a moment of terror that he was a fly suddenly landed in her web, but it passed as her smile grew wider.

He was probably still doomed.

At least it would likely be pleasant, whatever that smile promised.

He turned his attention to Kathra instead.

The Commander also had a knowing smile on her face, but it didn't seem as predatory, if you wanted to split such hairs. Now was not the time to take her aside and ask, so he just turned to greet Wyll and let the many women of the comitatus thump him on the back, hug him, or plant a kiss on the top of his head.

Welcome home, as it were.

Because he and Kathra had already talked at Ogrorspoxu. Bound mentally as well as emotionally, as was necessary to keep him sane, when most of the women on *SwiftStar* didn't have the time or energy to truly babysit him and all his night terrors.

Daniel turned to Wyll, caught both eyes momentarily

centered on him, when Anndaing generally only used one, rarely turning their heads slightly to look directly at you.

But again, he and Wyll had talked at Ogrorspoxu when he was there, but nothing deep nor dangerous. Mostly a delivery of free books from someone's library collection, written in an obscure Ovanii style that machine translations could not do justice to.

Daniel felt weird, training machines to do a better job of translating delicate, Ovanii emotions onto paper, but it was at least something he could do to honor their memories.

Wyll nodded across the short distance, but remained otherwise closed.

"Everyone, Ebube will have lunch for us in the dining hall," Kathra announced in a serious voice. "Then we will talk."

Daniel shivered at the woman's tone. She would not be joining them in the coming war. Her and Erin would be moving to a new phase of their lives, with newly-born daughters possibly already walking if *SwiftStar*'s next mission was as long and interesting as Daniel expected it to be.

Instead of asking now, he followed the others. Tried to follow the others, but a bubble of women formed around him and almost silently seemed to chivvy him along, so he did not linger in the hallways of his old home.

Around the curve and up a deck to the comitatus hall. The place that been his home, however briefly, just as the same room on *WinterStar* had been his temple. His retreat.

Ebube emerged from the kitchen as he entered. In the past, he had always seen the quiet woman as nearly transparent, especially compared to the other chefs he had known.

It was almost like she could turn sideways and vanish, so little did her personality come out.

As a cook, he had found her solid and good, but lacking

that indescribable element that made Ndidi so amazing. Perhaps that was it. Ebube was merely a chef, while he and Ndidi were artists?

Daniel got a hug from the woman and suffered to be placed in the spot of honor, across from Kathra and Erin, between Ife and Ndidi on this side. All the other women surrounded them, leaving he and Wyll, on Kathra's other side, as bullseyes in a sea of martial femininity.

Food was good. Not up with the best meals that he had cooked on *SwiftStar*, but above the worst as well. Rotini in a brown sauce and then baked as a casserole.

Simple. Elegant.

Comforting.

Perhaps there was hope for Ebube to come into her own, without him and Ndidi to overshadow her.

Daniel caught a similar reaction in Ndidi's eyes as they ate. The others groused good-naturedly about the terrible food, but nobody was fooled.

He and Ndidi had left them in good hands.

The band of intense ice that had been around his heart seemed to melt, apparent now only because it was gone.

Kathra smiled knowingly. But then, she knew him probably better than he did, since she could see through the blind places he had erected over the years to keep his sanity.

As one does.

Eventually, the plates, dessert, and coffee got cleared from the tables, with Ebube and her assistants retreating to the kitchen and closing the space off.

Privacy, such as it was.

All of the comitatus were here. Plus several other women Daniel knew, not all of them human. But every single one was somebody that Kathra trusted.

And two forlorn males, one Anndaing and one *Rabic*.

Outsiders by definition, but that was okay as well.

It was Kathra's war. He was just a chef who served in other ways.

"Some of you have been on Kanus," Kathra spoke up over the suddenly-dying murmurs, leaving the room silent as a tomb. "And thus do not know that *SwiftStar* located and destroyed what we believe is the forward base from which *SeptStar* originally launched the raid on Ogrorspoxu."

Cheers and whistles, even from the women who did know. But it was a serious blow against the Sept, from women who had spent their lives living in fear of retribution.

It must feel good to deliver some.

"Further," Kathra continued, "we have good reason to believe that we can locate other such bases and do similar amounts of damage, eventually forcing the Sept to either commit massive amounts of force to protect such places, or abandon them until they can return in significant enough numbers to hold that line against us. Against you. I won't be out there with you, since I promised the old women that Erin and I would be safe."

Heads nodded in a silent rhythm. These truths were known. The Mbaysey would have a new generation of leaders soon. Another generation of warriors that would uphold Yagazie's dream.

Daniel wondered if Kathra would order him to make contributions to the eventual cause.

It was a better, cleaner form of immortality than Urid-Varg had intended.

"Now, we begin the next piece," the Commander intoned, looking around until her eyes fell on him.

Daniel felt like a mouse in a room filled with cats. But Wyll probably did, too.

His lot was to serve.

"I will send *SwiftStar* on a much longer mission next," Kathra continued. "True piracy, because Ndidi wishes to take prisoners from the Sept, instead of just collecting ears as trophies. That means ground combat troops, drawn from the comitatus, the Mbaysey, and what volunteers pass my standards."

Her eyes took on a sympathetic hue, as Daniel stared at her. Nobody else was probably in the right spot to see. Nor did they know her as well as he did.

"With those needs, I will move myself and *SeekerStar* to Kanus on a permanent enough basis," Kathra said. "At the same time, to maintain the illusion we create, Ife needs an alien to appear as ambassador to the Upynth, so that they do not realize that *SwiftStar* is a human vessel. I am sending A'Alhakoth with them. With Acqueir Chanthraphone and Tanuss Barleyne along we should be able to fool them. Kam, Nkechi, and Iruoma will lead the ground warriors that I send, along with enough alien recruits to keep the game going for a while."

She paused and studied every face in here. Daniel felt the weight of those eyes return to him.

"Eventually, we will need to break the Sept," Kathra said in a voice almost too quiet to be heard, but for the utter silence around her. One finger emerged from a fist and tapped the table between the two of them. "This is where it begins."

Daniel could have dropped a slice of onion on the floor and heard it bounce.

He turned to Wyll, almost as if Kathra was mentally controlling him.

"Wyll Koobitz," Daniel asked in a loud, hard voice. "What can the Anndaing and the Merchants Guild do to help?"

That shark blinked and his whole hammer flinched as he turned an eye towards Daniel.

Wyll knew the truth about Daniel. Few others outside this room did.

The Anndaing merchant's eyes both narrowed. His nearly-lipless mouth took on a hint of a grin. The nostrils above his hammer flared ever so slightly.

"Nothing, officially," he replied, waiting for the groans and rude comments to subside before he continued with a bigger smile. "You folks are just barbarian pirates running rampant in someone else's back yards, after all. But none of them have filed any sort of official complaint to date, so we won't believe such rumors. I presume you'll wish to recruit here and places along the way to your next trade venture. I might know a few people to chat with."

Yes, the Merchants Bank wouldn't want to take an official position here, especially not if the Anndaing were stirring up a war on someone else's home turf. A race war, since the Sept were dominated by a human-supremist cult intent on subordinating everyone else beneath their heels in layers of alienness.

"The storm is coming," Daniel reminded him.

"I've known that since the moment Crence Miray showed up on my station with you and Joane aboard, Daniel," Wyll replied, nodding to *SwiftStar*'s nerdy Assistant Engineer seated a little ways down the bench. "But convincing the Board to Call the Armada is not something done quickly."

He paused a beat to turn back to Kathra.

"Even if I agree that it will be necessary sooner than anyone outside this room probably expects," he continued. "That's why I'm here."

TWENTY-FOUR

"Where the hell are we?" Crence asked as they dropped out of jump.

Again.

None of the stars looked right, but he was so far from Anndaing space already that he was getting used to that.

Crence'd been counting very carefully, each time they reappeared. *Koni Swift* had ended up jumping seven times now, with one or the other of those human pirates appearing somewhere close enough that Dane had them on a scanner as the ship jumped. At least the first four or five times.

Nobody was supposed to be that good.

Jine turned his entire hammer to look, letting Crence see both blood-shot eyes instead of the one normally pointed this way. It had been one hell of a run, the last few hours.

"Hopefully, completely, freaking lost," he said with a heavy breath. "Dane, don't bother trying to triangulate, as you won't believe the system when it tells you."

"What did you do, you sarky bastard?" Crence asked.

He liked Jine. Had hired that crazy shark for the

immensely stupid things Jine might do when *Koni Swift* got into trouble.

He had never seen this particular smile on the nightflier's face before.

"If you don't care about consequences, you can actually sit inside the jump corridor and ride the gyros," Jine said tiredly. "Everything's relative anyway, since physics are different over there. Everybody flies straight because they think that way."

"Consequences?" Crence prodded.

"Jump five," Jine said. "We had turned inside the tube before we landed. Dead aft from what we had been. Landed. Charged. Leapt. Same as all the others."

"They stayed with us on that one still," Dane piped up.

"Yeah," Jine agreed. "But they were facing the wrong way and had to stop and rotate themselves after we left. That takes longer than they planned. Then I did it again on six."

"Okay, same question," Crence asked, letting a little of his panic out now as gruffness. "Where in the Hells of Morh are we?"

Jine responded by pulled up a projection on his board and then filling the front section of the bridge with it.

"This is Tavle Jocia," he pointed to a light and changed it to red. "And here's the first place we jumped."

A second light appeared, probably out of scale, since it was visible and the first jump had been measured in Standard Stellar Units rather than light-years.

"Dane plotted my crazy-fin maneuvering from that first jump," Jine continued. "After that, it was a tail chase into the darkness. Not the first pirate to try that. Not the last, either, since they did such a bad job of it."

"They stayed with you through five, at least," Crence noted dryly.

"You can do that when you are a warship, if you're not

firing anything and instead pumping all your energy into the engines," Jine noted. "Even human drives. But that's a problem when you have to try to maneuver at the other end and somebody just pulled a bootlegger reverse on you. And then did it again."

"So we lost them after five?" Crence asked.

"I was pretty sure," Jine flexed everything now, and not just his hammer. It had been a hell of a day already. "Six was just in case."

"And seven?"

"You can never be paranoid enough," Jine nodded sharply now. "Not with pirates."

"So where are we?" Crence asked, yet again, never having gotten a straight answer from these two goofballs.

Jine typed a few commands and a new sphere appeared. A huge one, too, covering a lot more than the sixty light-years Jine had promised earlier.

Dane growled a particularly pungent obscenity at nobody in particular.

"Willing to bet you that we're in the top half, inward third, spinward side," Jine said with a grin. "Won't know until Dane runs enough star scans to lay down our actual current location, but I've got a gut feeling."

"So we lost them?" Crence asked. "And us?"

"Them," Dane snapped tartly. "I'm never lost for long, even with this goofus flying."

"I need a nap," Jine sighed. "Dane, you got this until later. There's an emergency jump plotted, all you have to do is trigger it and we'll go a half light-year, with a ballistic arc that looks fifty times longer. Somebody fix dinner, and then wake me up."

He didn't even look back as he exited the bridge, but Crence didn't begrudge the shark that much. He'd been pretty sure that the humans would catch them this time.

This hadn't been pirates out for a quick strike. Nobody would have chased that hard and that long, regardless. Especially as *Koni Swift* was carrying human goods that were pretty common here, rather than the crap the humans had treated like it was platinum-plated on the way here.

Dane fixed him with both eyes now.

"How long do you need?" Crence asked, stretching his own back by twisting it one way and his hammer the other.

Dane shrugged.

"Wouldn't have taken that bastard's bet," he replied. "Because he's probably right. I'll start there and if he is, we have it in about two hours."

"How long to just find me the Core?" Crence asked. "I need that much so we can start inward. I don't even want to wait the two hours."

"Give me zwölf or two-zwölf minutes and I can rough that in," Dane replied "Why is that important?"

"I need to get to Ogrorspoxu now," Crence said. "We can leave buoy messages at the usual meeting places to warn everyone else, but Wyll Koobitz and Obaj Gendrah need to hear about this as soon as possible."

"What about Omezi?" Dane asked.

"Her especially," Crence noted. "In spite of me invoking the Armada on you goofballs, this really was not an act of piracy. This was war."

TWENTY-FIVE

THE MEETING WAS COMPLETE. Daniel had retired to the suite that had been his before *SwiftStar*. Ebube could have taken it over, since it was marked on the plans as belonging to the comitatus chef, but she had stayed where she was.

Saving it for him, she had said.

Daniel was just glad that the rest of the women assumed that he would be returning one of these days.

He had his own doubts on the topic.

The room had not changed. Probably been closed off and ignored except for the occasional cleaning pass to make sure no dust accumulated.

A bed wide enough for two friendly people, as long as they touched when they slept. It was tall enough for an Mbaysey woman, so it always made Daniel feel like a child sleeping in his parent's room when they were on a trip without him.

Nightstand where he had once left his personal effects from his pockets, back when he did such things. A single reader slab claimed the space forlornly, next to the clock he had found in a pawn shop even before *WinterStar*.

A chair where he had draped his jacket, wearing just the standard black shirt underneath, itself covering that obnoxious lime and white bodysuit that Urid-Varg had always considered the height of fashion.

And the gem that was part of his soul now.

Dresser and closet with what little clothing he had accumulated from the days when he traveled entirely out of that same duffel bag he still used five years later.

Everything was generally black for the kitchen, even though Kathra had presented him with a set of the tangerine pants and jacket that the women of the comitatus wore. He'd kept the pants on *SwiftStar* and added the turquoise jacket that seemed to fit his mood better when Ife required him to look like a grown-up.

This meeting had gone longer than he had expected, but mostly he had answered questions for Wyll and Ife so they could plan.

Kathra already knew his soul.

He sat on the edge of the bed and wondered if he should go find himself a glass of chewy, red wine to take some of the edges off. Lord knew his head was still ringing with the noise and conversation.

Getting up sounded like too much work. Even to walk the thirty or so steps to the kitchen where Ebube no doubt still had a wine rack stashed off to one side for celebrations and need.

Even in poverty, the Mbaysey had understood wine. Fresh fruit lasts for days. Dried fruit for weeks. Canning extends that to months. Fermenting it gives you years.

So they made wine from anything that they could, usually feeding the must back into other dishes. Or to whatever animals they had around.

The fish on Kathra's two WaterStars never complained.

But his butt wanted to grow roots on the bed. He felt like a bear preparing to hibernate for winter.

The door alarm chirped politely.

Daniel considered all the ways that answering constituted a stupid idea, and rose anyway. Whoever it was knew where he hid. And they were all at least as stubborn as he was, which was saying something truly impressive to a random outsider.

Deep breath. Contain the sigh.

Do not revert to that night when you helped Kathra kill Urid-Varg. Or however one might describe it. Areen, Erin, and Ndidi had been there, too.

He paused and stared at the blank, steel panel, willing whoever it was to leave him alone, but not actually reaching out and doing anything.

The Left Hand of Evil always started with the tiniest thing.

He closed his eyes, counted to one, and opened them.

A hand found the switch unerringly and opened the door.

Tiny.

He was used to the Mbayscy, where even the small women tended to be at least his size, while the tall ones were like Kathra.

A'Alhakoth came up to his nose. Physically.

As a force of nature, she was comitatus only surpassed by the Commander, as one would expect.

They were not close enough to dance. Yet.

Fear grabbed hold of his stomach anyway.

"*Bon jour,*" he said, turning to one side and gesturing her into the room.

She paused, studying him for some sign, and then entered, not stepping too close, nor taking a wider path around him.

Daniel close the hatch and walked past where she had stopped, grabbing his jacket and turning to the closet to hang it.

That would free up the chair for one of them to sit. Otherwise, they both ended up on the bed.

Daniel allowed himself no assumptions. Nor hope.

Instead, he leaned his weight on the back of the chair, as if it was a shield that he could use to deflect the tiny warrior from whatever she had come to take from him.

She was not nervous, at least outwardly. None of the body language, close enough to human, conveyed that.

A'Alhakoth stood with her weight on her left foot and her hands hanging at her sides, like they had encountered one another in the hallway outside and wanted to gossip about something trivial.

Daniel was not fooled.

They studied each other for long moments. This woman had been inside his mind, his soul. He had done the same to her, but never deeply.

Always at as much of arm's length as he could, once he realized that she was always watching him.

Deadly, serious eyes.

She turned and sat on the edge of the bed silently. Not poised to run, but also not kicking off her boots and sliding back to put her weight against the bulkhead wall.

"Sit," she gestured to the chair, as if she understood that Daniel might run from his own room if she spooked him too much.

Merde, I really am out there, aren't I?

He slid around the chair and rested, making sure to actually sit on it, much like she was on his bunk.

More silence. Navy blue eyes he might drown in, except they were a calm lake today, rather than a stormy ocean.

"Why do I frighten you?" she finally asked, cutting away

all the deflections and perambulations he might have considered. Had prepared.

Blunt. As only the cutting edge of a yanagiba knife might be, flensing otoro tuna for lunch.

Daniel swallowed his objections. His denials.

She had been inside his mind like a burglar seeking jewelry already, while he had never gotten past sitting in her salon for tea.

It was weird, being on the receiving end.

Might as well offer up the truth now.

"None of the other women want anything from me," he replied, trying to keep his voice from cracking. "Or rather, whatever physical needs they have might be handled in any other number of ways. I just happen to be handy. That's a rude way to put it, as they all seem to enjoy themselves, but all of them leave when we're done, or first thing in the morning."

"And me?" She leaned forward a little.

He thought he could smell her scent better when she did that, like those few centimeters were meaningful for olfactory impact.

She reminded him of stargazer lilies.

Hopefully, it was all in his mind.

"You want more," Daniel nearly despaired aloud.

"And you're afraid to offer it?" Those calm eyes got darker, focused on him now. Pupils started to slit down as though she was about to pounce, like a particular tabby he'd had in his kitchen for several years.

"I'm afraid to be your first," Daniel retorted. Carefully. Fearfully.

That much, he had seen in her. She might have been young, and a touch reckless, but A'Alhakoth ver'Shingi had still been a Jarl's daughter. As far as Daniel knew, no Kaniea male had ever impressed her enough for the woman to even consider experimentation.

"Or only?" she asked in a quiet, deadly voice that was like a punch to his stomach when he hadn't been looking.

Daniel lost all his breath.

"Especially only," he managed once he got air back in his lungs.

"You've only ever been a dilettante," she stated, somehow not making it sound like an accusation when she did. He didn't understand how she did that, either.

"Most of the women I knew in that former life were fragile creatures, A'Alhakoth," Daniel replied, finding some footing in the anger that had originally driven him from Genarde. "Expensive, glass sculptures. Pretty to look at, but easy to break if you handled them at all roughly."

"And now?"

She seemed even closer now, like she had kept somehow leaning into him, even as she never moved.

"Now I am surrounded by *comitatus*," Daniel said simply. "All of you are tougher than I am. And that's okay. I never claimed to be a warrior. I'm here because Urid-Varg was a fool, and nobody else could be trusted with that power once Kathra killed him. Once Kathra's done with me, I'll go back to being merely a chef and be happier."

"Will you?" she probed, like she knew things he didn't.

That was even more frightening than the thought of finally casting all his ghosts into a star someday and only being human again.

If that was what would happen. He would not know until that day passed. Nobody would.

"Tomorrow, if I thought that the wars could be won any other way," Daniel's voice took on some of the fire threatening to scorch his soul. "Until then, I have people to kill yet."

She blinked and suddenly was leaned back again, even though she hadn't moved.

"You said you weren't a warrior, Daniel," she offered, perhaps just a touch confused now, rather than a predator stalking him in his own den.

"Nobody else will be able to kill Hadi Rostami, A'Alhakoth," he explained. "Short of annihilating the ship he is on and making sure no escape pods survived the destruction. He doesn't have my suit, or the gem, but he has my mental powers. I'm still the only one that can walk naked in space. I have to kill him. Or at least grapple him while one of you has the knife."

"And you still don't see why I'm interested in you, Daniel Lémieux?" she smiled wryly.

"Oh, I see it," he retorted. "I'm just not sure which of us is the bigger fool."

"You could tell me to leave." Her smile got serious, even as it never wavered.

"That would make me the bigger fool," he summed up.

"So you want me to stay?" she asked, her face softening now.

He understood her fear, but dealing with his own was almost too much.

"More than almost anything," he said. "I'm afraid of not measuring up to what you expect, whatever that might be."

"And not just waking up next to me tomorrow?"

She held out a hand. He leaned forward enough to take it, but didn't do anything more than enjoy the feel of her skin. Three long fingers to his stubby four. Periwinkle to brown.

"The day after tomorrow," he whispered. "Of thinking I could be what you needed, and failing you."

"You can't," she whispered back. "I've been you. I've gone far deeper into your soul than you ever imagined, Daniel.

Almost deep enough to meet that chorus of voices that haunts you. You were too busy trying not to pry, to invade my privacy. Erin went there inside me but you stopped at a threshold. Kathra went there. Others. Never you."

"I have my reasons," he grimaced.

"The left hand of evil, I know," she said, smiling warmer. "I've been Urid-Varg through your eyes."

He found his breath gone again. Not even Kathra had delved that deep, as far as he knew. Only Ndidi, and she had no interest in ever having a male touch her.

That was what made them an effective team, because he could treat the Shield as a sister. A niece. Maybe a daughter.

Nothing where either of them would ever be a threat to the other.

A friend.

A'Alhakoth ver'Shingi would never be only a friend.

He took a deep breath and lifted her into his mind. Into that salon where all the comitatus women had visited so regularly, when they needed to understand him. To contain him and his fears.

"I've been here," she said, looking around.

She was standing by the window. He had seated himself on the couch.

Daniel gestured to the wall of books that occasionally graced the place. All his fears. All his dreams. All his memories.

Plus Urid-Varg and a thousand others.

"I don't need that," she waved a hand. "I've already read them."

He felt his breath fail again.

She had already read them? All of them? And still knocked at his door?

"Then what can I give you, having already offered my soul?" Daniel asked.

She waved a hand and they were back in his bedroom. A'Alhakoth had understood that she could choose to sever the link herself. Not many of the others had gotten to that level.

She stood. He never moved.

She smiled. He waited.

She reached down and grabbed the edges of her shirt, pulling them over her head and tossing it to the side. He gasped.

Kaniea were externally human enough. Lithe and light, for the females, where the males were broader, taller, and much heavier. Built more like a dancer, even compared to the women of the Mbaysey, to say nothing of the other warriors of the comitatus.

Periwinkle blue skin. He had never paid that much attention to her lips except to note in passing that they were more indigo. Her nipples were the exact same hue.

She had small breasts. Upturned. Even now, a small voice in the back of his mind yelped nervously that she looked more like a teenager than a grown woman, but that was a human comparison. And a bad one.

A'Alhakoth ver'Shingi was comitatus.

She held out her left hand and he took it.

She pulled, and he stood.

Her right hand went under his shirt to feel the muscles on his side.

"I want your skin," she said simply. "You. Not you and the gem, or you and your memories. None of that. I want to feel your flesh pressed up against mine. I want to feel you inside me. I want to wake up in the morning with you wrapped around me, keeping me warm. Is that more than you can do?"

He gulped. Looked deep into the oceanic depths of those navy blue eyes.

Daniel reached down and pulled the black T-shirt over his head, landing it close enough to hers for scoring.

The gem seemed happy to detach, which struck him as insane with whatever shreds of sanity still lingered. Usually he had to force it to disconnect from his sternum.

It went onto the nightstand atop the book he probably wasn't going to be reading tonight.

The lime and white shirt came off just as easily as his T-Shirt had, again surprising him, as it always seemed to stick awkwardly when he removed it.

She wore heavy boots. He knelt at her feet now and removed them, peeling socks at the same time. He rose when she did and kicked off the slippers he wore on decks.

Suddenly, she was nude. But not naked.

He was frightened on her behalf, because she seemed so utterly fearless right now that he could not fathom it.

All her hair was cobalt blue, including the places he had only dreamed about. Again, externally human in all the ways that mattered.

And she had a scent. A heady musk human enough as it bored into his mind like a drill trepanning his skull.

Daniel joined her a moment later, reveling in the feel of her pressed against his flesh.

A'Alhakoth turned and pushed him onto the bed. He pulled down the single quilt he normally slept with and she crawled into the darkness with him.

He realized that he had never even kissed the woman, so he remedied that.

Then let her decide how things would proceed.

TWENTY-SIX

Kathra studied Ife, seated across from her. They had retired to her office and sent everyone else to rest, after four hours of planning, explaining, and occasionally quarreling with people.

Interestingly, she'd had to argue with her comitatus to tone some things down, but they had been released, both mentally as well as emotionally, by Ife defeating even a single Sept Patrol. Many of them had wanted now to salt the earth, at least metaphorically, with Sept blood.

Ebube had delivered a carafe of coffee and disappeared. It was just the two of them now.

"How did Ndidi do?" Kathra asked.

She'd already asked Ife that question, back at Ogrorspoxu, but enough time had passed for the woman to digest and reconsider her answers. Neither of the women were her original comitatus, pilots and warriors, but the rules had been different in those days.

As had Kathra's needs. Most of her Spectre pilots simply weren't suited to commanding major warships in battles.

Even Stina had needed to relearn how to fight, before Ife let her walk that deck.

"Ndidi has the potential to supplant Erin, among all your women, Kathra," Ife answered quietly. "Yes, she is young. And half-blind without her glasses. But she has the ability to shift gears mentally, from aggressive to sneaky, in the space of a heartbeat. And does not have the bad habits Stina or the others have overcome, so she will only get better from here."

"How good is she?" Kathra asked.

Ife paused and reflected, her eyes losing focus on the external world.

"One more long mission, like the one we anticipate, and she will probably be good enough to take over command of *SwiftStar*," Ife said. "Or build out the crew of a new vessel, although that is a more challenging task. Her years in the kitchen work to her advantage, as she understands how to get along with people, while at the same time commanding them. You need that among your officers. Who you would give to her as Shield, Sword, and Pilot will need to be given a great deal of thought for that reason. She would succeed, but it might take time to gel them together."

"Good," Kathra nodded, sipping at the mug of coffee, thankfully decaffeinated. She would need to sleep yet. And the little one had been active today, kicking and thrashing. "How is Daniel holding up? And what will it do to the rest of the crew, adding A'Alhakoth into that mix?"

Ife had a knowing smile on her face. A wry pursing of the lips and eyes swelling outward a bit.

"A'Alhakoth may need to understand that she has to share him," Ife chuckled. "I'm not sure she grasps that yet."

"Share?" Kathra asked.

"You supplied me with exceptional women, Kathra," Ife nodded, also drinking as she found words. "Hard, stubborn, brilliant, and competent ones. Tanuss might fuss. Acqueir was still working herself slowly up to the point of interspecies communication when we arrived here. None of them are human, including A'Alhakoth, so they all have the same level playing field for his attention."

"I never imagined my petite, *Rabic* chef would become a sex object for my comitatus," Kathra shook her head and grinned. "He's short, irascible, and the wrong color."

"And brilliant in a field of competition that none of your women can match," Ife replied. "Except Ndidi, and she's so utterly repulsed by the thought of a male touching her that she's not a threat to the others."

"What about you?" Kathra asked. "Would you consider a male?"

"Any other male? No," Ife shuddered. "But Areen has said nothing bad about the man, and she would. I might have to get extremely drunk, so I could pretend he was a girl. And he'd be on his own to satisfy his own needs afterwards."

Kathra laughed.

"I agree," she said. "He's almost good enough to be a woman, but only almost. And we are also Mbaysey. Much of the rest of the galaxy approaches their sexuality in a more binary pattern, however silly and backwards that might be. I will rely on you and Ndidi to protect him from the predations of the other women on your crew. Do not forbid it, but let them all understand that there are rules, and he will make the decisions, as hard as that might be for him."

Ife shrugged.

"He can be stubborn about some things," she said. "But he has submitted. Do you see him telling any of those women *no* if they came to him with demands?"

"Probably not," Kathra agreed. "He and I have already talked about A'Alhakoth. She is old comitatus, and has looked into his soul. Tanuss and Acqueir are newer, and not part of that inner circle. They do not yet have my utter trust, like the rest of you do. But at the same time, you do have my trust, Ife. If you think that those two, or others, should be initiated into the mysteries of Daniel Lémieux, then I expect you to act and command accordingly."

She watched Ife recoil, ever so slightly. Flinch. Not from fear, but from awe, if Kathra was reading the light in the woman's eyes correctly.

"Comitatus," Kathra reminded her sternly. "And more than that. I cannot command in the field. Perhaps ever again, or at least until my daughter is old enough to step into command if something did happen to me. That means you, Ifedimma Ogu. As Erin has been my mighty right hand, my Sword for so long, now she must become my Shield, as Ndidi does for you, while you become my Sword. And all the things that go with it."

"You told me that a year ago," Ife breathed. "I thought I understood it then. I was wrong."

"Indeed," Kathra agreed. "But not so wrong as to go astray. Merely to dream too small at the time. I need you to dream bigger now, Ife. I need you to act as though you were me when making those decisions. And knowing that I will support your decisions. If you went dreadfully wrong, the worst that would happen is that Ndidi would demand that you stand aside, and I might support her, but you would have to be so far off the reservation at that point that it would be obvious to everyone involved."

Ife nodded.

"Is it always like this?" she asked.

"This hard?" Kathra asked, waiting for the woman to nod. "It is. I wondered, time and again, how I would manage to fill Yagazie's shoes. Without Erin, I might not have survived. This little one will have a cousin who is her half-sister, but I also plan that she have little sisters. And perhaps a brother as well."

"A brood?" Ife asked, shock scribing her features.

"Poverty was the past, Ife," Kathra focused. "We could only have as many children as the tribe could support. As the ClanStars could feed. The Anndaing and especially the Kaniea, offer a wider future. Already, our trade with outsiders has tripled from what it used to be with the TradeStations at the edge of Sept space. It could go even higher, but there are limits right now to how much we can ramp up food production for all those exotic things that Kaniea and Anndaing have never eaten before. Still, they pay exorbitant prices for that, and we can, in turn, afford to buy more advanced electronics. Better educational tools. Eventually, more and perhaps bigger ClanStars, assuming that we retain the old patterns of spinning them instead of tying ourselves to Anndaing factories."

"Bigger ClanStars?" Ife gasped.

"Instead of one ring, perhaps two, balanced at the ends. Or three. More. Who knows?" Kathra asked. "Maybe a Stanford Torus. I even asked Wyll if they could put engines and jumpdrives on something like a Bishop ring. The look he gave me, after I showed him what such a structure was, was so utterly priceless I wish I could have taken a picture to hang on the wall behind you."

They shared a laugh. Even the sharks, thousands of years into interstellar culture, occasionally got themselves into ruts, but they were tied to planets. The Mbaysey were beholden to no star. To no man.

Nor to any alien, either. In her lifetime, the Mbaysey would never be planetbound, or even station bound. If it didn't have drives to leave a star system she considered too dangerous, Kathra Omezi was not interested.

They had not yet achieved the mythical forty years of

wandering from the ancient Earth cultures, but she would be happier knowing that her descendants might go four hundred. Perhaps four thousand.

"We will do the Ovanii proud, to have the service of one of their ancient ships," Kathra told this woman. "They understood what roaming meant, while those fussy merchants at Ogrorspoxu defend their little moats with fastidious energy."

"Will they continue to help us, after the Sept are dealt with?" Ife asked.

"I cannot imagine the Sept ceasing to be a threat to the galaxy, even in my daughter's lifetime," Kathra shrugged. "But the Merchants Bank and Guild will help us, because we are willing to blunt the Sept in any way we can. They have seen the truth from Daniel, so the fools who think that they can negotiate treaties the Keyaksar will honor will be shouted down or sidelined."

"Because of the Free Worlds?" Ife suggested.

"If the Sept take the Free Worlds and incorporate all that mass of humanity, with what they probably have learned about the Anndaing, then even the Armada might not dislodge them in time," Kathra said. "Eventually they'll come this way, and perhaps be inevitable when they do."

"What would we do if they come?" Ife asked. "When the Sept start conquering Free Worlds systems in earnest and truly threaten the Mbaysey?"

"Very simple," Kathra looked at the woman and smiled. "We take those stars away from them again."

TWENTY-SEVEN

Septagon *Singara*. The anchor of a force that would see them back into the Free Worlds.

Hadi smiled to himself as their shuttle landed on the flight deck, delivering him and Amirin to their new vessel. He knew Amirin Pasdar would have preferred *Vorgash*, but a new aspbad had taken command, and was still shaking down the vessel, even a year later.

It was a pity the new aspbad just wasn't as good a bureaucrat as Hadi. People forgot how important that was. He had no doubts that the man assigned to command had been a well-connected member of the Seven Clans, rewarded for a lifetime of warlike service by being given Amirin Pasdar's Septagon.

Once Amirin had told Hadi that he was not returning to *Vorgash*, Hadi had ignored the ship entirely, except to occasionally grin to himself when that Septagon didn't rank as well as it had on the quarterly reports in the various excellence categories.

Back when he had been in command.

But we all have small souls in our own way.

Singara had been the vessel that replaced *Vorgash* on patrol, when they first set off on the grand sailing quest after Kathra Omezi, slipping an entire warfleet of over fifty support vessels, including Patrol Tenders and freighters, through the dark, quiet corners of the Free Worlds.

Pasdar had determined that he could not take *Vorgash* on this mission, once he understood that Hadi had recruited some of the best officers to go with him on *SeptStar*, and then used them up like nails on the way home. Many of the men who had survived would never fully recover, and it was better to leave them be, rather than to face any subtle accusations and rumors that might require Hadi to destroy them later.

Similarly, Septagon *Uwalu* had never really recovered from what the chef had done to them in that nameless system where the Sept first came to understand the existence of the Star Turtle.

Hadi Rostami understood now the scream that had paralyzed four hundred thousand men. Shut down an entire Septagon for nearly a minute.

He could not replicate the effect on that scale, but neither could Lémieux, once *Vorgash* had killed the turtle and driven its helpless, dying body into the heart of a star.

Daniel Lémieux had survived, but he was weakened now. The Ishtan had survived as well, reduced to only four and forced to seek allies for the first time in their immortal lives.

Amirin Pasdar at first, and then him later.

Hadi Rostami was the last of the Ishtan now. Whatever that meant.

And however long he had to make use of these powers before they faded.

If they actually would.

He had been Ishtan when they died. Hadi still wasn't sure

what the implications of that merging were. Would he live forever? Live a normal life but retain their powers that whole time?

He had two tasks before he died. Kill Lémieux and help Pasdar overthrow the Sept and replace it with something else.

Even he couldn't say whether whatever they built would be better, except that all those scum on Rhages would be sent to the purifying fires of Hell. Hadi Rostami would no longer be embarrassed to call himself Sept, as he had been since he left the capital.

Kill them all, and *make Allah* sort them out. Even the All Merciful would likely be tempted to just cast them into the flames forever.

Next to him, Amirin rose as the shuttle finally shut down. Out a porthole, Hadi could see lines of well-dressed troops and officers as they filed into the bay and came to attention.

The old Amirin Pasdar would not have required such a ceremony. Might even have been mildly offended by the entire process, but the new man wanted to become Emperor of Humanity. The warrior had been put carefully to one side so that the politician could come to center.

It was already going to be enough of a disruption, changing dynasties. Pasdar needed to maintain the pomp and ceremony of the Sept, the old Sept, before the rot became so evident. He would need to maintain equilibrium.

It helped that Amirin had never married, always more committed to his commands than the social niceties. The two of them had identified several candidate wives that could be commissioned to cement the man's rule. Especially as the ancient texts, long ignored and frequently forgotten, allowed a man four wives, if he could maintain them and love them all equally.

Equally badly, perhaps, but Amirin Pasdar would not favor one over the other. All would be political alliances.

They were alone in the shuttle as the last of the various aides and flunkies filed out and took their places.

"You have a particular, mischievous grin that is frequently out of character, Hadi." Amirin turned his terrible gaze to this side and let his own fleeting grin appear. "What evil do you have planned now?"

"Contemplating wives," he replied. "Wondering if four would be sufficient, or if you should take seven at once in a grand ceremony, so that all the Clans are equally represented."

Amirin blinked with a moment of hesitation also out of character for the man.

"And that is just another of the reasons you have helped make me the man I am, Rostami," Amirin bowed his head slightly, but it conveyed great respect. "As Andarzbad, however, you will be in a similar position. Perhaps with a similar need. The Clans will wish you bound to them as well, especially as you will act as something of a Vizier, even if another holds that title."

Hadi felt his face go completely white. The gasp was almost inaudible, but this was Amirin Pasdar he was dealing with.

"What?" the naupati demanded suddenly in a harsh whisper.

"Children," Hadi replied.

"Of course," the great man nodded. "The next generation of the new Sept we will create."

"Will they inherit the power?" Hadi gulped.

"You said it would fade within a few years," Amirin turned accusing eyes on him now.

"That was what the Ishtan said," Hadi agreed. "But that was before. We cannot know what will come. The Ishtan were inside me when they died, and left their mark. Would my children bear it?"

They were alone in the shuttle, or Hadi would have jumped them into the other space to talk, but it was not necessary.

He watched his future emperor transform into a tactical genius in an eye blink.

"Children will be a necessity," the man said.

"Should they be yours instead?" Hadi offered shakily. "I can make the necessary alterations that I can never bear children, but the wives would have needs. Would they be willing to bear yours?"

It was Amirin's turn to gasp, but he was planning a campaign to conquer the entire galaxy now, in his lifetime. Everything became details and implications.

Amateurs study tactics. Professionals study strategy.

Conquerors study logistics and bureaucracies.

"We will speak of this again at a later time, but it does change some aspects significantly," he said. "You are sure?"

"No, but too many questions would be raised, in awkward circumstances," Hadi said. "If I am sterile for reasons never explained, then they might accept medical intercession. Or perhaps even personal. No other man could be allowed, lest my position as your ally be undermined. I could certainly fix the women appropriately with my powers, but again, that requires more planning than at this moment."

"Indeed," Amirin nodded sharply.

Hadi watched the man draw a breath, straighten his uniform out, and transform back into the grand, political creature that he needed to be for *Singara*'s crew, before he strode out of the hatch into the eerie emptiness of the deck, the silence broken only by the faint tune of the Imperial Anthem being played to welcome the new naupati.

They needed to see their new commander.

And be reminded of the power of their dread Emperor on Rhages.

It would not be all that long before those two men were one.

TWENTY-EIGHT

Ogrorspoxu looked so close that Crence was pretty sure he could smell it, even from the top of the orbital arc *Koni Swift* was following as they chased the station. He'd already sent a private message to Wyll and Obaj, letting them know he needed a private meeting.

"Hey, Crence," Dane spoke up. "*SeekerStar's* not listed on the local inventory. You always ask, so I added it to the data pull."

Crence turned to look at the other shark. Jine was too busy flying to pay much attention, unless the scanners pinged something and he had to maneuver.

At least once a year somebody got their piloting certs pulled for flying stupid, so you had to pay attention, especially as crowded as orbital space could get around this station.

"Interesting," Crence replied.

And out of character, but he didn't say that. There were some things he didn't even share with these two. Especially conversations with Wyll.

Kathra Omezi had been a topic of many of them over the last however long.

"Incoming message," Dane piped up now. "*Eyes only: Trademaster*. Huh, that's not ominous or anything."

Dane got sarcastic at times, but that was par for the course. Like Jine going totally laconic as they were being chased through jumpspace by human pirates.

Part of what made *Koni Swift* work so well.

Still, he didn't get those messages all that often.

"Take it in my office," he said, rising. "Route it there."

He rose as the other two glared at him, but he was feeling immune today. Almost bite-proof, truth be told.

Back in his office, he settled and called up his terminal, typing in the long code that would allow the message to be decrypted.

EoT messages were never a good thing. Usually, they came from the Merchants Bank, and not just the Guild. That meant Wyll or Obaj had something. If he didn't make such good margins being a spy, Crence would have gone legit years ago.

But where was the fun in that?

Message: *Wyll Koobitz off station and out system. Has traveled to Kanus aboard* SeekerStar, *in tandem with* SwiftStar. *Requested you travel there immediately if they have not returned before you did. Developments.*

Obaj

Well, tunashit.

It might have sounded like a request, but Crence wasn't fooled. Obaj might be a single, thin layer below Wyll in the overall scale of things, but from their rarified level, Crence was still dealing with demigods when it came to power in day-to-day operations.

Human goods wouldn't fetch nearly the margins at

Kanus that they did here, but that was Omezi's fault. She'd already started flooding the market.

Of course, her folks might be in need of some of the stuff he had with him. There was always that. Still, his crew would bitch.

More than usual, even.

He typed a reply and sent it over, letting the five light-second lag work in his favor.

Reply: *Acknowledged. Kanus-bound. Messages for delivery?*

Crence

The frightening part was that he got back a message from the station in zwölf-two seconds. Including ten seconds in flight.

Message: *Project* EveningStar *under consideration. Godspeed.*

Obaj

Double tunashit.

That didn't even sort of sound like fun.

Anndaing syntax didn't capitalize letters in the middle of a word. Even Human Spacer did it so rarely that they had to have a special term for it. Camel case, following after a human desert creature with a hump and a lot of fur.

There was only one place he could think of that was appropriate.

WinterStar. SeekerStar. SeptStar. SwiftStar.

What in the Hells of Morh was an EveningStar?

Crence closed the channel and erased the screen.

And sighed loudly.

Might as well go do this in person. Otherwise, one of the two of them would storm in here and get rowdy.

He rose, moving around his desk and exiting the office back onto the main bridge.

Jine and Dane seemed poised on the edge of a feeding frenzy when he got back into his chair and sighed again.

"Change of plans," he announced in a tired voice. "Set course for Kanus, minimum transit time."

It was educational, watching Jine stand up, dig into one of his pants pockets, and walk over to Dane, handing that shark a coin.

Dane smiled like he had just been served the freshest chutoro available.

"Seriously?" Crence asked the goofballs. "You two placed a bet on it?"

"Worse," Jine said in a despairing voice as he sat back down. "Where. I couldn't imagine them not even giving us time to land and swap cargo packs, since we were loaded with human goods from Tavle Jocia. The trademasters on station will throw a fit."

"They've already been overruled by Obaj Gendrah," Crence said carefully. "And keep that tucked under a fin. Wyll, Kathra Omezi, and *SwiftStar* are all at Kanus, waiting for us."

"Oh, shit," Dane whispered incredulously.

"Yeah," Crence replied. "Whatever corners you have to cut to get us there, do it and don't even bother to ask me. Just keep a log, so we can have Wyll pay for our maintenance fees at Kanus. This feels even bigger than my report to the Bank about the so-called *surge in piracy* at Tavle Jocia."

"Did the war start already?" Jine asked in a small, careful voice totally out of character for the brash pilot.

"The war started the moment *SeekerStar* hailed us, Jine," Crence reminded his unindictable co-conspirator. "Maybe the humans have finally realized that and decided to do something about it."

"*Koni Swift* going to go to war alongside the Mbaysey?" Dane asked.

Crence considered how much he should tell these two. Could tell them.

They'd both been with him for years, and had security clearances only one step below his, even if they didn't know it. Most of his crew had had their scales inspected with a microscope and laser micrometer before Crence could hire them. And then again annually.

Outsiders just thought he was an asshole when it came to hiring otherwise perfectly-qualified spacers.

Some of those folks had been spies. Others just didn't know how to keep their mouths shut in public.

A drunkard had no berth on *Koni Swift*, regardless of his or her qualifications. Same with anybody that could be blackmailed for whatever secrets Wyll Koobitz and his colleagues deemed unacceptable.

But Jine Riffin and Dane Roguez deserved some amount of truth. It would help them plan. *EveningStar* didn't sound any better, thinking about it here.

"If this is the next step that we've been expecting, then *Koni Swift* will be put up on blocks in somebody's warehouse," Crence said quietly. "Cold storage indoors, where it can't even be accidentally seen by someone wandering by with their sensors pointed the wrong direction."

"Oh, shit," Jine said this time, but Dane was no doubt thinking the exact same thing.

"Then what?" Dane filled in the gap when Jine's voice failed.

"We transfer to a different vessel for a certain duration," Crence acknowledged that there were some secrets they couldn't know yet. "I don't know which one, how long, or for what purpose. That's why we're going to Kanus. To find out."

He could look at both of them at the same time.

Humans couldn't do that, so they had to arrange meetings and bridge compartments to let them face each other.

Both sharks had gone a little pale under their scales. About like he had, and remained.

"It's gotten serious," Dane said in a voice barely above a whisper.

"This might be the beginning of the Call to Armada, sharks," Crence nodded. "The Anndaing/Human war."

TWENTY-NINE

IFE FOUND IT INSTRUCTIONAL, watching the comitatus combat women who had until recently been pilots, all of them now down on the ground on Kanus in a private training field not all that far from the ver'Shingi estate.

It was a rainbow of silliness, as she looked over things from her place in the stands.

Officially, she had no role here, except as a witness familiarizing herself with the operations going on in front of her. Unofficially, any of the people who survived the hell that Kam, Nkechi, and Iruoma were about to unleash would end up serving aboard *SwiftStar*.

Ife wanted to know what to expect.

As she would have been willing to bet, the Kaniea males had rallied when Kathra opened up enrollment in a ground combat force designed to operate in space. They tended to be big chaps. Erin's height or a little shorter, but broader and heavier, dense with muscles that neither human nor Kaniea females generally developed without adding all sorts of interesting chemicals to their diet.

In addition, Ife could see a smaller collection of Kaniea

women interspersed, along with at least seven other species. Many of them had arrived recently, so she expected that Wyll Koobitz had put out a quiet call before *SeekerStar* left Ogrorspoxu.

Iruoma was on a presentation stand, with Kam and Nkechi standing on either side. The prospective troops were lined up in reasonable formation in front of them. Looked like roughly a thousand, so Ife already knew that three quarters of them would be washed out of this batch.

Probably enrolled in some sort of force by the Anndaing Merchants Guild against future need. Or the nucleus of a larger fighting force.

After all, technically everyone here was a private citizen, with rumors swirling around that they would go off and be engaged in piracy.

It was even true, if you looked at it correctly. The Mbaysey had a formal trade agreement with Merchants Bank, but legally Ife, Kathra, and the rest were outsiders. Had the Sept any clue, they could have filed a formal complaint and at least driven recruiting like this underground.

Pity that they'd never gotten around to studying Anndaing mercantile law.

Iruoma of the grand scowl was in high dungeon today. Ife was enjoying herself, even as she imagined how uncomfortable some of those poor Kaniea males must be.

"Look closely," Iruoma gestured to the two women beside her. "I am Iruoma Emeka. If you survive, I will be your commander. Kamharida Nkiruka and Nkechi Okeke will be my adjutants. All of your officers will be women. All of them. If you men want to rise to command, walk away right now and form your own combat teams. Commander Omezi might decide to contract with you later, but if you stay, you will be subordinate to Mbaysey women. Period. Questions?"

She let the moment hang.

"I can't hear you," Iruoma upped the power of that scowl a notch, to the point Ife wondered if she would start glowing. "Questions?"

"No, ma'am," a few brave voices called back, raggedy and perhaps a dozen from that thousand.

"Louder," she snapped. "I thought you people considered yourselves a warrior race. Questions?"

"No, ma'am," the call returned, louder. Firmer. Almost competent.

"We are comitatus," Iruoma snarled so hard that the microphone pointed at her from off to one side hissed with feedback. "The very best Kathra Omezi could find, when she needed tough, capable killers. And we are human. Many of you think that Kaniea or Anndaing males will be tougher, stronger, perhaps even meaner. My women will cure you of that notion. Again, you will serve under us, with no path for promotion. Accept that now, or retire from the field."

She paused and Ife studied the candidates. She was aware of the basic qualifications Kathra had laid down, so all of the people in this group had some level of combat training. Many of them might even have seen combat along the way, as Anndaing Caravan Guards like Alten Rezal, aboard *Koni Swift*.

Ife wondered how many of them were as dangerous as a little woman like A'Alhakoth ver'Shingi, who had arrived aboard *SeekerStar* the trained daughter of a Jarl, knowing sword, hammer, stick, poniard, bow, and six forms of unarmed combat.

And then gotten trained up by Kam and Nkechi on how to be really dangerous.

They didn't teach anything like Greco-Roman wrestling to Kaniea or any of the Anndaing worlds Ife had researched.

Nkechi would probably have to break a few bones before these men learned how to resist her.

To say nothing of the weird amalgam of Hong Gia Kung Fu and the Kaniea Fluttering Hand form that Nkechi and A'Alhakoth had come up with.

Iruoma pointed to the stands now, to the cluster of folks down below Ife, right at the edge of the field.

"Some of you have heard of A'Alhakoth ver'Shingi," Iruoma called. "She is Kaniea, like many of you. She is also comitatus, like me. Commander Omezi has appointed her Ambassador to the Upynth. Those of you who survive my training and come with us will be assigned to guard her, but she will also give you orders. All comitatus will give you orders. You will obey them or be put ashore. Officers of *SwiftStar* will give you orders. You will obey them. At some point, we will begin raiding and capturing human ships belonging to the Sept Empire. You will know how to fight humans by then, because we will have taught you."

She paused now and studied the crowd. They were a little more animated than they had been before, but the morning was growing slowly cooler as a fall storm front came in from the south. Pretty soon, the forecast suggested rain, which was the weirdest part of being on a planet, and one they wouldn't encounter once they got back into space, like they belonged.

Ife could still count the exact number of days she had spent on the surface of a planet in the last three decades.

"This is war!" Iruoma continued, booming the worlds. "You are glorified Caravan Guards, but you will kill people because we tell you to. No other reason will be needed. I will point you like a gun or a sword, and expect you to kill whoever you encounter with absolutely no mercy until someone orders it. Again, walk if you are not prepared to kill without let up, hindrance, or provocation. Those of you who remain will probably become candidates to join the Mbaysey at some future date."

Ife smothered a smile as the recruiting speech ramped up. She'd heard Iruoma and Kathra working out the details for maximum stun value on the males of Kanus, who tended to think they were in charge.

Not on an Mbaysey ship.

"We give preference to women," Iruoma's voice dropped and got a little jagged now, a rusty blade sawing awkwardly at a limb. "The entire Mbaysey is eighty-seven percent female today. Most of the men are too soft and fragile to be warriors, but we keep them around so they can contribute to the sperm bank if they somehow manage to impress us."

Long beat as if Iruoma was studying the crowd. She might be. The woman was the fiercest person around, other than Kathra.

"None of you are comitatus, so you won't impress me," she said bluntly. "But we'll have Kaniea women. Anic. Wisp. Anndaing. Maybe you'll get lucky and they'll request you make a contribution to the freezer for immortality. Again, that's about as high as any of you will ever rise, so if you are secretly harboring some stupid delusions of adequacy around the Mbaysey, I suggest you join an Anndaing knitting circle instead, or start a bakery, because those are more useful than your egos."

She paused now and studied them. Kam and Nkechi were scowling almost as hard. It was a delightful performance and Ife was certain that it was being recorded by someone for Wyll Koobitz's records. And probably to play in front of the next batch of recruits that shark would be rounding up. Ife couldn't imagine it would be all that long before the war did ramp up and the Anndaing needed warm bodies who knew how to hold pistols and blades.

Especially with the sorts of things she had planned.

"I won't ask if you have any questions," Iruoma continued conversationally. "Because there is nothing any of you can say at this point that will impress me. Go bust your fins and asses in training, because only one in four of you will be here in a month. Dismissed to your barracks."

The three women immediately turned and walked this way across the platform as the larger mob began to dissolve into thirty-two big training teams, led by caravan guard trainers that Koobitz had supplied from somewhere.

Ife rose and moved down to the bottom of the stands, arriving as Iruoma did. Ndidi was down here, seated next to Daniel, with A'Alhakoth on her other side, and Acqueir and Tanuss beyond that.

Why Daniel was separated off from everyone by Ndidi wasn't anything Ife needed to worry about. The various women had all been quietly taken aside and given the conditions of continued service aboard *SwiftStar*, over and above Kathra's rules.

Ife wasn't fooling around. Ndidi let them know that.

The shock was probably only now starting to wear off.

She needed Daniel more than she did any of the others, including A'Alhakoth, who was just here as a masquerade to fool the Upynth for a while.

But she smiled as she joined them.

"A month?" she asked Iruoma as the group came together and headed backstage to where lunch should be about ready.

"That washes out the obvious candidates," Iruoma said with a harsh smile. "We'll load three hundred or so here, and then chuck the last group out when we pass Ogrorspoxu, assuming that there are that many bad ones left. Then we go play pirate."

She spoke that last bit to Ndidi, who nodded serenely.

Ife found it instructive that the two youngest women

here, Ndidi and A'Alhakoth, were likely to be the two most important as Kathra's war progressed.

Because she had no doubt that the Sept were going to get ugly before they were willing to admit that a woman was their better. Any woman.

Ife looked forward to teaching a few of them.

THIRTY

Kathra studied the shark closely. He was, after all, the first Anndaing she had ever met. Not the first she had ever seen, as Alten had come through the airlock first, but the first representative of Merchants Bank or the Guild to deal with the Mbaysey.

Crence looked tired. His scaly skin sagged a little on his bones, as if he had lost weight. Almost as if he had been ground down. He seemed more gray than he had been before as well, but that could be any number of things.

Impending galactic war was just one of the problems that shark might be facing.

But even seated next to Wyll he seemed a little ragged.

Today's meeting was a hurried affair, only because *Koni Swift* had dropped out of jump and immediately raced close to *SeekerStar*. Kathra hadn't been planning to go anywhere soon, but *SwiftStar* was a week or so from Ife's next mission.

Kathra looked at her warriors, assembled randomly around the table flanking the two Anndaing. Erin on her immediate left, as always, the two of them less than a month from giving birth and now showing tremendously. Daniel on her right. Ife and Ndidi.

The inner-most conspirators, as Kathra liked to think of them. She needed Wyll. Crence had turned into a valued ally and even a friend, in the times she had seen him since that first, fateful voyage.

The rest were comitatus. That covered everything that needed to be said.

"You're here," Kathra said to Crence as everyone settled.

There was tea, but it was still steeping, so quickly had everything come together to get them all on *SeekerStar*'s deck.

"We met pirates at Tavle Jocia," Crence replied. "Except that they weren't pirates. Not after as hard as they chased us."

Kathra listened to a blow by blow description of the chase and insane evasions that the nightflier Jine had taken. *SeekerStar* could never have done something like that. The vessel was too fragile.

But Kathra already knew that Jine Riffin was crazy.

When Crence Miray was done, they listened as Kathra explained *SwiftStar*'s next mission, and the reason she had moved her base here more permanently.

Crence whistled through his nose.

"Is there a lot of money to be made in Upynth space?" he asked his boss.

Kathra wasn't the only one to laugh out loud. The trademaster might be something of a warrior spy, but he was a merchant first.

"Yes, but you won't be the one to exploit it," Wyll replied dryly.

Kathra liked the sulk that came across Crence's hammer. She had been around the species enough now to see the subtle cues in body language.

"*Koni Swift* is a target now, Crence," Wyll said over the trademaster's grumbles.

"Garage time?" Crence asked sourly.

Kathra watched all the humans at the table perk up. She knew, but hadn't told everyone else what bits and pieces Wyll Koobitz had shared with her.

"Garage time," Wyll acknowledged. "Followed by you and your crew earning their keep as Anndaing Merchants Guild volunteers."

Interestingly, Ife and Crence snorted almost in harmony. But then, she had studied the Anndaing as a trademaster, even though she wasn't.

"What have you got for me?" Crence asked in a sliding tone of angst and depression that Kathra remembered from her and Erin's teenage years.

"A Scout-6, you lazy pirate," Wyll barked with a laugh. "So stop moping. Jine and Dane will be in heaven."

"Excuse me," Daniel leaned forward and directed his gaze at Wyll. "What is a Scout-6?"

"Think Cargo-6 just like *Koni Swift*, Daniel," Crence answered. "Only with more guns and better armor, plus the addition of a big sensor array replacing a couple of the cargo boxes aft. Ramp up the sneakiness by shielding all emissions better, and carry enough food and supplies to be gone for a long time."

"Keep your fin down and glide along below the surface?" Ife asked. "Are such ships tough enough to be pirates themselves?"

Both sharks turned to her with looks bordering on panic.

"We have three hundred and fifty combat troops right now," Ife smiled like she was the third shark at the table. Or seventh. "Fifty or so of those were going to get washed out next week. Another fifty were going to be left at Ogrorspoxu as not quite good enough for a slot. Does your Scout-6 need a boarding party? Maybe pull a supplies pod for a barracks and not be gone nearly so long? Or just plan to take food from people you raid? You already know human food and what to avoid."

Kathra laughed. Ife had the most innocent smile on her face, like they were talking about new breeding programs for tomatoes or something. Everyone else had leaned in so that they didn't miss anything.

Wyll's eyes got huge. Nearly popped sideways out of his sockets.

Crence Miray was also surprised, but a sly grin came over his face as his hammer pulled back just a bit.

"You know…" he said to Wyll Koobitz.

"I will consider it," Wyll interrupted in a dry, superior voice that suggested the two of them would be locked in a small room with good sound-proofing at some near future point so they could argue more vociferously at each other.

Ife turned deadly serious now.

"It is my expectation that a Scout-6's mission would be to secure my inner flank," she said to the two sharks, before turning her gaze on Ndidi and then Kathra. "Finding those waystations we didn't go after once we killed the first one."

She paused and Kathra smiled, seeing where the woman was headed.

"We know they exist, because Daniel learned enough from that Sept aspbad and we have *SeptStar's* as-built ratings," she continued. "There should be at least three layers of them reaching back to Sept space. At this point, one of them may have belonged to the pirates that tried to hit *Koni Swift*, if you wish to still call them pirates, rather than a forward raider operating for the Sept. You'd have to capture them and read their logs for the truth, but it doesn't really matter. They are bigger than a Cargo-6, and smaller than *SwiftStar*. The Sept will need the first ring to invade any depth into the Free Worlds, and the next ones to reach Anndaing space."

"Suggestion?" Kathra asked, taking a moment to assure herself that the two merchants still weren't used to thinking like pirates.

It took a subtle mind shift to do that. The Mbaysey had years of practice, trying to outthink such folks.

"If Crence can find them, we could meet up later and *SwiftStar* might have a go at a few," Ife smiled. "Ndidi did a lovely job on the first one, but we caught him asleep at the controls. I doubt the next ones will be such kittens."

"Can I have Daniel?" Crence asked.

He knew how *SwiftStar* had found the first one.

"No," Kathra said flatly. "He needs to be with Ife and *SwiftStar*. The Upynth as allies are more important than hidden bases that are probably proliferating like ticks as we speak. At some point, a larger Anndaing fleet will have to get involved."

"What are you suggesting, Kathra?" Crence asked, glancing over at Wyll in the way that the sharks did, the eye on that side rolling outward and back horizontally, like a human glancing sideeye.

"*SeptStar* staged a pirate raid on Ogrorspoxu," she smiled. "Go find one of their worlds or bases and return the favor. You have an exceptionally detailed map of Sept space and the Free Worlds."

"That would constitute an act of war, Kathra," Wyll spoke up.

"Only if it is officially sanctioned by Merchants Bank, Wyll." Her smile grew wider. "Maybe I should hire Crence and his new ship for a time."

THIRTY-ONE

THE NEWS HAD REACHED them in flight, but Hadi was not surprised as he studied the latest messenger delivering information to Amirin.

All bureaucracies work slowly. That is their nature and their power. The good ones temper the mercurial excesses of a dynasty or a fool.

Still, it was concerning as he read through the folder.

Forward Operating Base Urmia, still inside Sept Space, was well behind them. Naupati Pasdar had gathered his forces now at Ardabil, deep in Free Worlds space, hidden like a tick in a hunting dog's ruff.

Septagon *Singara*. A dozen Patrol Tenders, when they might normally have brought four. Eight patrols themselves, in addition to the two permanently assigned to *Singara*. Forty transports bringing food and supplies. Six transports carrying combat troops.

No doubt spies had noted the massive shifting around of forces that presaged the invasion, but the three men who might have sent on messages to the Free Worlds government had rediscovered their love for the Sept, under Hadi's questioning, and told him everything he needed to know.

Two of them had even been allowed to survive his interrogation. The third had made the Keyaksar looked like a mendicant monk by comparison. Hadi had enjoyed torturing that fool in the privacy of his own head, until he just willed the man's heart to stop beating.

Hadi read faster, but he had also gleaned some of the information he desired directly from the mind of the messenger seated across the table from him and the naupati.

It was just the three of them, as *Singara*'s aspbad was not a man either of them trusted enough to admit to the conspiracy.

The messenger had delivered the news of a pirate raid, far beyond Free Worlds space. A place *SeptStar* had departed from.

Finally, Amirin looked up from his reading and the messenger quailed, whitening visibly at the barely-controlled rage emanating off the naupati like a scent.

"And the other three?" Amirin started his interrogation in the middle, rather than bothering with niceties.

"Only the one savaran felt that his ship had the supplies to make it as far as Ardabil safely, Naupati," the man replied in a voice controlling its fright reasonably well. "As he was not senior enough to take command of the others as Marzban, the Patrol Commander, he technically mutinied against his superior officer and came here directly. The other three, as far as we know, were headed towards a Free Worlds system where they intended to acquire supplies and continue to return home as well as they could."

Hadi was shocked at the low, angry growl that emerged from Amirin. That sounded like the old Sardar who had nearly lost an eye to a rebel's blade, forty years ago.

"If they somehow are not arrested by a Free Worlds

bureaucrat along the way, make sure they are arrested here and tried for cowardice in the face of the enemy," he said in a voice like a stone for honing blades. "The ship that did bring us news, what is their state?"

"They operated on half-rations and minimal activity, Naupati," the man said. "The physical toll was extreme, but none of the men died from starvation. They did, however, cut things so finely that they had perhaps another two days before someone did. The crew will be perhaps a year returning to full health, according to the doctors that examined them."

"Mark them all for medals, and promote the savaran," Amirin said slowly. "Then transfer them home aboard the next vessel making the return journey to Urmia, with rehabilitation orders that get them as far as *Singara*'s home base. Or *Vorgash*'s."

"It shall be done, Naupati."

"Do we know who attacked Forward Operating Base Zabol?" Hadi leaned in now, hoping to deflect a little of Pasdar's rage.

This was a messenger who had drawn the short straw, not the fools in command who had been responsible. He didn't deserve to be shot. Hadi had looked inside his mind to confirm that much.

"We have the scans from the Patrol vessel, Aspbad Rostami," the man stammered, turning this way and perhaps relaxing, now that things were onto a tactical setting. "There are no vessels even remotely similar, anywhere in our records."

"And they did not communicate at any point?" Amirin also went tactical, rather than raging. "Just dropped out of jump and opened fire?"

"Affirmative, sirs," the man said. "The four vessels that did escape the carnage were all on the far side of the station when it made a raking pass. One ship was on guard duty and returned to engage, but was quickly annihilated by the firepower of the intruder."

Hadi flipped to the rear of the document for the statistics collated from the scanner logs.

"Ram Cannon-grade firepower on all the turrets that engaged you?" he asked.

"Correct, Aspbad," the officer nodded. "Individual Patrol vessels are outmatched, but a full Patrol should be able to give a better accounting of itself."

"I doubt that," Amirin pronounced gravely.

"Sir?"

Hadi noted the page that Amirin was studying and flipped to it. It required a moment before he saw the thing that had apparently jumped right out at the naupati.

But Amirin Pasdar was one of the best Imperial Sept combat commanders alive.

"Truly?" Hadi asked.

The messenger was lost, and wisely chose to remain silent.

"Ram Cannon is an approximation, but a misleading one," Amirin nodded. "That ship was engaging at a range when Ram Cannons would go myopic and lose effectiveness because they could not focus. Similarly, they also ranged farther, killing that last vessel before it could escape."

"Aliens?" Hadi asked. "True aliens?"

He thought back to the many civilizations that the Ishtan had encountered in their endless travels hunting Urid-Varg. And also to the species the snakes had called Anndaing, looking like an erect, bipedal version of a hammerhead shark from ancient Earth.

Nobody had weapons like that. Even the Ishtan would have noted something.

Amirin surprised him by shrugging.

"Unclaimed wilderness inward towards the galactic core beyond the established borders of the Free Worlds," Amirin noted, turning his attention to the messenger. "Not anything marked inhabited. There are species out there such as Upynth or Bhaorajj, from what I remember, but none of them are even as organized or powerful as the Free Worlds. These are either wandering marauders or our old friends."

"Old friends, Naupati?"

"Last we met them, Kathra Omezi had the assistance of a gigantic, alien turtle that was so dangerous to *Uwalu*," Pasdar smiled. "*Vorgash* killed it. Perhaps she has repeated herself, and found another group of aliens to help her."

Something in the man's eyes gave even Hadi pause. Amirin grinned ferally.

"We shall see how they deal with Septagon *Singara*."

PART THREE

MARAUDERS

THIRTY-TWO

Daniel preferred deep space.

Maybe it was just him, but being surrounded by masses of people for long periods seemed to grate on his nerves. It was like thousands of ants crawling across his skin, but he couldn't scratch, because they were inside his mind.

At times, he wondered if it was the influence of Urid-Varg, who had gone years without encountering another living being in his travels. Alternatively, the mental powers the creature had accumulated had driven him to solitude as a way to escape.

In the darkness, there were fewer minds around him so he could keep them at a distance.

SwiftStar had over five hundred crew now. Still far less than the three thousand or more that the ancient ship had once hauled, back when the quarters contained families as well as warriors, but much more than before, when it was just the fighting crew Ife had brought with her the first time.

He sat on the bridge in the dead of night and listened to the song of the stars.

Myler Bolazt, Stina's Anndaing Assistant Pilot, was in

charge, with the lights turned down as *SwiftStar* sat relatively unmoving, the ship's systems scanning the stars around them to confirm where they were. It was one thing to put a dot inside a holographic chart floating in the air in front of you. It was something entirely else to actually look at the stars surrounding you in real space and triangulate against them.

Every system moved. Usually, groups of stars moved in tandem with their neighbors, but there was still drift over time. Some of these charts might be over a thousand years old, because the Anndaing hadn't needed that level of accuracy, this far from Ogrorspoxu, and the Mbaysey had never come this direction.

The Upynth were only known because they occasionally traveled, but they weren't merchants like the Anndaing, or sojourners like the Mbaysey. Most of the hulls that called on their worlds were Se'uh'pal.

How many places did that describe?

Daniel had never really considered how much of human trade with other species was carried out by the folks some might insultingly call rabbits, if they wanted a rude pejorative. The Sept disliked anyone who wasn't human. But they still used the Se'uh'pal.

It probably helped that those folks had no word for morality in their own language. Just profit and loss. In that, they weren't all that different from the amoral bastards of the Sept, looking to extend an empire across all humans.

And maybe everyone else after that.

Daniel could see a future where Anndaing ships, representing the various species of that space, picked up more of the trade, crossing K'bari space in larger and larger numbers. Eventually the mixed, semi-human populations of the Free Worlds would hopefully have an alternative to Sept aggression. Maybe even some new colonies, either with the K'bari or filling in on worlds they had abandoned.

He wondered if he'd live long enough to actually enjoy it.

But Hadi Rostami was nowhere close by. That was good enough for now.

Sitting in real space, between those long jumps that *SwiftStar* was taking across the galaxy, he could listen for the man's voice.

Rostami had left Rhages. Or Earth. Wherever he had been for so long, while Daniel and Kathra had been at Ogrorspoxu and then Kanus.

By now, little Adaku Omezi had been born. Similarly, Kwento Uduik was also there and laughing at Erin's breast.

Would the future history of the Mbaysey start a new chapter with those two births, so closely aligned with *SwiftStar*'s mission to the Upynth?

Myler suddenly rose from his spot and stepped away from his station. Daniel recovered from whatever daydreams had occupied him and looked around.

The Pilot and a tech who had been supervising various systems went out the bridge hatch like a pack of wolves were on their heels, nipping.

Ndidi took Myler's spot and settled.

They were alone on the bridge of the vessel.

Daniel paused to look around nearby space, but *SwiftStar* was deep in the darkness between three isolated stars that existed as long alphanumeric sequences, not even names. None were marked inhabited, and the space was not known to be claimed by anyone since the days when the K'bari had walked these pathways.

"Am I in trouble?" Daniel asked with the slightest tease to his voice.

Ndidi turned to look directly at him, one eyebrow well above her glasses and looking like a stern matriarch about to discipline an unruly child.

Not that Daniel had had any experiences like that when he was young.

Honest.

"Have you done something that I should know about?" she asked, sounding more like the Shield of a warship in Kathra Omezi's service.

"Probably," he laughed. "I should spend more time cooking with the larger group feeding all the new soldiers. That will keep me too busy to cause problems for the rest of the crew."

"The only problems I'm aware of are setting up a rotation system for people wishing to seduce my chef," Ndidi suddenly grinned.

He smiled in a lopsided way, still unsure about all that. What was it about him that drew those women? All of them were tougher than him. Generally smarter, too.

A'Alhakoth had been made comitatus, back when that meant pilots flying Spectres. The first alien to have that distinction. Tanuss was an engineer who left Joane in awe with her technical abilities. Even Acqueir seemed on the verge of exploring a world where she didn't need to engage the Anic pair-bond.

A few other crew women had smiled at him more than usual lately, too, now that he put his mind to the task.

"Should you or Ife do something about it?" he asked.

Everyone involved were adults, even if it had taken Daniel some time to get himself to seeing the alien women as such. All of them were women he subordinated himself to, literally in the case of A'Alhakoth, who was comitatus.

"We have," Ndidi said simply, leaving it at that.

He had to wonder, but if she wasn't going to explain, he might have to ask Ife and see if the Speaker felt like enlightening him.

Daniel might be Kathra's bloodhound in some aspects,

but he was still just a chef around all these warriors and killers.

"Anything I should be made aware of?" he asked tentatively.

"No."

He occasionally had to remind himself in Ndidi's case that she was only twenty-four years Standard. The Sword sometimes sounded older than him. More poised and experienced than he remembered her being, but not in a bad way.

She had perhaps finally begun to grow into herself.

At some point, they would merge, and he could see more of that truth for himself, just as any and all of the comitatus women regularly inspected the insides of his own head and soul for any of the gathering darkness that might presage something evil taking root.

"Can I ask a personal question?" Daniel asked. "Friends, instead of comrades?"

She turned and smiled at him. It was warm, but also firm and distant in ways he had a hard time articulating.

"Why have you never had a procedure done to fix your eyes?" he continued. "Why retain the glasses? The Anndaing have the medical technology to give you better vision than I have. And one of these days I will use it, when my own eyes start to fail."

She sat in silence. Contemplative. He'd known her long enough to see the channels of logic and emotion she pursued.

"They define me," she finally said in an adult voice he didn't think he had ever heard from the woman. "For my entire life, those glasses marked the limits of what I could achieve, back when every girl wanted to grow up and join Yagazie's comitatus. Or later Kathra's. I couldn't because I needed glasses."

Daniel sat in perfect silence, wondering at who this new

woman was that he felt he might have never met before, occupying the flesh of the precocious teenager who had been his closest friend in the galaxy for the last few years.

"I don't need to be able to see like that to serve on a warship, Daniel," Ndidi continued. "To be *SwiftStar*'s Shield. There is great power in that."

"I don't understand," he puzzled, aware of the immense cultural gap that separated a *Rabic* Algerian chef from an Mbaysey warrior.

"There are little girls out there now who will never be tall, Daniel," she smiled proudly. "Never athletes. Maybe half-blind, like me. Something."

She paused and took a breath. Daniel could feel her standing on the same sort of cliffs he frequently had been called upon to climb, like starting both of his restaurants on nothing but the conviction that he could create something so much better than anyone else that he would succeed where everyone else failed.

"I am *their* symbol, Daniel," she finally said. "They can dream about growing up and being like me. There are many more young girls like that in the Mbaysey than there are like Erin or Kam, to say nothing of Kathra. Does that make sense?"

"It does," he said, finally understanding. "But I was such a dreamer. I realized one day that I wanted to cook, more than anything in the world, and my parents eventually understood that I was serious. After that, it was patience to learn all the rules, and then an understanding of how to break them. And a willingness."

"I got myself to *WinterStar* because I identified a gap I could fill," she nodded in agreement. "A place where others would not be as committed to excellence as I was. A need. But for you, I would have eventually had your job, and maybe earlier than I did."

Her own smile got a little lopsided, too, like a strange mirror held up to him.

"Of course, without you, we'd all be dead or slaves again now," she said, her tone serious but her smile intact. "Because Urid-Varg would have probably gone on and started conquering the Sept by now."

She paused, reflective.

"How long would it have taken him to capture the Sept and eventually destroy them and humanity as well?" she asked.

Daniel leaned back, caught off guard by her question. Several of his ghosts appeared at the edges of his vision, like they were physically haunting the bridge of this warship with him.

"A decade, perhaps," he replied. "From Kathra, he would have learned enough to head straight to Rhages and depose the fool currently seated on that throne. From there, I can only imagine the terrible crusade that *salaud* might have unleashed across the Free Worlds and other places. Knowing what I know, the Anndaing would have encountered them soon. Possibly *Koni Swift* and Crence Miray on the very voyage where we found them, had they gone on to Thrabo or maybe F'Dashua."

"So you saved all of us," she said.

"I am not a hero, Ndidi," Daniel felt his tone get hot. "Not a messiah, nor a prophet. I am just a man. A chef."

"You are much more than that, Daniel," she chided him. "The Left Hand of Evil tells me that much."

He shrugged rather than offer more defense.

Honestly, he was just a cook. Urid-Varg had been a rapist waiting to engage a whole new harem of mindless victims, on his way to perhaps forging yet another empire.

Daniel had been forced to stop that *branleur*.

Maybe that was enough.

"And now?" he asked, wondering where the conversation might go next.

"I just wanted to check on you," Ndidi said. "I know you come here frequently at night, as a way to meditate away from the rest of the day's problems. Especially when someone might come knock on your door. This is sacred ground if you will, by agreement."

He grunted, vaguely aware of something along those lines, but that wasn't why he did it.

Here, he could be surrounded by the people who were the beating heart of *SwiftStar*, as they went about their own duties to keep everything moving along.

Because he could see where they were headed.

THIRTY-THREE

HADI WAS NOT the aspbad of Septagon *Singara*. The man who held that position was another glory-hound son of a distaff branch of Clan Aghaei.

Personally, Hadi had decided that the aspbad had been promoted beyond the level of his competence already, and was only protected in that position because the previous naupati had been a commander that Amirin Pasdar would have respected as a professional.

Hadi ignored Aghaei most of the time, except to look inside the man's soul occasionally, hoping for something, anything more sophisticated than women, whiskey, and racing horses.

He had yet to be anything but disappointed along those lines.

They were all three in the Command Node of *Singara*, that long causeway a deck above the men who commanded this mighty war machine. None of the ones below were men Hadi had promoted to these positions, so he had to rely on the fact that they served in command of a Septagon as an approximation of their competence.

Mechanics had installed a third command throne for him, opposite Aghaei's. It would have added a pleasant symmetry to the Command Node, but they had not recentered everything, so it left the space awkward.

Hadi had simply reached into Aghaei's mind and twisted the necessary components to get the man to shut up and serve, that first time his reedy voice had begun to suggest snidely that Hadi Rostami didn't need to be here, as a mere aide to the naupati.

Maybe the man needed to suffer a heart attack or other medical emergency that utterly debilitated him, and then Hadi could take over? Except that he and Amirin were only going to be here for a short period.

The long term campaign to conquer the Sept Empire began at Tavle Jocia. Act One barely ended on this ship.

"Is the fleet in readiness?" Amirin called to the room as he rose from his throne and began his habitual pacing, down and back the long axis of the Command Node.

"All vessels confirm readiness, Naupati," one of the men replied in a professional tone so at odds with the idiot aspbad in nominal command. "All Patrol vessels and tenders are showing green on my boards. Resupply squadrons have already been confirmed onsite for staging."

Hadi watched Amirin stop and turn slowly in place, as though studying the Command Node and the men he had inherited. Hadi understood that long moment of reflection.

This would be the last time the legendary Naupati Amirin Pasdar commanded a planetary assault from the Command Node of a Septagon.

Assuming, of course, that it wasn't necessary to set a Septagon in orbit of Rhages and use the Axial Megacannon to annihilate targets thinking they could somehow resist. Such a play to overthrow the emperor would be neck or nothing, but Hadi and Amirin were already past the point they could walk away.

Honor, if nothing else, demanded a change. Pride and vanity drove the two men to demand it be Amirin Pasdar, and not someone else.

None of the Emperor's advisers, councilors, or relatives that Hadi had met or heard rumors about were worth more than the time it would take to hunt them down and shoot them.

Amirin's eyes found his from across the space. Hadi could see all the same thoughts in that man's mind, but they had merged personalities enough by now that Hadi wasn't really sure where each ended.

Both men had been touched, altered by the Ishtan, something that only Daniel Lémieux could understand. Amirin had escaped with most of his sanity intact, at least.

Hadi continued to doubt his own, but he had Naupati Pasdar to direct his folly. To kill the men that needed to be removed from Pasdar's path to power.

"*Singara* Assault Fleet," Naupati Pasdar announced in that bold, deadly voice that reminded everyone who he was, "initiate your jumps. Next stop, Tavle Jocia."

THIRTY-FOUR

"*GORBAK*," Crence cursed under his breath. "Are those numbers real?"

He studied his scanner board and read the statistics again. Commander Omezi had told them what they would be facing, but in his heart Crence hadn't ever really *believed*.

Septagon.

What tuna built a seven-sided building in space? That wasn't a ship. It was an architectural statement.

Crence had spent enough time around humans to be able to think in human measurements, bizarrely off-kilter as they might be. He would have called it a ziggurat, but the sides didn't step. The main hull was seventy decks tall, because everything they did was in sevens, it seemed. Three hundred meters vertical, with flat facings. Thirty-two hundred meters on one of those facings, from edge to edge. A little over seven thousand meters from that bowsprit barrel to the rear edges of the center engine wells.

Seven Ram Cannon turrets on each facing. Zwölf-two of what Kathra Omezi's notes had called Heavy Particle cannon turrets to engage smaller vessels foolish enough to not run immediately when a Septagon appeared.

And that Axial Megacannon on the bow. What xenocidal bastard builds a weapon that can destroy cities from orbit, and then puts it on every battleship in their fleet?

Trick question. The Sept Empire.

They had built that empire by offering folks the starkest choice possible. Surrender or die.

The Commander's notes indicated how many hundred Septagons had been built. Even accounting for the size of Sept space, they could put together a fleet big enough to give the Armada pause. Crence still didn't know what the Merchants Bank had planned.

He was just happy that their blacked-out, nameless Scout-6 could hide so well from that monstrous collection of firepower and insanity over there that represented a Sept invasion fleet.

Septagon *Singara*, from the arrogant transponder telling everyone within range who to fear.

Zwölf-two full Patrols of ten vessels each. One hundred and forty of the *salauds*, plus a zwölf of what his new notes called Patrol Tenders. Milk-cows, as it were, hauling all the supplies and repair facilities that the little warships could not transport themselves.

Crence salivated at the astonishing number of unarmed transports hauling food and equipment around, wondering if it was worth actually going pirate on a few of those if he could isolate them.

Nobody said espionage couldn't be profitable, after all.

"I tripled checked my systems, Crence," Dane finally spoke up. "They all agree with what the Mbaysey sold us for intel. You suppose she knew this was coming?"

"Absolutely she knew," Jine chimed in. "Don't let that calm, black exterior or the scaleless skin fool you. That woman's the nastiest shark I've ever met. Or you. Maybe even heard about. We might not be safe, if she decided to take a bite out of Anndaing space."

"She's the best ally we've got," Crence reminded both of his goofuses. "Without her, we might have sailed into someplace like Thrabo one of these days and come under the guns of a Septagon like that before we even knew what had come out of the depths at us."

"Yeah, but what in the Hells of Morh do we do against something like that?" Dane asked. "Or a whole group of them?"

"They're slow and defensive," Crence said. "Keep that in mind. They waddle deliberately, worse than Jine does first thing in the morning, trying to get to the kitchen or the head. That's why they need those patrols. Those things are much faster, but can't range far because they have those silly grav field inducers the humans use and no internal space for food as a result. At least until they buy better systems from us."

"Will they build more *SeptStar*s?" Jine asked now, smiling with greed.

"Maybe," Crence shrugged. "It didn't do all that well in its first battle, but they probably didn't realize Ife was any good. I don't think anybody realized how sharp that woman was."

"Can anybody resist *that*?" Dane gestured with one fin out the forward ports at the monstrosity that was getting itself organized to go ruin somebody's day.

Maybe everybody's, considering that the closest Free Worlds system of any value in that direction was Tavle Jocia. Right where Kathra Omezi had suggested the Sept might take a bite, if they wanted to completely shatter the Free Worlds as an independent entity.

That battle fleet looked like enough trouble to take and

hold the place, but it could only hold. One Septagon could do that. If you brought two, you were looking at your next target after this.

Crence remembered all his lessons from Merchant Marine academy.

"Nothing that the Free Worlds has, Dane," Crence replied. "But the Sept can't really hold a world, so much as own orbital space and install new governors for the planetary system. Eventually, the locals either accept a *fait accompli*, or stir up so much trouble that the Sept have to either withdraw or commit a stupid amount of forces to occupy the place."

Dane was typing furiously, so Crence looked over.

"According to Omezi's notes, all of the Free Worlds fleet might be needed to push out something this size," Dane said. "And that involves stripping the border worlds all the way down, including piracy patrols. All you'd have left was search and rescue boats. What do we do now?"

"We follow them," Crence replied, turning his other eye to his nightflier until Jine nodded. "Sneak in after that fleet and confirm everything that's just supposition at this point. Gain all the tactical and strategic intelligence we need for the Merchants Bank Board of Directors to decide what they want to do."

"Anything short of the Armada stop that?" Jine asked, disbelief evident in his voice.

EveningStar, but Crence didn't say that out loud. Not even to these two. He only knew that much because Wyll trusted him enough that Obaj could send a message along. And Crence had asked his boss what the term meant.

If he didn't spread the infection of knowledge to Jine and Dane, they'd be better off, because that idea was utterly insane at a level that made even a crazy-fin shark like Crence nervous.

"Maybe," he temporized instead.

Crence turned to Jine.

"Assuming Tavle Jocia, and this is as good a guess as anything, can you get there ahead of them and go quiet?" Crence asked.

"Sit in the darkness like that last *verk* that chased us out when *Koni Swift* left?" Jine smiled.

"Just so," Crence nodded. "I'm going to assume there are more like that. Pirates in Sept pay, or maybe Sept ships camouflaged to look like pirates. I'd camp a set of them around the outside like that, so that people trying to escape with a normal hop to the edge of the system maybe came under guns before they could recharge things. Nice way to help with radio silence, if nobody can escape to bring help immediately after an invasion."

"We've got better guns and armor than *Koni Swift*," Jine smiled hopefully.

"And no reason to use them, except firing over our dorsal fin at someone as we run like hell, Jine," Dane snapped, showing that he at least understood their priorities.

Not that a nameless Scout-6 might not plot Sept freighter paths in and out, and take one along the way, just to be a shit. But that was tomorrow's conversation.

"Yeah, yeah," Jine groused. "I know how Tavle Jocia Flight Control prefers things. We're probably better coming out deeper anyway. Only four-zwölf light-minutes out, instead of way out in the darkness like most folks. We'll still be way off scanners of anyone not hammering the vicinity looking."

"Do it, and keep ready to shoot and run," Crence ordered the nightflier.

He paused and looked at Dane.

"I need you to plot me two courses out of here," Crence said.

Dane nodded, like maybe he already knew what was

coming, but the shark had flown with him long enough, so maybe he did.

"One, minimal-time-course to Ogrorspoxu," Crence said, before taking a breath. "The other to Narlpynth, the Upynth homeworld. We may need to grab Ife and *SwiftStar*, if this goes down the way I think it might."

"What would *SwiftStar* be able to do against a Septagon, Crence?" Jine suddenly seemed far more perceptive than that shark normally was.

"I can't tell you, Jine," Crence replied, turning to the other shark. "Or you, Dane. I'm not supposed to know myself. But Wyll has a plan."

"Is it a good one?" Dane asked.

Crence shrugged.

"I can guarantee you nobody's going to see it coming."

THIRTY-FIVE

Ndidi studied the orbital space around the planet Narlpynth from her station on the bridge of *SwiftStar*. They were out a ways from the planet itself, just observing the system for surprises before committing themselves to arriving in any sort of public way.

The so-called *land of the builders*, where *u-pynth* meant *people who build*. Historically, ancient humans might have compared them to the Romans of western EurAsia and their roads, or the Chinese who had built the ancient great walls and canals.

But the Upynth weren't aggressive conquerors like humans. They built roads and cities, but didn't set out to colonize and master all the systems around them as part of some greater empire.

Not like humans.

There were six worlds in what was considered Upynth space. Nothing, really, in the face of even the Free Worlds, to say even less of the Sept Empire. It would be like comparing the Kaniea to the Upynth for relative size.

But they were free. And builders.

Ndidi had never visited the homeworld of the Humans. She hadn't even been born yet when the Mbaysey left Tazo for life in space, so she had only images and stories to compare the Upynth to the zebras of her ancestral homelands.

Or unicorns, since Ndidi had seen skulls of the z'lud that Urid-Varg had kept aboard the turtle, flensed of flesh and sealed against time. The z'lud didn't have that horn in the forehead that the Upynth did. Or the Wisp aft in engineering now, in the form of Tanuss Barleyne, although the Upynth could stab you with theirs.

Bipeds, along a fairly generic model, but Ndidi had read somewhere that the design tended to be the most efficient arrangement of limbs for a mobile, tool-using species. The skull was long and oval shaped, with wideset eyes on the front corners, where they could zero in forward, or protect the creature from being snuck up on.

Green and brown stripes were largely vestigial these days, much like the horn. And they had a mohawk even more serious than Erin on her fiercest day, either buzzed short or running long and draped over one shoulder, depending on fashion.

Smaller than humans, generally, the males would be about her size, while the females were not much larger than A'Alhakoth. Most of the human crew would appear as giants, as would the Kaniea males and a few Wisp and Anic combat troopers of either sex that were Kam or Nkechi's size.

Ndidi took a deep breath and turned her head both ways, aware that everyone was watching her, either directly or surreptitiously, including Ife. But the Speaker had made it clear that she was in charge right now.

Training day, as it were, except that it was more like final exams.

Ndidi reached out and keyed a line to the office where

A'Alhakoth was seated. The woman appeared immediately, but it took Ndidi a moment to understand why she looked different.

A'Alhakoth was wearing Kaniea makeup today, when normally she didn't. It was a subtle shading and shadowing that made her face seem even more like a triangle than normal. An arrowhead pointed at the speaker, if you would. Her lips were brighter and outlined. A'Alhakoth had pulled her longish hair back into a braid and communicated fierce with her expression.

Mbaysey didn't do the warpaint that other human cultures seemed compelled to explore, so it was even more alien than usual, as much as A'Alhakoth was something of a sister to her after the last few years.

"Ready?" Ndidi asked unnecessarily. "We're about to make the final jump in."

A'Alhakoth nodded, eyes narrower than usual, which complimented that horizontal slit to make her seem a predator.

Ndidi turned to her Sword now, fixing Ngozi with stern eyes.

"Unlock your guns, but only fire on my order," Ndidi said simply.

The older woman nodded professionally and clicked a few buttons, like she had everything aimed already and just needed to clear the safeties.

All around the ship, the gun teams were prepared to step in and fix guns that overheated, broke, or otherwise failed in battle, but Ngozi controlled everything from here.

Ndidi turned to Stina Carte.

"Confirm your course, Pilot," Ndidi said.

"We will come out of jump low," Spectre Sixteen replied, her eyes glowing with an internal fire. "Unlike any other culture currently operating. Same rough distance for safe ship-handling, and a spot currently unoccupied by any vessels, but within range of many weapons on the various stations, as they have left no obvious gaps in their defenses. We will be moving relatively slowly, compared to orbital traffic, and three escape jumps have been programmed, depending on your needs."

Finally, Acqueir, on sensors.

"We will rely on you to protect us against surprises," Ndidi said simply.

The Anic woman smiled as fiercely as Iruoma might.

Ndidi nodded and smiled back at the woman, watching those internally-lit eyes glow with excitement.

The flight here from Ogrorspoxu had indeed been enough time for the Anic woman to overcome her own specist inhibitions and knock on Daniel's door.

And had returned a second time, so apparently they had come to an understanding.

Ndidi would never let a male touch her, but it was good to know that the weird heterosexual members of her crew could find pleasure and fulfillment.

She turned to look at Ife one last time, giving the woman a chance to say something, but Ife did not. Just stared at her with hard eyes.

Ndidi tripped a switch and waited a moment for the system to beep at everyone for attention.

"All hands, stand by for transit into Narlpynth orbital traffic," she said slowly. "Pilot, make your jump."

THIRTY-SIX

As planetary invasions went, Hadi was almost disappointed in the fools running Tavle Jocia.

Of course, Naupati Pasdar had already spent considerable time in-system when they had originally commissioned and built *SeptStar*, and that time had not been wasted on idle debaucheries, unlike many senior Sept commanders might have done. Hadi had cataloged the entire system with a level of detail that probably would have frightened the locals, had they access to his notes.

Singara had come out of the jump on a corner where they were set to pivot and either destroy the command node station where the governor lived, or shatter the naval base where a few anti-piracy vessels were always stationed, along with a variety of warships that might make up larger forces.

All of them had been caught so flat-footed that Hadi wondered if he could have landed ground combat troops on the skin of either station and gotten through their airlocks before anyone even realized that they had a problem.

Fourteen full Patrols of Sept ships were such overkill right now that they ended up standing around looking tough to the eighteen vessels that might have been able to engage them or flee.

Three had managed to escape, but only because they took one look at the arrival of such a tremendous fleet, *AND* a Septagon, and ran like hell.

And even that number was lower than Pasdar's battle plans had expected as a best case outcome.

Seriously, where were the intelligence-gathering forces that might have noticed an impending invasion?

But then, nobody had ever done something so deeply out of character as this.

The Sept were methodical commanders, for the most part, Amirin Pasdar excluded for all the obvious reasons. The Free Worlds were most likely expecting another one of their border worlds to be attacked rather than a commercial center so far behind the lines.

Nobody would ever be able to sneak up on a Free Worlds target like this again, but that didn't matter. The damage would have been done by tomorrow. Either the Free Worlds initiated a significant build-up of naval forces, or they risked whole sectors being spalled off by a vastly rejuvenated Sept Empire.

How bad had it gotten?

Hadi had to stop and wonder if the rot at the core in Rhages had reduced the entire war to a desultory affair, haphazardly undertaken by both sides and almost aimless.

He turned to Amirin and nodded that secret nod. Amirin returned the gesture after a moment.

They could afford a few seconds as the local military and political forces got themselves organized enough to at least surrender competently.

In an eyeblink, the two men were back aboard *Vorgash* at the peak of its era as the finest warship in the Sept Empire. A peak long since passed.

Hadi tried not to dwell on the symbolism inherent in that observation.

"What worries you?" the Naupati asked as they were alone.

"Tavle Jocia was not prepared for us, in spite of the uptick in piracy as our forces hounded the Anndaing vessel *Koni Swift* and others," Hadi replied. "We might not have needed *Singara*, except as an exclamation point."

"The Free Worlds have grown decadent and foolish," Amirin announced.

"But so have the Sept," Hadi noted. "When was the last time the Sept fleet did something non-linear and surprising, when you weren't the man in command?"

The Naupati opened his mouth to reply hotly, and then closed it. He blinked, and began to pace.

That was a good sign. Hadi had bounced the man out of the tactical situation of invading a hostile system, and up to the strategic, as a good aspbad should do from time to time.

Amirin paused at the far end of the Command Node.

"Years. Maybe decades," he snarled angrily, stomping now as he paced, his rage directed at the plates beneath his feet. "Gods, the decadence has taken even us in its grasp and begun to drain the life from everything. We have become boringly predictable, because I am the only Naupati left who is pushing the margins for newness."

"Not just stasis, but entropy," Hadi offered. "That was why the Ishtan could accurately predict that you would make an attempt at Empire. Nobody else was capable of challenging you and giving you a reason not to."

The man's response was a wordless growl.

"Tides, Amirin," Hadi continued. "The Sept was rotted from the inside out. Perhaps the Free Worlds knew that and hoped that with enough time, we would fall in on ourselves. Or to initiate the very civil war that might have been your next step, without the mental powers of the Ishtan to help you."

"I was always going to attempt it," Amirin said.

"Yes, the aliens knew you would try," Hadi noted. "They said as much, but they were also expecting to live longer than they did, so perhaps they wished to observe your campaign, were it necessary to continue to help, so they could stop the chef and his allies with the full force of the Sept."

Amirin continued to pace as Hadi watched.

"This changes nothing about the invasion and capture of Tavle Jocia," Amirin finally stopped and faced Hadi.

"Correct," Hadi agreed. "But it changes the timing of the next steps."

"It does, indeed," the Naupati nodded. "Tavle Jocia becomes so much less relevant to things, and so much more."

"More?" Hadi asked, surprised.

"I have not forgotten about the Anndaing," he said. "If the rot of the Sept is so great, we will need to make sure they cannot fall on us from behind while we contest Rhages."

"So?"

"So we will need to plan an invasion of their worlds," Amirin Pasdar, future Emperor proclaimed. "The merchants of Tavle Jocia can quickly grow rich, if they wish to assist me by building new warships for that effort."

THIRTY-SEVEN

A'Alhakoth had already been Kathra's Ambassador to her own people, and had traveled all the way to human space at one point, so dealing with a whole new species of aliens she had never met before wasn't that far of a stretch. She hadn't crossed into the Upynth systems from Bhaorajj space, but that was pure luck of the draw on which ship she had ended up working.

How might things have turned out if she had ended up on an Upynth station instead of a human one, so many lifetimes ago?

Things we can never know.

But she was here now. In the office aboard *SwiftStar* that Ife had assigned to her as Ambassador. At some ancient point, an Ovanii of equivalent rank and authority had sat at this very desk, with a much different chair, and dealt with other vessels in their fleet.

A'Alhakoth presumed that the important leaders rode in the gigantic vessels, so this man or woman would have been a clan leader perhaps. Another one like Udo Zalman or Nkiru

Okeke, back with the ClanStars, most likely. Someone tough and competent.

She could fake it.

The internal comm system came live with Acqueir's voice.

"I have a line to the biggest station," the sensor's officer said. "They are politely demanding to know what the hell is going on, but haven't locked any weapons on us yet. I'm sure everything is passively aligning as closely as they can with optics, but nobody is currently painting us with ranging lasers."

"Make sure Ndidi knows there is trouble before I do," A'Alhakoth said. "She'll take command at that point anyway."

"Noted," Acqueir replied. "This line will beep and then you will be live with Station Control. They're speaking the human Spacer language, so my rudimentary fluency already has them convinced we're far from home, as did my eyes."

A'Alhakoth chuckled. Not many species had eyes that glowed. That would certainly cause excitement.

The line beeped and changed timbre.

"This is A'Alhakoth ver'Shingi, Ambassador to the Upynth," she said in the Spacer she had learned on her way to meet Kathra and Daniel.

"Ambassador?" the creature replied as the screen finally flickered and caught up with the transmissions. The lag wasn't that great. Maybe a second. *SwiftStar* had indeed come low and then inserted into a trailing orbit, rather than get any closer.

At least before talking to the locals.

The person was Upynth. Fur, eyes, and that mythical unicorn horn the humans and Kaniea shared in their ancient legends.

"Ambassador," she confirmed. "My Commander sent just this one vessel, in order to convey an ambassador and begin negotiating treaties of peace and trade with your worlds."

Which was all the Mbaysey had ever wanted. It was the rest of the galaxy that didn't want to let Kathra Omezi be.

"What species are you?" the Upynth at the other end asked, possibly a touch less politely than they could have.

A'Alhakoth presumed she was dealing with a female, but that was just a gut instinct, rather than anything about the voice or face that was obvious.

She still wasn't used to species covered entirely over with fur. Kaniea and humans had hair on their heads, but not many other places. Anndaing had scales. Anic and Wisp were equally weird.

"Kaniea," she answered, trying to smile and not have it seem angry. "My kind are from far beyond Bhaorajj space."

That caused the female to blink those big, brown eyes and narrow them. Like she had heard of folks from over there, and maybe even encountered stories.

As far as A'Alhakoth knew, she had gone farther from home than any other Kaniea, but it was possible a few had made it this far over the last two centuries.

Or that the Se'uh'pal had spread some stories.

"We thought you people were human," the woman said.

"I speak a few human tongues," A'Alhakoth replied. "As well as many others. My Anic communications officer assumed you would also be familiar with the languages of the Free Worlds and Sept, as your closest galactic neighbors."

"I see," she said, pausing again. Absorbing all those implications, perhaps. She even smiled ever so slightly. "I am Mara Ermendrud, representing the Upynth Trade Authority. Welcome to Narlpynth. Do you need a transport, or will you bring your own?"

"We will arrive by our own transport, with a small force of diplomats and a few guards for security purposes,"

A'Alhakoth replied. "My team will contact you for docking instructions, presumably following Free Worlds standards?"

"That will be adequate, Ambassador," Ermendrud noted. "I look forward to meeting you in the flesh and finding out more about a mission that might have brought you such a great distance."

She cut the line and A'Alhakoth took a deep breath.

Now was when things would get tricky.

THIRTY-EIGHT

CRENCE HELD HIS BREATH UNNECESSARILY. In the depths of space and distances measured in light-minutes, nobody would hear him breathe, but it was an unconscious thing.

He'd been to Tavle Jocia several times now, but always as a trademaster making points on his margins by having new stuff that the humans and their allies couldn't get enough of. Now, he was quietly waiting in the darkness as ships deeper in the system maneuvered noisily, or fled quietly past.

They'd been right about pirates camped in all the usual landing zones. Several freighters had been taken by ships suddenly pointing a huge number of guns at somebody trying to recharge their drives.

Yet another reason why *Koni Swift* was such a useful ship. He'd escaped that sort of trap because he could move faster than the other folks could chase.

"Crence," Dane murmured from his side, like he was also hiding in the deep water from something big and hungry swimming by.

Crence looked over and watched the shark's board.

"I'm scanning roughly a zwölf of what we'd call pirate

vessels behind us," Dane continued. "Guessing another zwölf hiding for tuna to emerge."

"More than I thought they'd have," Crence grimaced, feeling his hammer droop.

How did a Scout-6 take on a battle fleet of such enormity?

He didn't. That much was obvious. He ran home and got help, hoping that there was something the Merchants Guild and the Bank could do to stop the Sept humans from taking all the Free Worlds over the next decade or two and being almost as bad at Urid-Varg, even without that maniac *salaud* in charge.

Small favors.

"So if I do the math right--" Dane started to say, but Jine interrupted.

"Take your boots off first," the nightflier riffed from his own silence. "More than zwölf here."

"That's my point," Dane countered. "I'm looking at something closer to five hundred thousand humans that just landed in this system, with all the support vessels. Even with freighters that are a box, engines, and a tiny life support cabin, there are more people here than anybody can reasonably expect to feed."

"I presume the *branleur* in charge over there isn't going to trust the locals he just invaded to supply him with food, even if he pays the going rate," Jine opined.

"Yeah, lots of food transports," Dane said. "Any value to them?"

"Only destroyed," Crence smiled at his top sharks. "I'm guessing the smaller ones, running about the size of a Cargo-12, are the ones hauling important stuff. Mechanical replacements and electronics."

"Yeah, but they must have slobbering amounts of stuff stockpiled on a Septagon," Dane said. "Look at the sheer volume enclosed, even for a crew of three hundred thousand."

"Okay, so what are you suggesting?" Crence asked. "Hit the food trucks instead of the valuable stuff?"

"We've got no place to store anything," Jine noted. "You took Omezi up on her offer and loaded in the combat teams. So you could take something, but not steal all their stuff and load it here."

"Don't need to," Dane said. "Blow a few up and we've thrown a net into their lagoon with weights attached."

"Until they come hunting for us," Crence replied. "Since they'll know where the ships are supposed to sail, they can also escort them, or even convoy some. Not worth the effort. We need to bring back somebody like *SwiftStar* or maybe Wyll has some Gun-6 or Gun-12 vessels we could enlist."

"It was worth a try," Dane shrugged, his hammer flexing.

"And it is a good idea," Crence nodded. "Keep watching them for patterns, because I got a feeling we'll be coming back and raiding this place at some point. Whoever is in charge will want to review your logs to see how humans swim."

He didn't dare tell them what insanity Wyll had suggested. Had planned.

EveningStar was so far beyond everything the galaxy would never be the same afterwards.

But they'd have to do something. Even the power emissions given off by the Septagon frightened Crence. But that ship down there, the biggest, nastiest whale Crence Miray had ever seen move under its own power, was a statement.

Even Kathra had called an invasion of Tavle Jocia something of a longshot, but an important one, because another Septagon, *Vorgash* instead of this new creature called *Singara*, had spent so much time in the system before. And it had the shipyards to build *SeekerStar* and *SeptStar*.

And a notorious Anndaing merchant vessel named *Koni Swift* had called on the place a number of times, possibly scouting it for a counter-invasion at a later date, when the Free Worlds woke up and decided that they needed allies. Or overcame their specism to ask.

Humans against the galaxy only worked for the overseers holding the lash. Everyone else were just pawns to be used up and discarded.

And Tavle Jocia had stopped belonging to the Free Worlds about six hours ago.

He made up his mind. Dithering wasn't going to help at this point.

"Jine, get us to Narlpynth as fast as you can," he said, turning to the nightflier as the shark blinked in surprise.

"Now?" Jine asked. "I thought we were going to watch for a while."

"I've seen everything I need to see," Crence announced with a heavy breath. "Get us gone."

Crence wondered if the entire Free Worlds had just stopped being free.

THIRTY-NINE

DANIEL LOOKED at the Upynth and saw z'lud in his mind. Urid-Varg's second empire, after he had wiped out the rest of the Mnapyre he had shared a heritage with.

The Upynth looked like z'lud, roughly. In much the same manner as most erect bipeds on the human model that originally evolved from tree-dwelling rodents had.

The snout was shorter on an Upynth and the eyes smaller, but both were more equine in origin than humans. The ears were indeed horse-like in their upright mobility, but Daniel didn't know their body language well enough to treat them like a semaphore.

And the Upynth had that horn that made them look almost like unicorns.

In his memory, he always thought that it should have been the other way around, with the forever-lost z'lud having the unicorn horn, since they were just a fable now. He'd asked them a few times to be sure, but even Daniel's ghosts didn't think that the z'lud as a race still existed, including several representatives who had been mounts of the terrible conqueror in his day.

They were all in a meeting chamber that conveyed a certain level of meadowness, in much the same way that the Anndaing rooms suggested calm lagoons. The dimensions were wider than necessary, wasting a lot of space around the edges. The carpets felt twice as deep as a human might have done, so soft and springy underfoot. The ceilings were nearly four meters, when they needed to be barely more than half that, and had extra lights in them that conveyed a warmer yellow light than most people preferred.

Feeling like a home they had lost, perhaps? Were they really native to Narlpynth? He didn't know.

At the same time, Daniel had never realized just how boring and mechanical human meeting halls were until he spent enough time around radically-alien creatures to see how they did things instead.

And he was the only human here.

A'Alhakoth was in charge on this side of the table, with Acqueir and Tanuss, plus a handful of Anndaing and Kaniea caravan guards standing behind them, just to make everything look exceptionally *weird*.

Seated across from an Upynth where he could see them both, the horn of a Wisp was more like a semi-rigid tentacle, while the Upynth conveyed an ivory hardness.

And everybody looked slightly askance at Acqueir. He wondered if she could make her eyes glow brighter than normal in the same way that a Wisp might. Tanuss was relatively dim right now, but Acqueir was a cat staring back at headlights.

The smile on her face didn't help.

The locals were all Upynth, which saddened Daniel in ways he couldn't really explain. Anndaing space was a mélange of interesting folk, all working together for the common goal of getting rich. The Free Worlds were less so, at least until you got clear out to places like Thrabo, where humans were only a majority of the population on some days, depending on which ships were in harbor.

Narlpynth was boringly mono-species. They didn't tend to have many outsiders, and much like the Sept they structured their laws to keep the icky, alien weirdos at bay.

Daniel wondered if they had a level of specism underlying it all and it was just not talked about in polite company. He had encountered a few Upynth back when he lived on Genarde, but they tended to be travelers, rather than builders. There were more in the Free Worlds ports he had visited with the Mbaysey, but not many.

Six worlds weren't going to stop the Sept Empire, when those *salauds* decided to come this way.

Mara Ermendrud was studying him from across the way. Daniel had taken a spot on A'Alhakoth's immediate right, and had been introduced as a translator, if one was necessary.

For the last year, Kathra had ordered as much communication as possible be conducted in Anndaing, even aboard *SeekerStar* and *SwiftStar*. A'Alhakoth might be rusty.

He doubted she would be, but it made for a good reason to have a strange human accompanying all the alien folks talking to all the other alien folks. At least he could speak any language that the Upynth knew.

Probably not a good idea to let them know that he also was fluent in Upynth itself, a result of one of his ghosts. The second to last mount that Urid-Varg had ridden had been a scholar and a linguist.

Plus, the K'bari named Arsène who had traveled widely, a thousand years ago.

"So what brings the Kaniea across the vast darkness beyond Bhaorajj space to Narlpynth?" Ermendrud asked as everyone got settled.

She was looking directly at him rather than A'Alhakoth,

but that was an easy enough question that everyone here probably got the general gist, even if only from her tone.

A'Alhakoth turned to him to answer anyway.

Merde.

"What do you know of the recent events in Free Worlds space?" Daniel asked in Anndaing, deflecting things a little.

"The Se'uh'pal have talked about the arrival of many more Anndaing in those sectors," she answered, one eye and one ear flickering up to indicate one of the caravan guards standing along the back wall, probably flushing with embarrassment under her scales right now.

Most of them were soldiers. Well-trained, but operating without Iruoma or the others and relying on A'Alhakoth's report to see how much trouble they might be in later.

Merde. Again.

"Have they mentioned the significant increase in piracy in and around places like Tavle Jocia and Thrabo?" Daniel asked, understanding that maybe the locals had already seen through everything Kathra had wanted to do here. "Or the long time that Septagon *Vorgash* spent at the former, commissioning new warships to attack Anndaing systems without provocation?"

Maybe stretching it the slightest bit, but hey, might as well see just how deep in a Sept pocket this woman might be, before the lies got complicated and messy.

At least the blink of surprise he got from Ermendrud was an honest emotion.

"How can you be sure?" she asked, perhaps the tiniest bit more belligerent.

Daniel caught the glance to the aides on her side of the table.

Like maybe Sept diplomats had left out a few tidbits when they had come through?

"Because I was on board an Anndaing Cargo-6 when one

of those Sept raiders attacked us, coming out of jump above a major Anndaing world," Daniel leaned forward just a little, opening his otherworldly senses to read the woman's emotional makeup closer than he had before. Studying instead of just watching. "Local Anndaing military forces managed to chase the pirates off before my ship was destroyed."

He paused for a long beat, relying on some of his helpful ghosts to get the timing just right.

"The Anndaing are a little put out at the Sept right now," Daniel added, leaning back and smiling frostily at the woman. And her assistants.

"Do you represent the Anndaing?" Ermendrud asked, her eyes taking in the entire table.

"No," A'Alhakoth finally stepped in, having probably gotten things where she wanted them, with him just representing her stalking horse.

The woman had a dangerous maturity beyond her years, once he'd gotten over himself to see her as a person and not a symbol. More the fool him.

"I represent the Mbaysey Tribal Command," A'Alhakoth continued sternly. That she did so fluently in human Spacer was just frosting at this point. "And also various trade houses on Kanus, my homeworld. They are looking for trade with folks who are not human, on the presumption that the Free Worlds might be filled with their own problems shortly."

"Problems?" Ermendrud asked, clearly knocked off center now and losing some of that antagonism.

But then, the six worlds were perched off in a corner, probably hoping that the titans on the battlefield would miss them when the apocalypse finally came.

They had been too unimportant for Urid-Varg to notice in passing, even when he spent several centuries hiding from the K'bari civil war and wandering into the dark places.

"A Septagon attacked me not far from Tavle Jocia," A'Alhakoth replied calmly. "Those require significant logistics trains to maintain in the field, especially with the massive number of patrol forces accompanying them on that raid. My current vessel has already destroyed the Sept base from which they launched their assault on Anndaing space. Other allies are currently looking for some of the bases from which the attack on Tavle Jocia had to have originated."

She paused and swept the entire Upynth side of the table with her disdainful gaze. Daniel watched the emotional impact, especially on Ermendrud. It was like a tide coming in.

"Those bases are most likely located along the outer fringe systems of the Free Worlds," the Ambassador continued. "That means they aren't all that far from the Upynth space, or the Bhaorajj, if the Sept decided to come this direction."

"And you're here to save us?" Mara Ermendrud almost sneered the words.

"Oh, no," A'Alhakoth smiled back. "We'd like to find allies and trade with you, but if the Sept want your worlds, there's nothing my people would do to rescue you. Or liberate you later without some level of agreements. That is, unless destroying the Sept Empire itself counts."

"Destroying the Sept?" Ermendrud didn't speak the words so much as breathe them heavily.

Her aides were all trying hard not to let their ears point all the way backwards at the staggering implications. Especially as the Ambassador had arrived in an Ovanii Dueler, and not something larger.

What might the Anndaing or Kaniea have available, if the war did come this far?

Daniel had a hard time not laughing or smiling. Another

being might be tempted to reach into a mind like Mara Ermendrud and tweak things to get her to see the threat.

It was unnecessary. She was already quite aware of the implications of a Sept raid on Tavle Jocia. That main trade route that ran parallel to the border with Sept space, the one through Tavle Jocia, more or less pointed at Narlpynth at this end. Just as there were other aliens closer to the edge of the galaxy with whom the Free Worlds traded the other direction.

Nobody was as big as the Sept though, except the Anndaing Merchants Guild.

"Destroying the Sept," A'Alhakoth repeated, suddenly smiling. "Are you the correct person with whom to negotiate trade and friendship pacts, madam?"

FORTY

A'Alhakoth had retreated to her quarters aboard the Upynth Trade Authority station. The locals had shifted gears and begun to treat her like a true Ambassador coming out of that first meeting. The one filled with all the fire.

A week had passed since and things were achieving a rhythm now.

More meetings. More negotiations.

More time to appreciate how well her father had prepared her for a life beyond some estate on Kanus, beyond raising a happy brood of pups like her sister E'Elbarth.

How had he known? Anybody on Kanus claiming to see the future was usually just a witch teasing children, but Linga ver'Shingi had approached her education with a deliberation that still left her breathless some days.

But then, Erin had looked at her soul and decided immediately that she would be welcome in the comitatus.

Tonight, A'Alhakoth was tired. Everyone was. They'd been running dawn to dusk for eight days now, dealing and detailing things.

Then dinners and state visit sorts of things, where the

Upynth had started to treat the Kaniea and Mbaysey like serious folks, rather than beggars come to the side door for the traditional charity on Kanus.

A'Alhakoth knew she was making great progress, but personally, she was drained. She had the lights turned most of the way down and the room's porthole window set to block ninety-nine percent of sunlight when they were pointed the right direction.

It was as close as she could get to being back at home on Kanus, in the room where she had grown up, a tower overlooking mother's garden on a late spring day where the windows would be open all night to let in air but not so cold you had to have a quilt over you to sleep.

The moonlight had been just about the same.

She sat on the bed with her legs folded under her and her pistol on the nightstand.

Comitatus. That meant the same uniform everywhere, matching the pants, boots, and black shirt of *SwiftStar*'s officers, but with the tangerine-flame jacket where they wore turquoise. It looked particularly bright against the periwinkle of her skin.

A'Alhakoth sat and meditated for a time, decompressing from the day. Friendly Upynth just meant that the verbal fencing wasn't backed up with any vitriol. If anything, the last week had let them actually start teasing each other a little.

It was a start. A good one. One Kathra would be proud of.

And Linga.

Plus, it would give the Mbaysey another place where the ClanStars could trade. A'Alhakoth could see some of the clans buying or building smaller vessels. Cargo-2's maybe, until they could afford something larger, then ranging their trade outward to compete with the Anndaing and the Se'uh'pal.

Nobody really traded directly with the Upynth. The Sept worlds were generally the closest, but that border was largely closed. The Free Worlds had a corridor, but the distance was great. The Bhaorajj hated everybody equally.

And nobody but Daniel knew what might lie beyond the Upynth sectors.

She wondered if he was awake. A'Alhakoth grabbed her comm from where she had dropped it at the edge of the bed and sent him a quick ping. Nothing more. Just a question mark he could choose to ignore if he felt like sleeping.

Or wasn't alone.

He replied almost instantly with his own question mark.

Who is coreward or east of the Upynth? she sent back.

The long pause suggested that he was consulting his ghosts. She had met a few of them, but Daniel had explained that they rarely surfaced to that level, and she would have to accompany him all the way to the bottom of his being to perchance encounter the larger group.

She'd never worked up that much courage.

Legends, Daniel replied after a time. *Awake?*

Company would be nice, she sent.

The old fussy hens on Kanus would be utterly appalled at her behavior, and with an alien no less.

None of them mattered. And she was no longer Kaniea.

A'Alhakoth ver'Shingi was Mbaysey. And comitatus. She would determine what constituted correct behavior. Or Kathra would draw other lines if she felt it necessary.

That Ife and Ndidi had not done so since the beginning of the voyage just meant that all the women interested in Daniel had stayed within bounds. She could share him with them, since the alternative would be giving him up entirely by making demands that the man was not prepared to deal with.

That much, she'd seen in his soul. In his memory. She remembered the human woman known as Angel almost as well as Daniel did. Perhaps better. And had seen the night when Angel broke his heart, and then rubbed his face in it.

She would never do that to him, but he knew that as well.

A tap at the outer door brought her back to the surface.

"Enter," she called.

She heard the door to the suite open, out in the main chamber.

"A'Alhakoth?" he called after it closed.

"In the sleeping chamber," she called back. "Do you need light?"

"*Non*, this is good enough," he said.

She listened, but he moved in utter silence, finally appearing at the open door to the sleeping chamber.

"I would say I am amazed you are still awake, but I could not sleep either," he said, stepping into her personal space. "What imperative drives you this evening?"

"Sit," she pointed at the chair. "Strange questions of allies and enemies."

He drew the chair around to face her. Upynth thighs were shorter than human or Kaniea, relative to the rest of their body, so she always felt like she was perched on the edge of their seats precariously.

The alternative was having him join her on the bed. It helped that they were both clothed, but she was comfortable here and didn't want to have to turn to face him next to her.

"So the Upynth sector is on the edge of a galactic arm, such as we might measure those things," Daniel explained. "The darkness is not complete, but far fewer stars lay behind Narlpynth for a considerable distance that way. Similarly, they are in something of a pocket, with few stars around them that have inhabitable worlds, unless you wish to spend enormous effort terraforming them, when there are others far easier and more accessible."

"So they are at the edge of a swamp?" she asked, visualizing the map as his words drew it.

"More or less," Daniel nodded in the dimness. "My ghosts have a few suggestions, but Urid-Varg went another direction when he fled the K'bari civil war, so their memories of the area are seven and eight thousand years old."

"But they might know?" she asked, unsure why it felt important to her, but unwilling to let the thread go.

"They might," he shrugged. "Going that deep would take time, and I didn't know if you needed an answer tonight."

"Maybe," she shrugged in turn. "Tonight, I really needed to be around my own kind. I've been around aliens constantly."

His mouth pursed, as if he was about to sarcastically point out that neither of them were the same species. Or that the only Kaniea around, male or female, were a handful of guards and some sailors over on *SwiftStar*.

But they both knew that. And she'd been merged with him enough times that he didn't need to say anything.

He wasn't alien. He was comitatus. Same as Ndidi and Ife. Same as Tanuss and Acqueir and a few others would be, one of these days.

"Would you like to ask them yourself?" he offered instead.

"Would they answer me?" she gasped.

What he was offering her was an intimacy deeper than mere flesh. It was something only Kathra and Erin had done.

Even A'Alhakoth had quailed at the prospect at the time, happier instead to start with knowing his body before she uncovered all of his soul.

She already knew more than most people.

Daniel held out a hand, but she shook her head.

"No," she said, shifting around and grabbing her various things to put on the nightstand or the floor. "You hold me here and we'll try."

A flash of something crossed his face, but it was too dark and gone too quickly for her to catalog it.

Fear, most likely. Daniel had never gotten over being afraid of himself and what he might do in a moment of anger, ecstasy, or thoughtlessness.

Urid-Varg might be dead, but his legacy of evil still lurked at the edge of Daniel's soul.

However, he rose and stepped close. Daniel paused for a moment to pull things from pockets and his belt, resting his comm next to hers along with a few trinkets he had accumulated.

They would do this dressed. She might get lost in her own needs to have him pressed against her with no cloth in the way. Still, she shifted so he could slide in behind her, against the wall, one arm under her head and the other around her chest, nestled carefully between her breasts without touching.

"Ready?" he whispered into her ear.

She nodded, and fell out of the universe.

FORTY-ONE

Daniel fell into himself, carrying A'Alhakoth with him as he descended into the bowels of hell. Or however you wanted to describe the place where he had to go when he wanted to talk with all of his ghosts, and not just the friendlier ones who would come to him on the surface.

It felt like traversing a waterfall, top to bottom, especially the pool of chilly water they struck.

But it didn't drown him. Or her.

Instead, it became a fog that thinned as he watched, revealing bits and swatches of a much larger place as it burned slowly off, perhaps in the heat of the woman he had brought with him.

None of the people he saw here were real, so height had no meaning. Every being Daniel had encountered had been his own size. It wasn't until he realized that he could look A'Alhakoth in the eyes that he could marvel at the possible size range of his ghosts back when they were living.

Urid-Varg had been a biped, Mnapyre, so all of the creatures he had taken later had been as well. No Vida or Bhaorajj, as interesting or weird as that might be.

Just creatures mirrored darkly around him as the fog drifted away.

Arsène greeted them first, the K'bari scholar who had in some ways begun Daniel's adventure into the alien realms, by teaching him the first of the ancient languages he knew.

Three eyes across the face, with the nose below that stretched into a snout halfway between feline and canine for size. Green, with a yellowish-tan fur and petite horns that swept back from his forehead and outward, rather like an ox.

The K'bari scholar studied them both, but Daniel could tell that most of his attention was on the woman, only the third person he had ever brought this deep.

"A'Alhakoth ver'Shingi," Arsène greeted her, bowing his head politely. "We are Daniel Lémieux."

She was holding Daniel's hand, standing beside him, so he felt her turn towards him questioningly, but Arsène spoke.

"That is the legacy of Urid-Varg, Seeker," he continued, addressing her by a much different title. "Each of us is layered atop the next, like a pearl being formed."

"And you are all one?" she asked, nearly breathless.

"We are the gem," Arsène replied. "If Daniel chooses, there may be others later, but he may also be the last of his kind."

"I come seeking your collected knowledge," A'Alhakoth replied.

Daniel smiled that she didn't ask them for wisdom. That sort of thing was simply the culmination of bad decisions that hadn't proven fatal at the time, so it was more luck and timing than anything.

Most of the beings here could already tell her that much.

But they did contain an impossible wealth of memory. Daniel had lost track of the number of forgotten languages he might learn if the need arose. Not even the Anndaing held some of them in the most ancient libraries.

One of these days, Kathra willing, he had a list of planets he would like to visit, to see what, if anything, might have survived on some of the cultures he knew.

Or what trophies he might dig from the ruins.

The fog was suddenly gone.

In a blink, all of the ghosts were there, even back to the Mnapyre that had been Urid-Varg's first victims, surrounding them like a Greek chorus about to call down the doom of the gods upon his head, except that they were different today.

The air had a taste he classified as *helpful,* a scent he could only identify today, having never encountered it before in his life. Neither Kathra nor Erin had provoked such a response, but they had come here for other reasons.

And neither of them had seen him as anything but a threat that first time.

In that, A'Alhakoth was much different.

She sensed it. There was a jolt of recognition he felt in her hand.

These men would answer her.

"We stand at Narlpynth," she said to the assembly in a conversational voice that still somehow carried to the furthest corners of the round space. "What lies beyond? Or whom?"

The heads stirred and all turned to look at a particular ghost.

Daniel felt his breath catch as he recognized the species, if not the being. With several thousand to know, not all had ever chosen to interact with him.

But this one would answer A'Alhakoth.

Roahrt. A semi-mythical culture from early Anndaing days, closer to the galactic core and somewhat along the line of Urid-Varg's passage when he abandoned the dying z'lud empire to live in the wilderness for a while.

Daniel paused to reconsider Urid-Varg. Twelve thousand years was such a long period that he had to remember gaps of as long as two millennia where the Conqueror had lived like a hermit instead of an Emperor, taking a new mount every generation or so, but not capturing entire species or smashing cultures.

Daniel flashed back to the Star Turtle, lost now, but once an impressive museum of technology, culture, and biology.

If a being plans to live forever, what does he do to fill his days?

That question could wait. The Roahrt stepped closer now, standing next to Arsène before them. He somehow conveyed immense height and strength, despite being the same size as the rest of the ghosts. It was as though in life he had towered above even the Ovanii, frightening as that might be.

As far as Daniel knew, the Roahrt had faded from the galactic stage eight thousand years ago. Before humans had even understood bronze.

"We have our own legends," the man began in a voice best suited to Sunday morning sermons in a tiny church in a southern French village, where he would bring the strength of love, rather than the fires of damnation, to fill his pews.

"Tell me," A'Alhakoth prompted.

"Urid-Varg spent a time at the knee of an ancient creature," the man said.

He had a name now, although Daniel did not understand how he knew, except that he was also the Roahrt once known as Pheryoutl.

"We studied power," Pheryoutl continued. "The creature was a female, so Urid-Varg could not threaten her or possess her, but he could learn from her. She was Byormi, and the last of her kind to remain behind."

"Behind?" A'Alhakoth asked.

"Roahrt legend says that the others had *Ascended* by then, but she stayed for a time, an oracle on a lonely world left to return to wilderness," Pheryoutl said. "We studied her power and her mind for a time, but she was as much in advance of Urid-Varg as he was the rest of us, so little could be learned."

"Did she leave prophecies behind?" A'Alhakoth asked. From the way her hand moved in his, she was turning to engage all of Daniel's ghosts, and not just these two.

"Only one yet unfulfilled," Arsène spoke up now. "In answer to his quest for immortality and godhead she quoted something similar to one of Daniel's favorite poets. The translation itself is more complicated, and the human poet did a much greater justice, so I will repeat his words instead.

…and on the pedestal these words appear:
'My name is Ozymandias, king of kings:
Look on my works, ye Mighty, and despair!'
Nothing beside remains. Round the decay
Of that colossal wreck, boundless and bare
The lone and level sands stretch far away.

"Just that?" A'Alhakoth asked.

"Urid-Varg knew a terrible rage at her words," Pheryoutl picked up the thread. "But he was as dangerous to her as a fly, so he left, consumed by equal parts fear and hatred. A commitment to indeed live forever and carve his name on as many worlds as he could find, so that he was never forgotten."

"The Mnapyre, z'lud, and even K'bari are gone now," Arsène said. "A few beings remain here and there, but the cultures that raised starships to the heavens are gone, replaced by others. Nothing remains of that colossal wreck."

"Even the Star Turtle is gone," Pheryoutl observed. "We few are all that remain of Urid-Varg save the wreckage."

"And beyond the Byormi?" A'Alhakoth asked into the great silence and despair that surrounded them.

"We do not know," the elder replied. "Urid-Varg lived for twelve thousand years and visited many worlds, but the galaxy is a huge place. We could mark every star the Conqueror visited on a map, and you would be aghast at how small the area encompassed."

"So traveling beyond Narlpynth would be an adventure into the darkness?" she asked, turning now to Daniel and including him in her wonderful smile.

"It would," he answered.

The entire chamber echoed the words in an immense, perfect harmony of voices that should have sounded ominous, but instead warmed him.

He intended to be the last, assuming he could not find a truly enlightened being capable of wielding the power and knowledge for good.

And how many Buddhas are there?

"Thank you," A'Alhakoth told the assembled men.

In the blink of an eye, they were back in her bed, her bottom snuggled back against him for warmth and his nose buried in her hair.

"You got the answers you sought?" Daniel asked.

She turned inside the circle of his arms, until their noses were touching in the warm darkness.

"I did," she replied. "Thank you."

"So now what?"

"I've already tricked you into my bed," she grinned. "I should take advantage of that while I can."

"I see," he kissed her with a smile. "This was all a conspiracy. I should have known."

She kissed him back, arms coming up around his shoulders.

Both comm units began to beep madly at the same time,

a sound designed to wake someone from the deepest sleep or summon you from the warmth of your shower.

A'Alhakoth untangled herself and turned her back to him again. Daniel took advantage of the moment to slide a hand inside her shirt as she grabbed both units and silenced them.

"This is A'Alhakoth," she said into her comm. "Daniel is with me."

"You both need to get dressed and prepare for transit to the ship," Ife replied simply, as if she already knew where she'd find the two of them.

But then, the comms might have a proximity sensor to each other, so maybe she did.

"What's happened?" A'Alhakoth asked as she wriggled away from his wandering hands to the edge of the bed.

Daniel sat up and slid over to join her.

"Crence Miray and his little scout just came out of jump and sent us a private, coded message," Ife said. "The Sept have invaded Tavle Jocia. With a Septagon."

FORTY-TWO

IFE WAS TORN between the need to depart Upynth space as soon as possible, getting *SwiftStar* someplace where it could help in the war that she felt was imminent, against the risk of leaving A'Alhakoth here alone as a diplomat, when the woman would become a target as soon as Sept spies could report home.

Ife had no doubt that the Sept would send assassins after the woman. They did that. Daniel would be the only one who could protect her, and he would be needed elsewhere.

She had allowed herself to be talked into returning to the station for consultations with the locals, even though she probably should have sent Ndidi instead.

The younger woman was currently in command on *SwiftStar*, ready to unleash all the hounds of hell if the Sept had somehow managed to follow Miray and his Scout-6 to Narlpynth.

They'd better bring a Septagon themselves, if they did that.

Mara Ermendrud was seated across from A'Alhakoth. Interestingly, the sides were not drawn other than that.

Several Upynth aides had joined them in this conference room. They were mixed in with her and Daniel. Crence Miray had even joined them, once she assured the man that the locals needed to hear his tale.

Perhaps the embassy had achieved some level of success after all, in the week they had been here.

Septagon *Singara* had probably just about hit Tavle Jocia on the day *SwiftStar* called on the Upynth. Ife tried not to dwell on the apparent symbolism there.

Crence's hammerhead swept the room like a sensor antenna.

"Everyone here needs to know, Crence," Ife reminded the shark.

She spoke in Spacer. He focused one eye on her and the other on Daniel, until the chef nodded.

"Very well," he sighed, turning his nose to the Trade Representative. "The Anndaing Merchants Guild sent my vessel to scout around Free Worlds space at the same time that *SwiftStar* came here. We encountered a huge Sept fleet at one of the places that had been calculated for them to hide a secret base. Following them to Tavle Jocia, we were there in time to watch them invade, conquer, and occupy the system. They showed no signs of leaving, so it was not a raid. This was the start of a new war."

He stopped there and Ife watched the way his hammer flexed up and back, so he must be filled with such great rage right now that speaking politely to strangers was a chore.

"Scouting?" Mara Ermendrud asked. She sounded innocent and polite with her words, but Ife wasn't fooled. "Scouting what?"

"We're spies, Madam Ermendrud," Crence replied testily. "The Sept already attacked my capital. We have not yet chosen to return the favor, although the vote was apparently close. *SwiftStar* was hired to destroy one of their bases, but the Mbaysey subsequently chose to open trade negotiations with the Upynth instead of hunting others. My superiors sent me to find those other bases that the Sept had to have built, in order to send a Septagon to Tavle Jocia the first time."

Ife leaned in before Crence lost his composure and bit the woman. Metaphorically or literally.

"They are aware of the attack on *SeekerStar*, Crence," Ife told him, in a tone that suggested he unflex his hammer a bit and maybe breathe through his nose while he thought.

She turned to Ermendrud now and focused on the woman.

"I can map the base we destroyed," she offered. "Crence obviously found the original one from two years ago where they chased us into Free Worlds space. There are five or nine others, depending on which Sept base they used as a starting point, but the first raid was Septagon *Vorgash*, so we started our scouting assuming the chain would lead to the *Vorgash* system."

"Those are human problems," Ermendrud snapped back at her.

Her aides were likewise dismissive.

Ife decided to play a little rough. She could let A'Alhakoth be nicer to them afterwards.

"Crence, how far was the predicted location of *Sept Base Four* from Narlpynth, direct sail?" she asked, turning to the shark and feeding off the rage that had his dorsal fin as straight as it could get in a chair that didn't have a fin-gap in the middle.

He paused, appearing to do some math in his hammer, but Ife wasn't fooled. The trademaster probably had forty systems in his head right now, depending on the need to flee or trade with whatever locals he encountered.

She knew the shark that well.

"Five days, for a slow fleet," he said. "Perhaps nine, if a Septagon sets the pace."

The effect on the Upynth was electric. Eyes got wide. Manes stood up straighter. Fur ruffled hard as skin got goosebumps. A few mouths even dropped a bit before being slammed audibly shut again.

"Nine days, direct sail. It's only a human problem if the Sept choose to ignore you, Mara Ermendrud," Ife smiled coldly at the Trade Representative. "Continue to ignore you, that is. How long would your forces resist a Septagon?"

The Upynth woman had no answer, but Ife wasn't surprised. There wasn't much in the galaxy that could take on a Septagon. Even threatening to ram them with the flaming remains of *WinterStar* had only driven *Vorgash* off for a time. It wouldn't have killed them, had A'Alhakoth succeeded. Merely injured them probably worse than anybody else ever had.

Nothing could stop the Sept, except the Anndaing Armada.

And the Mbaysey.

Ermendrud looked like she was grinding her teeth, from the way her jaw muscles moved.

"And what would you have us do?" Ermendrud countered, her voice getting rough and sharp, suddenly sounding like the sort of person you might encounter in a dark corridor on a station.

Ife respected that. The diplomat was merely a cloak the woman wore in polite company, rather like Ife's uniform.

Underneath, they were both brawlers. She let the woman see the same fire in her eyes now.

"The Sept have just captured a world from which they could operate forward fleets that are a threat to the Anndaing," Ife said with a grim, hungry smile. She gestured to A'Alhakoth with one hand. "The Mbaysey and Kaniea came here seeking trade, but the Anndaing are likely to be looking for allies for what might turn into a war, Madam Ermendrud. I cannot leave an ambassador here without significant forces to protect her, and those are not available. It becomes necessary for me to withdraw A'Alhakoth and hope that we will be able to continue on some future date from the great progress I have already been briefed on."

"And what can *SwiftStar* do against a Septagon?" Ermendrud asked.

"Nothing," Ife admitted. "But the Anndaing are already making preparations, and the Mbaysey are allied, so we will help them fight the Sept."

"What do you want from me?" she asked, her voice growing quiet.

"You could send a representative to Ogrorspoxu and Kanus, Madam Ermendrud," Ife offered. "I would be happy to transport an embassy of Upynth to continue the negotiations and provide introductions to the Anndaing Merchants Bank. The Se'uh'pal are, as I understand it, a Sept ally, so they might decide to punish you economically when the wider war starts. You might desire allies in the Anndaing."

"What about the Mbaysey, Speaker Ogu?" Ermendrud asked.

Ife smiled now.

Even Crence might have flinched a little.

"The Mbaysey are going to go destroy the Sept Empire," Ife said. "Commander Omezi has already declared that."

FORTY-THREE

Kathra had returned to Ogrorspoxu aboard *SeekerStar.*

She had Erin with her today, along with Obi, Yejide, and Elyl, all acting as bodyguards for the two of them and the infants both currently asleep in clothe wraps the two women wore around their shoulders and one hip.

A messenger from Wyll Koobitz had framed this trip as an invitation, but Kathra was canny enough to recognize a summons for what it was, however polite the message inscribed.

And Wyll had been polite. Insistent, but courteous.

SeekerStar rode in orbit, trailing close to the main station, the place some sharks roguishly called the Central Bank. Her ship would be safe under the guns of the station, if another Sept raider suddenly appeared.

She could only hope that Daniel was safe as well, but there had been no news from *SwiftStar.*

Kathra wondered if Crence Miray had returned with important news. Certainly the local traffic control had been sharper and less laconic than usual, according to messages relayed from Obioma.

Something must have happened. The system had a militant air that had been lacking on previous trips.

The look on the first Anndaing caravan guard's face as the entire group emerged from the SkyCamel dock was utterly priceless. She'd often wondered if their eyes really could bulge far enough out of their heads that they would pop loose. The hammer was mostly cartilage, with only a thin ring of bone running out each direction to provide strength.

But his eyes only bulged, seeing sleeping human children for the first time.

Kathra smiled at the thought of what would happen when either Adaku or Kwento woke up fussy and started to cry.

At least both daughters were dressed in comitatus flame today, cute little onesies the crew of *SeekerStar* had worked up from spare fabric.

Seven Mbaysey women, taking on the galaxy.

You blink first.

The guard led them to a door, opened it, and stepped smartly aside with a bow. Like he had been warned the human women were dangerous and he needed to mind his manners.

Kathra wondered how maternal a female guard might have been instead. Anndaing women were externally nearly identical to the males, without the dimorphism humans or other species had. They didn't nurse their pups. At some point, presumably, Kathra would encounter a female with Adaku in tow and could ask.

Both Wyll Koobitz and Obaj Gendrah waited inside the room. Interestingly, they were alone, without even their own aides, to say nothing of bodyguards.

Wyll held up a finger to them for silence, so she and Erin sat with the little ones in their laps, and the other three women took up positions on the walls as the main door closed.

A moment later, an inner door opened and Crence Miray stepped out, taking a spot next to Wyll.

Kathra let an eyebrow convey a wealth of questions, until one of these men could explain.

Must be good.

Wyll cleared his throat, which was apparently just loud enough, or just something enough to wake Adaku. Or maybe the fierce, squawking, little woman was just hungry again.

Kathra unbuttoned her new pocket on the shirt so the ravenous beast could drink her fill, gurgling happily and falling quiet again as Kathra held her.

Three sharks were at risk of losing eyes even worse than the caravan guard.

Kathra smiled.

"Gentlemen?" she asked, throwing in the most innocent look she could manage.

Kwento was likely to wake up shortly, also hungry.

If you thought I looked strange, wait until the utterly martial killer known as Erinkansilemi Uduik is breastfeeding her own daughter in front of you.

"Uhm," Wyll managed unconvincingly.

Kathra waited. Erin grinned at them. She was willing to bet that Obi, Yejide, and Elyl were, as well.

"There's news," Crence began with a disgusted sigh, casting serious side eye at the others, as only an Anndaing could do justice.

Kathra turned her attention to the trademaster.

"Septagon *Singara* attacked and captured Tavle Jocia about a month ago," Crence continued. "With a massive fleet bigger than anything we expected."

"Just one Septagon?" Erin asked.

"Just the one, yes," Crence confirmed.

"Then they are defensive for now," Erin nodded, leaning back lest she disturb her own beast.

Kathra agreed.

"Have you told Ife?" Kathra asked.

"We went straight to Narlpynth from Tavle Jocia," Crence nodded with his whole hammer. "They are a few days behind us, because my Scout-6 could move so much faster through jump and I figured speed was more important. I expect them tomorrow, give or take."

Kathra paused to listen as Crence gave them a deeply abbreviated rundown of everything that had happened at Tavle Jocia and points after. It was sobering news.

"I see," Kathra said as a placeholder when he was done, turning to the other two sharks now and fixing them with her glare. "And what did you think an Ovanii Dueler like *SwiftStar* could do against a Septagon?"

"Nothing," Wyll replied. "That's not why I asked you to join me here."

Again, Kathra noted the pains to be polite. To ask, when they both knew that a shark like Wyll could order things, even from an Mbaysey Commander who didn't nominally answer to him or the Anndaing Merchants Bank.

"None of you will be surprised to learn that we have sent a number of spies and scouts into Free Worlds space, as well as the Sept Empire," Wyll continued, showing just a hint of a grin with his lipless mouth and lively eyes. "While you have been wonderful guests, we did indeed need to take things with a pinch of salt, to use Daniel's phrase."

"Indeed," Kathra nodded, including Crence in the gesture. "That was why I made you such a good deal on a map of human space in the first place. Best you learn for yourselves what I and mine have known in our bones. Tazo is never going to be forgotten. Certainly never forgiven."

"Just so," Wyll nodded. "Over the last year and a half, the

Merchants Bank has been adjusting old plans to new scenarios. Without sufficient details, we have always assumed that we would eventually encounter another K'bari. Or perhaps an Ovanii. Humans were just a more interesting shape to the threat. The Free Worlds are not even a threat, but perhaps the greatest trade and marketing opportunity in the last five hundred years. If not longer."

Kathra watched. Wyll had obviously given much thought to this speech. It would be a pity to derail it early with questions he was getting around to answering.

"However, the Free Worlds are not an organized political entity, as many would frame such a definition," Wyll continued. "Even less so than Anndaing space, because we at least have the Merchants Bank as a supervisory board of directors to keep things in fin."

Wyll paused to study the two of them. The four of them.

The seven of them.

"The Sept Empire is a threat of a different nature," he said heavily. "Not an unmanageable one, but diplomatic overtures have been rebuffed, as have trade negotiators. This did not surprise us, as it fit in with the general consensus among our contacts in the Free Worlds, as well as things you have told us, Kathra. But Tavle Jocia represents an existential threat."

"Existential, Wyll?" Kathra asked.

"They built *SeptStar* there," his gaze bored in on her now. "They can build more. The system is wealthy enough to support a Septagon fleet such as Crence observed. In short, Sept control of Tavle Jocia, even if they do not attack any other Free Worlds systems, gives them the fin up if they want to consider attacking places like Acran, to say nothing of eventually coming to Ogrorspoxu or Kanus. None of our worlds could currently resist a Septagon with anything less than drastic measures."

"How drastic are we talking?" Kathra asked, looking at Obaj now.

He represented different directors on the board. His authority in the overall scheme of things might be a hair less than Wyll Koobitz, but the difference was negligible.

"Even more drastic than you imagine, Commander," Obaj replied, his face as serious as she had ever seen one of the sharks get.

"Oh?" she leaned back now as the little one seemed done.

She took a moment to clean Adaku up and burp her as the room fell into silence. Quickly, the little princess of the Mbaysey fell back asleep, smiling happily with one tiny hand wrapped around Kathra's finger.

She looked up finally and stared at Wyll.

"How serious do you intend to get?" she asked.

"Something like the Call to Armada, Kathra," Wyll replied after a heavy breath. "Both more and less at the same time."

The Commander nodded rather than speak, unsure if she would enjoy where they were going.

But the Anndaing had provided her and Mbaysey a safe harbor. Not even the Free Worlds had been able to do that. And they had sold her *SwiftStar* at a ludicrously cheap price, but that was just a measure of their concern.

After all, if the Sept Empire was coming, better to have a well-armed pirate out there raiding things for you, with plausible deniability in the deal.

Kathra was certainly not one to shy from killing Sept troopers in whatever numbers she needed to, in order to save her people and the rest of the galaxy from those *salauds*.

She would listen.

And then judge whether or not her own future path continued to travel with the Anndaing, or if they would need to take a different fork in the road.

"Ife and her crew have now made two major voyages aboard an Ovanii vessel," Wyll said. "Fought a major battle. Sailed to new systems. Proven themselves at the same time they have proven the technology."

"They have," Kathra agreed, leaving nothing on the table for the men to read.

"We would like to discuss leasing you a second vessel, Kathra," Wyll said. "And supplying a significant portion of the crew, while you will supply the officers to command it."

"Lease?" she noted the very specific term.

Wyll Koobitz had *sold* her *SwiftStar* in fee simple, with expectations attached, but no conditions spelled out in the contract.

Not that she needed prodding to send a killer after Sept forces.

A lease suggested all sorts of legalisms would be involved. The Anndaing were trademasters, after all.

"Lease," Wyll confirmed with emphasis. Interestingly, he turned to Obaj now with an air of expectation.

The other shark pulled a small projector from his jacket pocket and placed it on the table between them. He did not turn it on.

"An Ovanii Dueler like *SwiftStar* is a fast, dangerous escort," Obaj said. "Lethal on its own, but designed to act in concert with others. The Sept do not have a single vessel of a comparable class, as they are largely a police force, rather than a military. At least as my understanding of such things goes, from the books Daniel translated for us into Anndaing."

Kathra nodded. Human histories and biographies for the most part, as well as some fiction, but all of it enough for Anndaing scholars to quickly grasp a better understanding of the Sept. To see this new entity that swam just off their flank, threatening to take a bite out of them if they weren't careful.

Sharks understood sudden bites from unexpected angles.

"Instead, the Sept have the standard Patrol, made up of ten vessels, either operating from a fixed base, or from a Patrol Tender vessel," Obaj continued. "If more force is needed, they simply send a second Patrol, or even a third. *SwiftStar* would be at serious risk of being overwhelmed by two Patrols. Three would probably be sufficient to either seriously damage the vessel, or force it to flee."

"Yes," Kathra agreed as a prod, wondering if they were going to offer to lease her an Ovanii Assailant.

Those were the larger warships of the Ovanii, the ones that the Dueler was built to escort. They also were more pure warships than a Dueler, since the smaller vessels were designed to help carry the entire tribe on their collected decks, much like heavily-armed versions of her ClanStars.

"We expect a war, Kathra Omezi," Obaj said, reaching out his right fin's big finger and triggering the projector. An image appeared. A ship, but one whose lines were unfamiliar to her. "It behooves us to recruit warriors like you, especially as most of the Anndaing Merchants Guild are trademasters first. Our kind might and might not have ever even encountered a pirate, let alone fired on one. The Armada works because all of the trademasters understand that sacrifices might be necessary to destroy a bigger foe."

Erin's sudden gasp caused everyone to turn to her. And woke Kwento hungry, so she needed to wave everyone off while she took care of her own daughter.

"What?" Kathra asked in a whisper anyway.

"That," Erin pointed with her off hand. "He's nuts."

Kathra turned to Obaj Gendrah and let her eyebrows frame the question.

"She may be right," he agreed with a grimace. "But as Wyll noted, this might be an existential threat, so we should approach it as such."

Kathra studied the image and finally recognized it with a jolt of energy.

"You are insane," she whispered in a voice with no emotion behind it, turning to all three of the sharks. Crence at least had the courtesy to turn gray and let his jaw drop open in shock.

The ship that was rotating slowly in the projection, so small that she could have covered it with both hands, was an Ovanii Battlemaster.

Those had been the core of the invading fleet, when the ancients had come to Anndaing space and thought that they could push the sharks around.

"We are not yet desperate, Kathra," Wyll took up the thread now. "But we also recognize that it would not take much to push the Merchants Bank into desperation. This is a calculated stratagem on the part of the Board of Directors, expected to yield certain results that should actually help us in any future war. Especially if we need to start one right now by preemptively attacking a Sept base."

"A Battlemaster?" Kathra asked, just to confirm.

"We captured zwölf-three on that day," Ohaj said. "Since then, we've built eight more to the same specifications, while keeping all twenty-three up to date with advances in technology. Daniel might recognize them when he sees one, as the last time the Grand Fleet of the Armada saw battle was assisting the K'bari rebels to free themselves from Urid-Varg. When the Conqueror was gone, they were retired to base, but still make training cruises."

He paused now, like the weight of the entire cosmos was on his shoulders. His hammer hung forward with the stress of the words.

"We would like you to take command of one."

"No," Kathra replied simply.

The entire room goggled at her, even worse than when the Anndaing males watched her breastfeed Adaku.

"No?" Wyll seemed almost angry.

Obaj was shocked. Crence might be on the verge of passing out.

"No," Kathra reiterated, going so far as to smile. "I promised those fussy, old crones on the ClanStars that I would outlive all of them. I cannot do that on the deck of an Ovanii Battlemaster intent on destroying a Septagon in single combat."

She paused for a beat, but that was just to hammer home her point now.

"However, I will accept your offer in the spirit in which it was given, with some changes to the eventual proposed deal," she continued. "Instead of me or Erin commanding, I will provide you a Speaker of such note that she will impress the rest of her crew. And your Board of Directors. One I trust as much as I do Erin, Daniel, and very few others. You will be pleased."

"Who?" Obaj managed to gasp out, finally gaining control of himself again.

"Ndidi has been Ife's Shield aboard *SwiftStar*," Kathra said. "And I instructed Ifedimma Ogu to train the woman to replace her. It was always my intent to grow the squadron larger, as my war with the Sept would not be over in my lifetime. Ndidi is even better than Ife is. The voyage to Narlpynth was to make sure that she had all the skills and experience she needed in order to take command of her own Dueler one of these days, when you got desperate enough to do another deal with the Mbaysey. The Sept will learn the meaning of fear itself if Ndidi Zikora *Speaks* for an Mbaysey Battlemaster, my friends."

Wyll shivered now, almost as badly as Crence did, but both of them had been into that interesting gestalt that

Daniel could create, when he needed to carry several others into his mind. Obaj had been there, too, but he was an ally, rather than a friend.

That made a tremendous difference with Daniel. Kathra understood.

And Ndidi had finally learned the truth about Tazo, those things that Kathra had instructed the elders to whitewash as much as possible, so that the current generation did not grow up with the scars of their elders. Erin's tattoo, immortalizing Granny Ezinne, would hopefully be represent a distant memory by the time Kwento was old enough to understand what it truly meant.

"Can Ndidi handle it?" Obaj asked in a quiet voice, striving mightily not to give offense.

"She is *Comitatus*," Kathra replied grimly. "Erin might have to give way to the woman in a few years. That's how good she can be, given the opportunity."

The room fell into silence.

"What is the name of this Battlemaster?" Erin spoke up, always the warrior. "The one you think to send after a Septagon."

"EveningStar," Wyll replied. "At least as it would translate into Anndaing and fit your naming standards for vessels. The Ovanii term is much longer and also refers to a homeworld they had long-since left behind."

Kathra nodded. And then smiled.

"That will never do," she replied.

"No?" Crence finally managed to find his tongue.

"That suggests a pining for yesterday, Crence," she turned to him. "For the Mbaysey, that would be a reminder of the Tazo we intentionally abandoned. The place we had to flee so that we could find our freedom in the darkness where no Sept court could decide later that the paper granting us freedom could be set aside. Nor decide that Mbaysey daughters could again be taken as property by rich Sept lords, for whatever perversions tickled their fancy. We do not wish to remember or immortalize Tazo."

"Then what would you call it?" Wyll leaned forward, finally grasping that everything would work out, just not in the way he had originally anticipated.

"A new beginning in Anndaing space," Kathra said. "A place where the day holds a promise of peace and trade and happiness. Gentlesharks, we will name it MorningStar."

READ MORE!

Be sure to read all five books in the Star Tribes series.

WinterStar
SeekerStar
SeptStar
SwiftStar
MorningStar

Available from your favorite retailers!

ABOUT THE AUTHOR

Blaze Ward writes science fiction in the Alexandria Station universe (Jessica Keller, The Science Officer, The Story Road, etc.) as well as several other science fiction universes, such as Star Dragon, the Dominion, and more. He also writes odd bits of high fantasy with swords and orcs. In addition, he is the Editor and Publisher of *Boundary Shock Quarterly Magazine*. You can find out more at his website www.blazeward.com, as well as Facebook, Goodreads, and other places.

Blaze's works are available as ebooks, paper, and audio, and can be found at a variety of online vendors. His newsletter comes out regularly, and you can also follow his blog on his website. He really enjoys interacting with fans, and looks forward to any and all questions— even ones about his books!

Never miss a release!
If you'd like to be notified of new releases, sign up for my newsletter.

I will never spam you or use your email for nefarious purposes. You can also unsubscribe at any time.

http://www.blazeward.com/newsletter/

Connect with Blaze!

Web: www.blazeward.com
Boundary Shock Quarterly (BSQ):
https://www.boundaryshockquarterly.com/

ABOUT KNOTTED ROAD PRESS

Knotted Road Press fiction specializes in dynamic writing set in mysterious, exotic locations.

Knotted Road Press non-fiction publishes autobiographies, business books, cookbooks, and how-to books with unique voices.

Knotted Road Press creates DRM-free ebooks as well as high-quality print books for readers around the world.

With authors in a variety of genres including literary, poetry, mystery, fantasy, and science fiction, Knotted Road Press has something for everyone.

Knotted Road Press
www.KnottedRoadPress.com